DUET

Patricia Collinge

A KISMET™ Romance

METEOR PUBLISHING CORPORATION
Bensalem, Pennsylvania

For my husband, Frank, whose love and encouragement supported me; for Betty, Carol, Darcea, Ethel, Gayla, and Joe, whose words inspired me; for Julie, John, and Alan, who can't quite believe it; for Howard, a dear friend; and most of all, for my mother, who taught me to follow my star.

PATRICIA COLLINGE

Though Patricia Collinge has enjoyed careers as a classical musician, college instructor, glassblower, florist, and small business consultant, writing has always been what she loved to do most. Now her varied background is a rich resource for her career as a novelist. Patricia has three grown children and lives in Tacoma, Washington, with her husband, Frank, and Kitty, a fat white cat.

PROLOGUE

"I won't do it, Robert! I can't possibly agree to that kind of arrangement." Marina stopped her restless pacing and turned to face the man seated at the desk. Leaning forward, she gripped the edge of the desk.

"It's a world premiere, Robert. A *world premiere!* If Fletcher wants to perform with me, he'll have to get here so we can rehearse. That's final!"

Robert Graves sat unmoving, waiting patiently for the tirade to end. His eyes met the furious icy-blue of her gaze with gentle forbearance. But the set of his mouth was firm, and Marina knew from experience that his calm smile indicated no suggestion of acquiescence.

"Are you through now?" he asked mildly.

Throwing him a furious glare, Marina hesitated. Then, with a sigh of resignation, she dropped into the chair beside the desk. Arms folded, she sat stiff and silent.

Robert watched her for a moment, his brow furrowed. Leaving his chair, he walked around the desk and stood beside her, his hands in his pockets.

"I know how you feel, Marina. But, hell, if you think *you've* got a problem, consider me." He observed her carefully, noting the slight relaxing of her shoulders and the nearly imperceptible softening of the rigid lines around

7

her mouth. "I've got to conduct a whole orchestra without rehearsing with him." He smiled wryly.

"Then why not . . ."

"Sh-h. Let me finish." Pulling a chair closer, Robert sat facing her. "Fletcher says we can pull it off, and there's no arguing with him. He's got us over a barrel. Unless we go along with him, he'll pull the score."

Marina's eyes narrowed.

"He wouldn't! Not with the hype the press has given this concert. *Chansons de la Nuit* is a newly-discovered Debussy work, for God's sake. It's the find of the century."

Robert shook his head slowly. "You know Fletcher's reputation. He's like a bolt of lightning. There's no telling what he might do." He shrugged, his face worried. "He could even refuse to honor his teaching contract." Rising, Robert walked over and stood in front of the window. "Do you realize how hard it is to convince people like him to abandon lucrative concert schedules for a whole year to come and teach for us?"

Marina started to speak, but Robert smiled grimly. The question was absurd. "Of course, you do. I had to call in every favor I ever did to get *you*, didn't I?"

A sympathetic smile flicked across Marina's face, giving way to a grimace of frustration. Her solo part in the premiere of this piece of music—a major orchestral work discovered only months ago in a Paris attic by Adam Fletcher—had promised to be a high point of her career.

"But, Robert, I've never even met the man. We've never spoken, never played together . . ."

Sitting again, Robert reached for her hand. Stroking it gently, he smiled, his eyes pleading.

"I know we can pull it off, Marina. I invited you here because you're the best there is. And Fletcher—well, we both know his work. Cellists don't come any better."

His eyes caught hers, and she looked away, unable to bear the worry she read there. It wasn't fair. It was extortion. He was putting the entire responsibility on her shoulders.

Robert's fingers tightened around hers.

"Please," he said softly.

All the fight went out of her at the hopelessness in his voice. Without turning, she nodded slowly, just once. Robert gave her hand a quick squeeze.

"I knew I could count on you."

Without answering, Marina withdrew her hand and stood up. She walked across the room and out into the hallway. Pulling the door closed behind her, she leaned back against it, shutting her eyes tightly to stem the tide of angry tears.

From the depths of her heart, she hated Adam Fletcher. Of all the arrogant, inconsiderate men she'd ever had the misfortune to get mixed up with, he was the worst. After this concert, she'd make sure never again to get in a position that allowed him control over her. Never.

Pushing away from the door, she straightened, furiously swiping an angry tear from her cheek. Before she was done with him, Adam Fletcher would know exactly what she thought of him and his blackmailing ways.

ONE

The small, expectant fidgets of the audience dropped off to a hushed silence as Robert Graves walked briskly onstage. A roar of applause greeted him, and he faced the blackness beyond the stage, acknowledging the welcome with a smile and a bow.

Marina kept her eyes glued to Robert, desperately focusing her thoughts on the music. She hadn't dared even a glance in Adam Fletcher's direction. She'd wait until after the performance to see what he looked like.

Hands clammy, she wiped one, then the other on her long black skirt. The silver of her flute glinted in the bright light, and she caressed the instrument with trembling fingers. Her eyes darted around the orchestra seeking reassurance. A sheen of moisture stood out on the French horn player's forehead. The first violinist gave a dry little cough.

Briefly, her attention fell on Jerry Haydn, the first cellist. She felt a pang of sympathy for him. *He* should be the one playing with her tonight, not Adam Fletcher. But Fletcher had made his imperial wishes known. And everyone had been forced to accede to him, without a rehearsal, without even so much as shaking hands. What self-centered, infuriating conceit!

Marina's eyelid began to twitch.

At the sharp tap of Robert's baton, her attention swerved back to the podium. Robert raised his arms and nodded in her direction, throwing her a brilliant, confident smile. Knees shaking, Marina rose and lifted her flute to frozen lips.

What if they didn't . . . Oh God, she couldn't think that way now.

She flexed her fingers, feeling them slip off the valves in a glaze of sweat. Sensing the undercurrent of excitement in the hushed, expectant audience, Marina took a deep breath, preparing herself for the inevitable descent of the baton.

Robert gave her a little wink just before a look of total concentration consumed his face. He lifted the baton in a delicate upbeat, then brought it down. With that motion, a palpable sensation of relief telegraphed through the orchestra.

The waiting was over.

The music began softly, with a delicate ripple of harp and strings, a muted tapestry of sound that filled the hall with subtle nuances of shade and color. Then, like a freshet flowing from a hidden source, the pure tones of Marina's flute floated out. They flooded the auditorium with fluid sound, weaving a haunting, sensuous melody through the gossamer veil of shifting harmonies. Clear and discrete, the notes hung in the air, hovering, waiting. . . .

The warm, seductive response of Adam Fletcher's cello began as a whisper, rising and spreading in an enchanting, engulfing tide. Its deep voice teased and tantalized, closing around the undulant, seductive flute tones as if seeking to grasp them in a lover's embrace.

At first Marina responded to the caressing sweep of sound with a dazed sense of wonder. Shyly, then with greater boldness, she allowed herself to be drawn deeper into the interplay, yielding to the seductive appeal with enthralled fascination. Her mellifluous flute tones took on a languorous, honeyed sound, as if captivated by the gentle cajolery of Adam's song. Transformed from demure maiden to provocative temptress, she teased and taunted, leading Adam to respond with ever-increasing urgency.

Mesmerized by the intimate interchange, the audience sat in rapt silence, abandoning itself to the electrifying drama of the musical seduction. Sensing this, Marina shed the last constraints of fear and uncertainty, leaving her spirit free to rove uninhibited in the exalted world of sound and sensation she and Adam were creating. The rest of the orchestra receded into the background, as the two wove their spell about each other, blending the voices of their instruments in a haunting, erotic ballet.

With rapturous abandon, Marina felt herself transported to a plane of exalted harmony she'd never known existed. A melting warmth began in the pit of her stomach, spreading downward in hot, liquid waves. Nothing touched her now except the moment and the mystical union of two unfettered souls. The notes soared to a rapturous climax and their music hung suspended, then gently drifted back to merge with the tranquil shimmer of sound and color that had been its wellspring. Gradually, the movement stilled and the music faded, slipping away until only a memory remained.

Marina remained motionless, eyes closed, flute still at her lips. The quiet, ending notes hovered in her ears, refusing to release her from the spell the music had cast. No sound broke the silence of the vast concert hall—not a cough or even the shuffling of a program. Over three thousand people sat spellbound by the performance they had just witnessed.

For a breathless moment the paralyzing enchantment prevailed. Then, as if on signal, the hall reverberated with thunderous applause.

The sound jolted Marina from her reverie and her eyes flew wide open. She lowered her flute, the other-worldly

daze of an instant before replaced by a new, keen awareness that she had to look at Adam. *Had* to.

She lifted her head, and her eyes strained to see across
the mass of musicians. For a moment, her vision blurred.
Impatiently, she shook her head, and Adam's face wavered into view. He'd taken off his glasses to mop his
forehead with a white handkerchief. As their gazes met,
his motion ceased. Marina froze, the blood coursing through
her veins, pounding in her head.

For a fleeting instant, she viewed him with crystal clarity. In that heartbeat, she caught a look of naked longing
in his face. Immediately, he looked away, jamming his
glasses in place—as if to conceal all evidence of the brief,
flaring exchange.

The musicians around Marina rose, smiling and clapping, calling out their congratulations. Cries of *bravo*
echoed from the audience, and Marina's startled gaze moved
to Robert, who frantically motioned her to the front of the
stage. Miraculously, a pathway opened, and in a daze
Marina moved down the risers to grasp Robert's welcoming hand.

"Incredible! Spectacular!" His grin threatened to split
his face as he led her to center stage. Somehow, Adam
was beside her, and the cheers and applause rose to a
feverish pitch.

A crackling static seemed to fill the space between her
and Adam. Marina turned, her chest tight. Unsmiling, he
took the hand she held out, gripping it firmly. Startled,
she pulled back, but Adam tightened his hold. Behind the
heavy frames of his glasses, his eyes gleamed, their smoky
depths black and guarded. Tendrils of thick black hair
curled over his high, formal collar and a damp curl clung
to his forehead.

With ceremonial formality, they bowed to each other.
Then, hands still clasped, they faced the audience to ac-
knowledge the continuing accolade. The galvanic charge
of his tight grip kept them welded together. Marina scarcely

heard the renewed swell of applause until an usher stood before her, offering her an armful of roses. Glowing like rubies against a bed of feathery green fern, they sent forth a cloud of fragrance that settled around her and Adam like a heady aphrodisiac.

She caught her breath, and moisture flooded her eyes, Adam freed her hand. She reached out, her smile trembling as she accepted the roses. Leaning forward, she kissed the usher on the cheek. Then she pulled a single rose from the bouquet and presented it to Robert. He gave her a light kiss. The audience went wild, renewing the clamorous applause and shouting.

"You're the one who deserves flowers," she murmured, stepping back. He held the rose up and gave her a courtly little bow, but Marina hardly noticed. Her mind had already leapt ahead to her next move, and both dread and anticipation pounded through her.

Taking another rose from the bouquet, she turned to Adam, suddenly uncertain. He watched her, his eyes grave. She held the rose toward him. The flower shook, and as Adam reached out to take it, she nearly dropped it. But his hand closed over hers, his fingers stroking her smooth skin. Nervously, she tried to pull her hand back, but he refused to let her go. He raised one eyebrow, his mouth quirked in a half smile.

"What? No kiss for me?" Though the words were a soft murmur, it seemed to Marina as if he'd shouted. She felt her face go pale and her throat contract.

He stood there, apparently at ease, but he drew her toward him with steel strength. Marina glanced around frantically. The applause continued unabated, and more shouts of *bravo* rang out from the audience. She couldn't resist Adam's demand without making a scene, but the thought of touching her lips to the warmth of his skin filled her with terror.

Stiffly, she smiled at him, forcing herself to appear unaffected. Leaning forward, she caught a hint of his unique, masculine scent: a fresh combination of soap and the piney fragrance of bow resin. As she drew closer, the aroma intensified, wafting around her in a dizzying, sensual cloud. Swallowing hard, Marina prepared to brush her lips across his cheek lightly and make a speedy escape. But Adam had other plans.

Her lips were just grazing the smooth, clean-shaven flesh when he turned his head, catching the kiss full on his mouth. A riot exploded in Marina's brain, like the blazing flare of a bolt of lightning. It sensitized every nerve in her body, and a tingling charge fused their mouths together, making it impossible for her to think rationally.

She tried to pull back, conscious of the thousands of eyes upon them. Instead, Adam's grip tightened, refusing to release her. Marina's eyes widened in panic, and her heart pounded with furious agitation. A cheer rose from the audience, and she felt her face flush with scarlet heat.

The few seconds trapped in his embrace seemed endless. But when he finally released her, Marina felt abandoned, cast free in space.

Dazed, she stepped back, eager to distance herself from him, making a desperate effort to appear calm and composed. Away from the chaotic distraction of his touch, a thread of anger began to work its way into her consciousness, eroding her shaky self-assurance.

Escape. She had to escape. Adam would be laughing at her. Deliberately, she kept her eyes away from him. With a final bow to the audience and another to Robert, Marina turned to flee back to her place among the woodwinds.

She never knew how she got through the final portion of the concert. Overwhelmed by the horde of emotions that still claimed her, she performed automatically. She felt an irresistible urge to look at him—to let her eyes rove over the well-defined contours of his face until she no longer hungered to stare.

Without even realizing it, she found herself reexperiencing the overpowering sense of unity—the perfection—she and Adam had achieved. It was a rare touching of souls—one that most musicians never experienced. The glimpse she'd had of his face just afterward—the stark, haunted yearning so quickly hidden—what did it mean?

Marina had to know. The strange pairing of arrogance and sensitivity puzzled her. So did the overwhelming effect he'd had on her. She'd have no peace until she understood it. With the realization, a sense of excitement came over her, bringing with it a quiet feeling of certainty. He felt it, too. She *knew* it. He had to be as eager to discover the secret as she.

Fighting the temptation to glance in his direction, she counted the final measures before her cue. Watching Robert carefully, she tensed for his signal, her mind relaxed and alert. Until the concert was over, she refused to let Adam Fletcher distract her.

When at last the closing round of applause ended and the audience began to leave, she finally allowed herself to look.

Adam was gone.

Disbelieving, Marina stood up, staring at the empty seat in front of the cello section. Other members of the orchestra came up to her, eager to offer their congratulations, but she hardly heard them. Distractedly, she peered over and around the mass of bodies, straining to see if Adam were nearby. Clutching the roses and her flute, Marina wanted to rush backstage in search of him, but she couldn't take two steps without someone stopping her.

"You were fabulous, my dear . . ." ". . . a thrilling performance . . ." ". . . absolutely electrifying . . ."

Marina tried to be gracious, accepting the warm compliments with harassed smiles and automatic responses. Her mind was on Adam. How could he have slipped off the stage without her noticing?

Frantically, she wove her way through the other musicians, until, at last, she reached the backstage area. It was impossibly crowded, and she saw that members of the audience had joined the milling throng. The need to talk to Adam had become an urgent, gnawing hunger. Scanning the press of people, she anxiously sought him.

Finally, she saw him standing across the room, coat on, cello in its case. A group of admirers surrounded him. The expression on his face was one of acute discomfort, as if each response to the eager questions and enthusiastic praise pained him. With his eyes hidden behind the heavy-framed glasses, he looked like a dark owl, poised to take flight.

A feeling of relief swept over Marina. She started in his direction. At that moment, Adam looked up. A chill shot through her body as their gazes collided. His face expressionless, he stared at her. Then, deliberately, he leaned forward, as if to listen more closely to what the woman in front of him was saying.

Marina stopped dead, stunned at his blatant rejection. Her heart quickened and a charge of adrenaline pulsed in her veins.

Who does he think he is? First, he bullies Robert into making me perform with him, and now he cuts me dead!

Propelled by anger, she started toward him again, pushing through the crowd, ignoring the sound of her name behind her. As she approached the group around Adam, the people fell back, allowing her through. She marched up to him, a smile fixed on her face. He turned to her with a polite, distant look. Marina glanced at his empty hands and the cello beside him. For an instant her mind contracted, then annoyance took over.

"Why, Mr. Fletcher, I believe you've lost your rose." To her ears, her voice sounded shrill and bitchy. She watched him carefully, noting the small, impersonal smile that barely twitched his lips.

"It would appear that way," he drawled, folding his arms across his chest.

The deep timbre of his voice sent Marina's heart pounding, and she felt a pulse begin in her throat. Abstracted, she observed the ebony depths of his eyes. A brief, uncontrolled flash of response immediately disappeared behind a murky veil.

Aha! Her heart leaped at the momentary reaction. With trembling hands, she drew another rose from the bouquet.

"Well, we mustn't let that happen," she said with forced lightness. "After all, you'll want to remember tonight's performance, won't you?"

Holding the flower toward him, she waited, scarcely daring to breathe, not taking her eyes from his face. A drop of moisture trembled on one velvet petal. Marina willed her hand to stop shaking.

"Are you asking for another kiss?" Adam's voice was so soft only Marina could hear. With a provocative smile, he leaned toward her, and Marina stepped back, thrusting the rose into his hands. A flashbulb exploded with blinding intensity, bringing the exchange to an abrupt halt. Adam threw his arm across his eyes and Marina blinked, momentarily lost in a sightless stare. When she was able to see once more, the shade had again been drawn tight over Adam's face.

"Miss Prohaska, Mr. Fletcher," a voice called from the edge of the crowd. Startled, Marina whirled around to see a bearded reporter grinning at her, a photographer at his side. Another flashbulb popped. Marina raised her arm, trying to shield her eyes from a third flash.

"Is it true the two of you just met?" A breathless woman, brassy gold hair piled high in corkscrew curls, pushed her way to Marina's side. "How did it feel to perform together tonight. It *was* the first time, wasn't it?" She gave Marina a bright, conspiratorial smile. Marina looked away, feeling distraught.

Everything seemed to be happening at once. The people gathered around them had doubled in number, and nobody was giving her time to answer the questions. Marina began to feel claustrophobic.

"How does it feel to premier such a masterpiece?" A

third voice materialized from somewhere behind the blond, and Marina craned her neck to see who had spoken.

"I . . . ," she began, but before she could speak, other voices cut in.

"Miss Prohaska, over here . . ."

"Mr. Fletcher, could you tell us . . ."

"How do you feel about . . ."

Confused and agitated, Marina tried to respond to the questions. She heard a rustle next to her, but in the clamor, she ignored it, determined to finish at least one complete answer for the microphones that had suddenly materialized in front of her. With her attention focused entirely on the reporters, it took her a moment to become aware of the unexpected silence that fell over the group.

Surprised, she looked up. The questions had abruptly ceased, and all eyes had swung away from her. Marina turned, her gaze following the others.

Adam Fletcher and his cello were disappearing out the stage door.

TWO

It took a second for the shock to sink in, then comprehension broke over Marina like a wave of ice water. Adam Fletcher had walked out on her! In front of the press, the television cameras, dozens of admirers, he'd turned his back and walked away.

"Adam!" She took a step to follow him, then stopped. What good would it do? Tears started in her eyes, and with a growing sense of outrage she blinked them back.

Slowly, she turned back to the mute crowd. Surprised faces regarded her, reflecting the stupefied bewilderment she felt.

She stood paralyzed, her flute clutched in one hand, the bouquet of roses drooping from the other, forgotten and unnoticed as they spilled out of her loose grasp to the floor. She swallowed convulsively.

"Well, well, well. I see the rumors about the temperamental Adam Fletcher are all true!" The deep voice of the bearded newsman broke the silence.

Marina glanced at him, thankful to have the crowd's attention diverted for a moment. Swiftly, she turned and started toward the dressing rooms.

"Miss Prohaska . . ." Turning, Marina found herself staring into the eye of a television camera. Her first impulse was to dodge around it, but whichever way she turned, it seemed to follow. Distractedly, Marina wondered if it had been there all along. Flushing in embarrassment, she felt like a bride left at the altar.

The thought brought a new, cold anger. Someday, somehow, Adam Fletcher would answer for tonight. Thrusting her shoulders back, Marina looked at the bearded reporter.

"I guess we agree on that score," she said tightly. The camera didn't matter any more. Nothing did, except getting out of there. She started toward the dressing rooms.

"Miss Prohaska . . ."

"Not now, please. Miss Prohaska will be available at the reception." To Marina's relief, Robert's voice cut through the rising protest of the press. Marina felt his hand at her elbow. He must have seen the whole, humiliating episode. Turning, she cast him a grateful smile.

"Thanks," she whispered.

A look of sympathy flashed across Robert's face.

"I'll hold them off while you get to the dressing room," he said in a low voice. "Then I'll pick you up for the reception."

Giving her arm a squeeze, he turned back to the press. With skill born of experience, he fielded the questions expertly. The sound of his voice faded as Marina hurried off. She knew the respite was only temporary. Even so, she felt lucky to have a few minutes to collect herself before facing the ordeal ahead.

Adam Fletcher leaned back against the luxurious upholstery of the chauffeur-driven limousine and closed his eyes. Removing his glasses, he rubbed his hand across his brow, slicking the damp hair back from his forehead before he folded the heavy frames and jammed them in his pocket. The tension of the last few hours began to drain away, leaving him limp and exhausted. All he wanted now was to get back to the hotel and the quiet of his room.

The limousine moved slowly, caught in the swell of

traffic leaving the theater, but Adam didn't mind. Insulated from the hubbub of the world outside, he sank into the cushions and let his weariness wash over him.

God, he was tired! He hadn't slept in—how long was it? Thirty-six hours? Forty-eight? Last night he'd played a chamber music recital in Paris, tonight a symphony concert in Vancouver. It was beginning to get him down, this constant jumping from place to place and concert to concert. And then there was that humiliating episode on the street in Paris three days ago. He threw his arm across his eyes, trying to drive the memory from his mind.

Maybe it was time to think seriously of cutting back.

He thrust the thought away. For a year, at least, he didn't have to travel. He'd take this time and get his life on track. *Then*, he'd deal with the future.

A feeling of relaxation crept over him and he let himself go, allowing his mind to rove back over the evening. He smiled, remembering the Debussy. The work was everything he'd known it would be.

From that first thrilling moment when he'd lifted the brittle, yellowed manuscript from the trunk, through the painful process of hand-copying the nearly indecipherable scribble, he'd been sure. The music was a rare treasure. And he, Adam Fletcher, had been the lucky one to discover it, and now to premiere it.

The limousine swerved to avoid a pedestrian, and the hard leather case holding Adam's cello crashed down on his knee. Awkwardly, Adam shoved it upright again. The chauffeur glanced in the rearview mirror.

"May I help, sir?" He slowed the vehicle, but Adam waved him on.

"It's all right."

Thrusting the instrument back in its original position, Adam fumbled for the seat belt. *That* would secure it. His hand brushed the rose, lying on the seat beside him. He closed his fingers around the stem. An unexpected stab of pain, the legacy of a lone thorn, jolted him. And with the momentary diversion, his mind locked on the one subject he'd been hoping to keep it away from.

The woman. Marina Prohaska. A vision of her loomed in his mind. When he'd glanced at her just before the music began, she'd appeared cool and professional. Her honey-gold hair was pulled back in a tight chignon and her eyes—their startling blue apparent even from his distance—glinted like glacial ice. His heart had dropped as he prepared himself to plod through the performance with someone who played faultlessly, but without warmth or passion.

But as the first clear, sensual tones of her flute filled the concert hall, he'd known he was wrong. Her music wrapped around him, luring and tempting him like a Lorelei's song. His response was immediate and powerful. And the moment his music joined hers, their spirits meshed.

His eyebrows drew together in a pained frown. The memory tortured him with its fresh reminder of what could never be. The incident in Paris, and Nina's reaction, had proven that. Jerking a white handkerchief from the breast pocket of his formal black tails, he wrapped it around his finger, stanching the tiny trickle of blood. He sat rigidly upright, trying to force his thoughts away from the woman. But no matter how determined his mind was to banish her, his body refused.

A deep ache came over him. The longing he'd suppressed with brittle sarcasm in Marina's presence now surged forth. The profound, almost religious, sense of exaltation he'd experienced swept over him again, shaking him to the very center of his soul.

An involuntary groan wrenched itself from his lips. This couldn't happen to him. He couldn't—wouldn't—allow it. Intimacy was for other people, not someone like him. He'd found that out long ago. Clenching his fists, he sat back, his eyes shut tight. He didn't notice when the long stem of the rose snapped from the tightness of his grip.

The limousine slowed, taking its place in line behind a row of other vehicles in front of the Hotel Vancouver. At the motion, Adam opened his eyes and peered up the block. The sidewalk and entry in front of the grand old hotel swarmed with elegantly-dressed people. Adam's limousine inched its way forward at a snail's pace, and his impatience grew at each tiny progression. Finally, with the vehicle nearly a half block from the entrance, Adam could wait no longer.

"Stop here."

"Here, sir?" Peering in the rearview mirror, the driver lifted a surprised eyebrow. Nonetheless, he eased toward the curb.

"Yes." The curtness of Adam's voice brooked no argument. Before the vehicle was fully stopped, he had reached around the cello to release the door handle.

Flustered, the driver hit the brakes, bringing the vehicle to an abrupt halt.

"Oh, please. Allow me, sir."

Without stopping the engine, he leaped out and opened Adam's door, removing the cello with the reverence of one accustomed to handling treasured instruments.

Ducking his head, Adam emerged from the limousine and fumbled in his pocket. He extracted a wad of bills, a mixture of francs and currency, both Canadian and American. He fished through the collection until he found several Canadian bills. Thrusting them into the driver's hand, he lifted his cello and turned to go.

"Wait, sir."

With unconcealed annoyance, Adam wheeled around.

"Well?"

"You forgot this." The driver held out the rose. The lower half of its stem dangled. He smiled almost apologetically. "I thought . . . well, maybe you wouldn't want to forget it." The look in his eye was one of hero worship. "You see, sir, I heard the concert tonight. And that new Debussy work—didn't it have a personal meaning for you? It seemed so—so . . . ." Suddenly aware of his presumptuousness, he stopped in embarrassment. "I thought—uh—

maybe this rose . . . ?'' When he spoke, an awed tremor roughened his voice. "It was a real privilege to attend the premiere performance. I'll never forget it."

Relenting, Adam accepted the rose and, for the first time since the concert, smiled.

"Thank you. I'll remember that." He watched the driver return to the limousine and pull out into the traffic lane. Then, with a sigh, he picked up his cello and started weaving through the people milling about. It must be some big do, to attract a crowd like this. Just his luck, to have to fight *more* crowds tonight.

He had barely entered the lobby when he heard someone call his name.

"Oh, Mr. Fletcher, the reception is this way."

The reception? Heart sinking, Adam realized the reason for the crowd. The gala celebration in honor of the premier of the Debussy work. They'd be expecting him to attend.

He looked around to see a middle-aged woman making her way toward him, a delighted smile on her face.

"I'm so glad you're here. We were afraid you'd be too tired to come, after the trip and the concert." Assuming he'd follow, she started toward a large doorway. Most of the crowd seemed headed in that direction, too. "Come with me. We have a secure room available for instruments."

Adam refused to budge. "I regret disappointing you, ma'am, but I *am* too tired. I'm here because I happen to be staying at this hotel."

The woman's face fell. "Well, surely . . ." she began, but Adam interrupted her.

"Madam, the *only* reason I'm at this hotel is to go directly to my room and get some sleep." He glanced quickly around the lobby. Unless he got out of there fast, *she* would show up. He didn't want another ordeal. Leaving the woman looking as if she might cry, Adam rotated ninety degrees and walked swiftly to the registration desk.

There, chaos reigned. The lone clerk was dashing about, trying to deal with a newly-arrived tour group. People and luggage blocked the desk and everyone spoke vehement French, cutting through the air with extravagant gestures. His testiness increasing, Adam searched for an opening so he could pick up his key, but it was like trying to breach a stampede. Finally, he gave up and stepped back, resigned to wait until the crowd thinned.

Minutes passed, and Adam kept glancing across the lobby toward the door, wishing he could make himself invisible. He couldn't take another encounter with *her*. Not tonight. But how could he hide? His cello was a dead giveaway. Shrinking into the collar of his coat, he tried to make himself as unobtrusive as possible. His mouth felt like cotton, and he swallowed convulsively, glaring at the noisy group gathered around the desk. Again, his thoughts settled on her. Marina.

Those eyes. Why couldn't he get them out of his mind? Though stark, icy blue from across the orchestra, at close range they had a tantalizing luminous quality, even when she was angry. And she *had* been angry when she found him backstage. If she was angry then, Adam could only imagine how furious she must be *now*.

A couple of bellhops arrived with carts and began piling the luggage from the tour group aboard. Adam watched the stacks grow higher and more precarious. One began to tilt and his breath caught. Just in time, a bellhop jumped to the rescue and rearranged the load. At last, the mob of people congealed around the carts and, with much waving of arms and excited babble, the group moved off toward the elevators.

"Sir . . . ? May I help you, sir?"

Adam had been so intrigued with the fate of the luggage that he'd forgotten his own situation.

"Uh—yes. Yes, of course."

Picking up his cello, he moved quickly to the desk and requested his key.

"Here it is, Mr. Fletcher." The clerk smiled at him, holding the key out. "Your luggage was taken to your room earlier. Would you like a bellhop for your instrument, sir?''

Adam shook his head and turned to go, eager to escape the exposed atmosphere of the lobby. Sooner or later, the press would notice him, and he had no more patience for such things tonight. Sticking the key in his pocket, he started for the elevators.

"Not so fast, Mr. Fletcher."

The low-pitched woman's voice had an ominously familiar sound. Adam froze, his chest suddenly tight.

"I don't believe we finished our conversation, Mr. Fletcher."

Adam hesitated. He must keep his emotions under control—keep the cool arrogance he'd managed before. *I can make her hate me*, he thought. Forcing his face into an impassive mask, he turned to face the woman.

"Really, Ms. Prohaska?" he inquired, dragging the "Ms." out. "You have more to say?"

He stared at her, allowing his eyes to travel slowly down her body and back to her face again. Her eyes widened at the mocking challenge of his gaze. Blue sparks, intense and stinging, shot from between her long dark lashes. Adam's fingers twitched with the need to reach out and touch the gleaming silk of her hair. He clutched the rose tightly, wishing he could put his hand in his pocket.

Marina took a step closer to him, nodding at the flower.

"I see you kept your rose this time."

"But, of course." With exaggerated motions, he bent his head to inhale deeply. "Such an appropriate memory of the evening." Lifting an eyebrow, he smiled at her, careful to keep his eyes free of emotion.

Marina also smiled. "I'm flattered you'd want such a memento. I have something else for you, too."

Not quite certain what to expect, Adam watched Marina come even closer and lift her hand. With detached fascination, he observed tiny details—the short, neat musician's fingernails, the sprinkling of golden hairs on her forearm, the tensing of muscles as the hand drew back. Then the hand flashed toward him, and the details blurred into a hard, stinging slap.

For a moment, Adam was too stunned to react. The rose slipped from his grasp and fell to the floor. Dazed, he lifted his hand to touch the fierce burning on his cheek. The cacophony of voices behind him and the flare of flashbulbs contributed to the surrealism.

Unnoticed by either of them, a CBUT-TV cameraman had come up and stood a few feet away, recording the exchange. Several reporters hovered nearby.

Marina still stood in front of him, her eyes blazing, her mouth set in a tight, furious line. Adam's eyes locked on hers and time stopped. For a brief instant, her mask of anger faltered, and in that millisecond she lay exposed. He glimpsed the pain that lay just under the surface.

Adam's breath caught, and he felt a dangerous flicker of response. But as quickly as it had slipped, the shield returned, and he again faced only hard, cold anger. Relief washed over him. Anger he could deal with.

The crowd he'd barely noticed before now seemed loud and stifling. The awareness that the entire exchange had been witnessed by the press—and no doubt recorded for posterity by the cameras—turned his face and neck a dull, brick red. His cheek still stung and he kept his hand over it, knowing the imprint of Marina's fingers would be vividly etched.

Taking a deep, careful breath, he stepped back, rising to his full height. Marina's head tilted as she kept her eyes locked to his.

Slowly, Adam took his hand from his cheek. A collective gasp rippled through the crowd of onlookers as the handprint flamed into view. Marina's face paled. Adam grasped the handle of his cello case and lifted it. With meticulous deliberation, he arranged the instrument against his hip, then stood for an instant, his eyes probing hers.

Her gaze shifted to the handprint, and the angry set of

her lips softened. When she met his stare again, her eyes were wide. She opened her mouth to speak.

Quickly, Adam seized his opportunity. His lip curled in a caricature of a smile and he made a small salute with his free hand.

"Touché, madame. You may be sure I won't forget *this* gift."

Not waiting to see her reaction, he turned on his heel and left. Moving swiftly through the crowd, he pushed aside those who failed to get out of his way. At the elevator, he jabbed the button furiously, ignoring the explosion of voices that followed his departure. He kept his back rigid, refusing to give any hint of the chaos he felt. The vultures had their story now. Maybe they'd leave him in peace.

The car arrived, and Adam stepped quickly inside, pressing the button for a floor two levels above his own. He turned to face the lobby, willing the door to close quickly. Several reporters were headed his direction with determined looks on their faces. After an agonizing interval, the doors began to inch toward each other.

A boy around ten years of age detached himself from the crowd and tore across the lobby toward Adam's elevator. He arrived just before the doors met and thrust his hand between them—the forgotten rose, now limp and lifeless, tight in his grip. Adam caught the door.

"Mr. Fletcher, you dropped this!" The boy peered anxiously through the opening.

Heaving a sigh, Adam took the rose out of the boy's hand. With a rueful smile, he held the flower up and nodded. The boy grinned.

"I knew you'd want to keep it," he said. He pulled his hand out, then reached in again. This time with a program and ballpoint pen clutched in his hand. "Would you give me your autograph . . . please? I'm going to be a cellist like you, when I grow up!"

Adam gave a chuckle, and suddenly the whole evening

seemed ludicrous. He took the program and scrawled his name on it. He started to hand it back, then stopped. "What's your name, son?"

The boy's eyes glowed. "Christopher."

Adam wrote "Best of luck, Christopher" above his name and shoved it through the opening between the doors.

"Oh, wow! Thanks a *lot*, Mr. Fletcher!"

"No," Adam said. "Thank *you*."

With a numb feeling, Marina watched the elevator doors close behind Adam. Her hand still stung from its contact with his face. But other than that, she felt like she was wrapped in cotton. Standing motionless, she waited, expecting a rush of triumph. But it didn't come.

All she felt was a sense of loss. And humiliation. Once again, the man had made her look foolish. The heady sense of angry righteousness that had sustained her faded. In its place a familiar, dull ache settled in.

It was the same old story. Her music was what people wanted from her, and that was all. The bright bubble of elation that had propelled her toward Adam flattened like a punctured tire. How could her instincts be so wrong? She *knew* their music had been the same exalting experience for him as for her. They'd touched each other's souls. How could he respond so deeply to her music, then reject her?

Wearily, she turned toward the reception room, ignoring the clamor of the voices around her. All she could think of now was getting through the rest of this miserable evening and going home.

A gentle touch on her shoulder brought her to a halt. Swinging around, she found herself facing Robert Graves. He regarded her soberly, his eyes sympathetic.

"Feel better now?" he asked softly.

Marina shook her head. She didn't feel better at all. The sight of Robert brought forth a powerful tide of remorse.

"Oh, Robert, I'm so sorry." Marina's eyes stung, and

she longed for the soothing flow of tears to bring relief. "I've embarrassed you and the Philharmonic." Her voice shook.

Robert smiled and, though he remained grave, Marina detected a hint of humor behind his seriousness. She rubbed her hand across her face tiredly. Robert threw his arm over her shoulders and gave her a quick squeeze. Leaning close to her ear, he whispered, "Don't take it so hard. He deserved it."

"But . . ."

"No buts. Just come in and enjoy the reception." With gentle persistence, he guided her toward the reception room, where a string quartet was playing and a large crowd stood around, champagne glasses in hand, chatting enthusiastically about the evening's concert.

"Marina!" Jerry, the rotund cellist Adam had displaced, wove his way through the people, a tiny, plain woman in tow. As they approached, Robert smiled and gave Marina's shoulder a brief pat.

"Let me find some champagne for us. Stay right here." With an encouraging smile, he wandered off into the crowd, giving Jerry and his companion a quick wave.

"Congratulations, darling. You were magnificent!"

Jerry threw his arms around Marina in a bear hug and planted a big kiss on each of her cheeks. Nonplussed, Marina stiffened, trying to draw back from the warm, friendly embrace. Jerry laughed, but released her immediately and turned to his companion, keeping his hand on Marina's waist with friendly ease.

"Marina, this is Annie Taub, harpist for the Philharmonic." Annie's face broke into a brilliant smile, and the plainness gave way to mischievous humor. She held her hand out. When Marina shook it, the grip was firm and confident.

"We saw what happened backstage at the theater . . ." Marina's face reddened. ". . . and in the lobby." Annie's voice shook with intensity. "Good for you!"

For a moment Marina couldn't speak because of the lump in her throat. Everyone was too kind. Her sense of guilt loomed larger than ever.

"I shouldn't have done it," she said softly. "I just . . ."

"Here we are," Robert's voice interrupted. Thrusting a glass of champagne into her hand, he grinned at her. "Drown your sorrows in this."

Marina smiled and took a sip of the champagne. It was delicately sweet, with an edge of tartness. The slight sting of its bubbles on her tongue created a pleasant, tingly sensation. She took another sip, and discovered a thirst she hadn't realized before. Because pre-concert nerves had forestalled any thought of dinner, the champagne now hit her empty stomach and settled there, producing a delightful warmth.

Draining the glass, she handed it back to Robert.

"Mm-m. That's good." To her surprise, she found her depression lightening.

"More?" Robert offered her his own untouched glass and she accepted it gladly. She drained half the contents in a single swallow. Robert and Jerry exchanged a look.

"Marina, you'd better slow down." Jerry laid a hand on her arm as she began to lift the glass again.

Marina giggled. "I'm okay—just a little thirsty." She finished off the rest of the champagne. "Is there some more of this stuff?" She wondered why she had dreaded the reception. Looking around, she saw a number of people who looked like they might be interesting to talk to.

"Here, hold this." Shoving the empty glass into Jerry's hand, she started toward a couple she'd noticed a few minutes before, a broad smile on her face. They looked the type to be benefactors of the Philharmonic, and she should thank them for making all this possible.

"Grab her!"

A hand clasped her wrist firmly and Marina came to an abrupt halt. Wheeling around, she found Robert standing close beside her, his grip tight and unrelenting. He slipped his arm around her waist. Jerry stood on her other side.

At first, Marina felt a twinge of annoyance. Then, seeing the worried expressions on their faces, she began to laugh. "Don't worry about me, you two. I'm fine now." She tried to move away from Robert, but he kept her firmly at his side.

"I have to leave you now, Marina." He looked at her uncertainly. "You know I have to circulate and shake hands with our patrons."

"I'll join you," Marina said promptly. With an unsteady finger, she pointed in the direction of the couple she noticed earlier. "I was just going to tell those folks how much I appreciate their support."

Robert blanched. The couple in question was the Premier of British Columbia and his wife. Robert threw a beseeching glance at Jerry and Jerry took Marina's arm.

"I've got a better idea. Let's get a bunch of the musicians together and go out for Chinese food."

Marina considered the matter for a moment, then airily waved him off. "I'd rather stay here."

Jerry didn't relax his grip. He smiled through clenched teeth. "Okay, let's stick around here, then." Behind Marina's head, he raised his eyebrow at Annie, and she immediately came to Marina's other side.

"Marina," she said, "have you met John Deering yet?" Through a serene blur, Marina saw a man approaching. It wasn't until he was right in front of her that she recognized him as the concertmaster of the Philharmonic. They hadn't yet met.

With a broad, friendly smile, John approached the little group.

"Greetings." He was short and compact, with a heavy black beard. Without the twinkle in his eye, he might have looked menacing. He exchanged salutations with Jerry and Annie, then extended his hand to Marina.

"So, *this* is the formidable Miss Prohaska!"

Marina drew back and gave him an appraising look.

"Formidable?" She began to giggle and groped for his

hand, shaking it energetically. "Formidable. I like that." Turning to Jerry and Annie, she grinned at them, weaving slightly. "Hear what he called me?"

Leaning down, she gave John a smooch on his whiskery cheek.

A waiter approached with a tray of champagne, and before anyone could stop her, Marina grabbed another full glass of the golden liquid. "I propose a toast!" She looked around at the others, her face expectant.

With dubious glances, each person took a glass. Marina held her glass high. The glass wavered and a few drops spilled on her hand. Switching hands, she shook the droplets off, then raised the glass again.

"To tonight." She took a healthy swallow and the others followed suit, looking uncomfortable. Marina raised her glass again.

"To all of you." She drank, and without waiting for the others, lifted her glass once more.

"And to the formidable—Adam Fletcher!"

Everyone froze.

"Marina, don't you think . . ." Jerry began, but Marina just laughed.

Turning, she walked swiftly to a large, potted fig tree a few feet away. Before anyone could stop her, she held her arm straight out and allowed the last golden drops of champagne to splash into the plant. Setting the glass carefully on the edge of the planter, she returned to the others. Weaving just a little, she faced them, hands on her hips.

"Thank you for joining me," she said soberly. "And now . . ." she looked from one startled face to the others with a slightly bleary-eyed grin, ". . . I'm ready for Chinese food!"

THREE

Marina awoke to pain—a dull throbbing sensation that consumed her brain. She lay still for a moment, then tentatively fluttered her eyelids, allowing a crack of light to penetrate. Brilliant sunshine tore in like a bullet. Marina winced. She'd never touch champagne again!

A gentle breeze wafted through the open window, bringing with it the pungent, salty fragrance of low tide on English Bay. In a minute, she'd get up and find some aspirin. Then she'd pull on her sweat pants and T-shirt and walk to the beach. It might help.

Gathering her energy, she shoved the covers aside and sat up. The room lurched and her stomach turned over. Above her eyes, a pounding began. Groaning, Marina fell back.

Immediately, memories of the night before taunted her. What had happened to the magic she and Adam had experienced during the performance of *Chansons de la Nuit*? How had it deteriorated to the tacky little scene at the hotel?

Her heart sank as she remembered the sensation of her hand coming in contact with his face. Oh, Lord, what a fool she'd made of herself!

Rolling into a ball, she closed her eyes tight and tried to

drive the thoughts from her mind. But Adam Fletcher's face, locked in that strange, vulnerable look she'd caught so briefly, remained etched on her brain.

As she lay there, the impact of her actions hit her. Last night's scene would probably be slathered all over the papers. What kind of repercussions might there be for the orchestra?

How could she ever face Robert? Kind, patient Robert. How could she face the other musicians? She pulled the blankets over her head, retreating to the dark, warm haven.

But there was no escape. Waves of guilt and remorse beat upon her like a storm-driven tide, refusing her the comfort of forgetfulness. Flayed by her thoughts, she lay rigid, moaning as another complication struck her.

There was a faculty meeting this morning.

She wouldn't go. Everyone on the Conservatory faculty played in the Philharmonic. Today, she couldn't cope with their anger—or worse—their disgust. Marina shuddered. She couldn't face *him*.

Her head pounded relentlessly, a steady tattoo of pain that tore through her brain, feeding on her distress. She was trapped. No matter how painful, how frightening, she couldn't escape the torture. Marina whimpered. In her distraught state, the long-repressed terror of a small child struggled through the bonds of her consciousness.

No! That was in the past. It didn't matter any more. With a convulsive movement, she burrowed deeper, wrapping the blankets around her in a tight cocoon. Here, sealed off from the rest of the world, she was hidden. Safe. But alone—so achingly alone. It was like . . . Oh, God, no!

Panicking, Marina tried to thrust the covers aside, but her arms tangled in the sheets, wrapping them more tightly. Dim memories of a helpless six-year-old girl, trying to hide from the unbearable world around her, rose from the past with horrifying clarity.

"Mama, Mama . . ." The thin whimper of the child's

voice reached Marina's ears, muffled by the tight wrapping around her head. Frightened and disoriented, Marina struggled to free herself.

"Mama . . ."

With a final thrust, Marina broke free. Ignoring the pounding in her head, she sat up, listening. But she only heard the thump of her heart. Gradually the quiet room settled into focus, and Marina knew it had been her own voice crying out, reawakened from the childhood she'd so carefully buried.

All the emptiness came flooding back, all her futile dreams. Her music was supposed to protect her from pain and loneliness. But now even it had let her down. Marina sat there for a long time, chest heaving, fighting back the terrifying memories that tried to surface.

Eventually, she calmed down and sat quietly, head pounding, staring out the window at the sunwashed world. At last, she rose and made her way to the bathroom. Stripping off her nightgown, she dropped it to the floor and stepped into the shower. The stinging punishment of the hot water felt good. She remained under its barrage until the water ran cold.

Shivering, she turned off the taps and stood for a moment, her cold, wet hair lying dank and dripping on her shoulders. Though the shower had cleansed her body, the aching depression remained. She felt exhausted and ill.

Gathering her hair, she wrung it out, reaching for a towel to wrap, turban style, around her head. She drew another towel around herself like a blanket. Gradually, the shivering stopped, but the enervating weariness remained.

Automatically, she went through her morning routine. First toweling her hair, then drying it with the electric dryer. She took out clean underwear from the dresser drawer and bent to step into her panties.

A glimpse of her reflection in the mirror stopped her. Walking closer, she turned slowly until her back was to the mirror. She closed her eyes for a moment. Then, without giving herself a chance to change her mind, turned her head and looked over her shoulder at the pale flesh of her back and buttocks. Faint white stripes crisscrossed the otherwise unblemished skin, from just below her ribs to the tops of her thighs.

Trembling, Marina ran her hands across the scars, feeling the ridges under her fingertips. It had been years since she'd dared look at them—ugly, disgusting reminders of her past.

No wonder Adam had rejected her. He must have sensed that the best part of her was to be found in her music. The rest was not worth bothering with. Closing her eyes, she tried to block out the memory that rushed into her consciousness. The memory of Ramon, who had taught her all too well—all too painfully—that men didn't want someone like her.

Thank God, Adam had sensed that. Humiliating as it was, thank God for last night. It had reminded her once more that she was only safe when she kept the wall between her and the rest of the world high and strong.

When she walked into the faculty lounge at the conservatory, the meeting was already under way. As the door opened, Robert stopped speaking, pointedly waiting for her to find a seat.

Embarrassed, she looked frantically around the room. Every seat was filled except one on the far side in front of the windows.

Directly behind Adam Fletcher.

Marina's throat went dry. Stiffly, she threaded her way through the maze of people and chairs, praying she wouldn't trip.

When she reached her place, she sank gratefully into the seat and fastened her eyes on Robert. The suggestion of a twinkle lit his eye.

"Comfortable, Miss Prohaska?" He raised an eyebrow.

Face burning, Marina nodded. She heard a chuckle

behind her. *Can't he just get on with the meeting?* she thought desperately.

"Have you sheathed your dagger, Miss Prohaska, or do I need to worry about a stab in the back?" An all-too-familiar voice drew her attention from Robert to the seat in front of her. Adam had turned and was regarding her over his shoulder. Though the words were murmured softly, he might as well have shouted. Jerking upright, she glared at him, but it was too late. He'd already turned back, his attention now on what Robert was saying.

Raging impotently, Marina sat and fumed. Damn the man. Why couldn't he have just ignored her? That's how she planned to deal with *him*. She directed her gaze to Robert, listening to his words with exaggerated concentration.

The agenda dealt with schedules and routines for the fall quarter, whose start was just days away. In addition to performing in the B.C. Philharmonic, Marina would be teaching individual students and handling master classes in chamber music and woodwind technique. A light schedule. Much lighter than she'd anticipated when she accepted the visiting-professor appointment.

The discussion droned on and on. Try as she would, Marina couldn't keep her mind on it. To make things worse, every time she looked toward the front of the room, Adam Fletcher's head got in the way.

Without realizing it, she found herself studying the way his hair curled in damp, black ringlets over his collar. An attempt had apparently been made to brush the shower-wet mane smooth, but it was drying in an unruly mass of springy tendrils. Marina felt a sudden urge to run her hand over them.

Most of the men sat upright and attentive, looking formal and uncomfortable in their suits and ties. But Adam, clad in jeans and a plaid flannel shirt, sprawled lackadaisically, one foot resting on the rungs of the chair in front of him. As time passed, he grew restless, frequently shifting his position—sometimes draping an arm over the back of his chair, other times loosely clasping his hands around his bent knee.

Each time he moved, the same fresh, soapy scent drifted into Marina's nostrils—a remembered fragrance that she found herself anticipating. It became almost a game, guessing how long it would be before he rearranged himself.

She tried to listen to the proceedings, but found herself distracted time after time by some newly-noticed detail of Adam's presence—the occasional glint of silver in his hair; the broad, powerful hands with their strong musician's fingers and clean, close-trimmed nails. At one point, he unbuttoned the cuffs of his shirt and rolled his sleeves up to the elbow. Marina found herself entranced with the dark tangle of crisp hairs that covered his forearms. Willfully, her mind zeroed in on the way the slightly rough texture of the hair would feel against the warm smoothness of his skin if she were to skim her hands over his arm.

She blushed. With determination, she fastened her gaze on Robert, straining to keep her thoughts on what he was saying. But her mind kept wandering back to Adam—his disturbing figure in front of her and the memories of the night before. Once again, embarrassment and humiliation thrust tormenting barbs into her consciousness, standing out in stark relief against the perfection of the musical experience.

Why? Why had he treated her that way? She closed her eyes, hoping somehow to drive the pain away by shutting out the sight of him.

The scraping of chairs on the wood floor made her start. The meeting was over. Opening her eyes, she stood quickly, poised to flee. But she found herself blocked in by others who seemed in no hurry. At this—the first meeting of the year, they chatted amiably—exchanging news and gossip from the summer break.

Keeping her eyes away from Adam, Marina waited for an opening to slip through, a stiff little smile plastered on her face. She knew he stood nearby. His scent permeated the air she breathed, sending her heart pounding. The hair on the back of her neck prickled, and when the deep timbre of his voice sounded close by her ear, she felt no surprise.

"Do you intend to stand there all day, or are you going to leave?"

With a guilty glance, Marina saw that the aisle ahead of her had emptied. She half-turned toward Adam, an apology rising to her lips. One look at him, standing with arms folded glaring at her, and the apology died. Without saying a word, she turned her back on him and started moving between the rows of chairs.

"Marina! Adam! Can you wait a minute?"

Marina whirled toward the front of the room to see Robert smiling in her direction. He beckoned to her from where he stood with two other people. She looked around at Adam, and found his eyes on her. Scowling, he moved a chair aside and motioned her ahead of him.

Marina pushed another chair out of the way, creating her own passage. Without a glance in his direction, she started forward, winding through the obstructing furniture. She felt Adam's eyes burn into her back.

Reaching Robert was like landing on a safe island in a turbulent sea. His hand on her arm gave her a sense of security and protection against the unnerving challenge of Adam's manner. Drawing her into the group, Robert smiled at Adam, just behind her.

"Marina, Adam, I'd like you to meet Ian Campbell and Jacob West. They're from the British Columbia Arts Foundation."

Marina shook hands with the two men, murmuring a polite greeting. She stood stiffly while Adam acknowledged the introduction. Now that his attention wasn't focused on her, he seemed quite friendly and charming.

"Mr. West, Mr. Campbell . . . ," he said.

Mr. Campbell beamed. "Ian and Jacob, please," he said, his voice warm and friendly. "We heard the concert last night. It was outstanding. Simply outstanding. Jacob and I agree that the two of you are a remarkable combination." He smiled into Marina's eyes. "One that we must capitalize upon."

Marina glanced at Robert. He smiled blandly, but his fingers tightened slightly on her arm. She opened her mouth, but before she could say a word, she heard Adam's voice.

"Thank you. It was a most memorable occasion." He gazed steadily at Marina, his eyes opaque behind his glasses. Marina looked uncertainly from him to Robert and the two men.

"Unfortunately, these gentlemen weren't able to attend the reception." Robert's eyes belied the regret in his voice. He took his hand away from Marina's arm and she felt her tenseness begin to drain away. Maybe the word hadn't got out. She was able to summon a smile.

"I'm flattered you were so impressed." She waited. The muscles in her jaws began to ache.

"Ian and Jacob have a proposition for the two of you," Robert said. Though he appeared to be calm and relaxed, Marina noticed a nervous tic in his left eyelid. She glanced at Adam. Silent, he watched the others, his eyes flicking back and forth between speakers. He had moved a few feet to the large, white-marble fireplace and leaned casually against it, one elbow resting on the mantle.

Mr. West glanced at his watch. "It's nearly one o'clock. Perhaps we could discuss the matter over lunch."

Marina's heart thudded. The thought of eating a single bite nauseated her.

"Sounds like a great idea to me," Robert said. He looked at Adam and Marina. "Okay with you?"

Adam pushed away from the fireplace. "I don't mind." His eyes chilled Marina as they came to rest on her. "It's up to the lady."

Marina felt trapped. The last thing she wanted was to endure his presence any longer than necessary. But what could she do? Wordlessly, she nodded.

Jacob smiled broadly. "Wonderful! I'll drive all of you."

Oh, Lord, Marina thought. *Couldn't it be someplace we could walk to?* At Robert's gesture, she went ahead of him—and alongside Adam—out of the building to the car.

The trip to the restaurant seemed endless. Rather than choosing an eating place in downtown Vancouver, their hosts took them across the Lion's Gate bridge to West Vancouver. Marina, Robert, and Adam sat in the back seat of Jacob's Mercedes, with Marina jammed between the two men.

Although the seat was spacious, Adam's large frame occupied nearly half of it. Marina squeezed as close to Robert as possible, but she couldn't avoid being crowded against Adam. The warmth of his body and the feel of his knee against hers teased her senses. Try as she might, she couldn't keep her mind from drifting to the response she'd felt from him on the stage the evening before. The memory was tantalizing.

It was torture.

After an eternity the car pulled up in the parking lot at the foot of the Grouse Mountain tramway. Jacob parked, then turned to the back seat.

"I hope no one's squeamish about heights. We have reservations at the Grouse Nest Restaurant." He beamed at them, and Marina felt her stomach turn over. Looking up, she gazed at the steep mountainside and shuddered. She *hated* trams. Even when she was skiing and *had* to use them, she hated them. Looking at the sheer incline, strewn with huge boulders and jagged granite outcroppings, she shuddered.

Chatting amiably, the others were starting ahead. Marina trailed behind, pretending to adjust her purse strap, gathering her nerve for the ordeal.

"Are you all right?" Robert asked in a low voice.

Marina nodded. Looking up, she saw Adam's eyes on her and felt her face go hot.

He raised one eyebrow and gave a knowing smile.

"Worried about something?"

Marina straightened and stared him in the eye. "Of course not," she said levelly. Moving quickly past him, she stepped into the cable car and sat down on one of the benches. The others followed her in, and in a few moments the doors closed and the car began to move. Marina clutched the seat and stared straight ahead.

When the car stopped at the unloading platform, she glanced quickly at Adam, but he was deep in conversation with Ian. As they left the car, he appeared oblivious to Marina's presence.

A group of Japanese tourists waited to board the tram, chattering enthusiastically, cameras in hand. Knees still shaking from the ride, Marina made her way through the crowd, and stopped to wait for the others.

The rest of the men had stopped a short distance away and stood in a huddle, talking seriously. Probably planning the proposal they were going to make, Marina thought. She had a sense of foreboding.

"Now, that wasn't so bad, was it?" Sarcasm tinged Adam's deep voice as he came up beside her. Marina stiffened. Deliberately ignoring his words, she turned her back and gazed at the view. But she couldn't keep her mind on it. Her senses tingled with his presence, as if an energy field emanated from him. Though instinct told her to flee, she could do nothing but stand there, gripping the rail in front of her, paralyzed by the voltage he emitted.

"Ready to go in?" Marina jumped at Robert's voice. In her preoccupation, she hadn't noticed when the conference broke up.

"Yes . . . yes, of course," she said. With a furtive look toward Adam, she saw he had already joined the other men.

Inside, they were escorted to a round window table. To Marina's dismay, the hosts graciously insisted that she and Adam take seats beside each other to enjoy the best view.

Marina slid her chair away from Adam, but with all of them around the table, she could only move a few inches. There was no avoiding an occasional brushing of arms or the potential of knees or feet colliding under the table. Her throat went dry at the thought.

She opened her menu and pretended to study it. But every cell in her body screamed out in awareness. Adam paid no attention to her. Instead, he charmed their hosts with extravagant compliments about the choice of restaurant and the view. They seemed pleased and flattered by his praise.

If only they knew what a rude, egotistical man he actually is, Marina thought. She sat with a wooden smile on her face, trying to act as if she were enjoying herself. But her stomach churned with nervousness. The queasy feeling she had awakened with returned full force. What was the proposition they were supposed to discuss?

She glanced at Robert and found him watching her. He looked away quickly. Marina's senses went to full alert. *He looks guilty*, she thought.

By the time the food arrived, she could hardly stand the thought of eating. She'd ordered a chicken salad, but the tender pieces of marinated chicken in their bed of romaine tasted like so much sawdust to her.

Although Adam pretended total preoccupation with his meal, his mind was only half taken up with the seafood platter in front of him. Marina's presence at his side made his nerves prickle with awareness. He struggled to maintain a calm demeanor. From the moment she arrived at the faculty meeting until now, he'd been trying to remain detached—to keep his senses aloof. But it was a losing battle.

The antagonism she radiated brought out all his competitive instincts, and his natural inclination would have been to defeat that hostility—to delve into the mystery he sensed beneath the surface and find out what made her tick. But he didn't dare follow his instincts. In penetrating her veneer, he might find more than he was prepared to handle. That would be dangerous. Their performance the evening before had already warned him of that.

After several bites, Marina could finish no more. She sat back in her chair and took a sip of the sparkling cider Ian and Jacob had insisted on. It was brisk and refreshing, with a pleasant apple tang. But after the first swallow, Marina nearly gagged. It was also alcoholic. Abruptly, she set the glass down.

Robert had been watching her, and signaled the waiter for coffee.

Silence fell while the others ate, giving Marina a brief respite. Now that Adam was busy with his meal, the pressure eased.

"How do you like our country, Marina?" Ian asked. Her sense of well-being abruptly dissipated as everyone turned to her.

"So far, I love it," she said. She felt self-conscious under the attentive stares. "Of course, I've only been here for a few weeks, but I'm impressed already." Nodding toward the window, she indicated the view beyond. "I've never seen anything so spectacular."

Ian and Jacob exchanged a look. "That's why we brought you up here," Jacob said. Leaning forward, he smiled proudly. "And this is only a small part of what British Columbia has to offer."

The waiter came with more coffee. At Ian's signal, he left the pot on the table, taking the empty plates away with him. A few minutes later, he returned with a cart of pastries and desserts. Marina's stomach lurched at the sight of the elaborately-decorated cakes and filled sweets. She shook her head and looked away.

Adam selected a large slab of devil's food cake piled high with white, fluffy frosting and coconut. After the meal he'd polished off, Marina couldn't imagine how it would be possible for him to finish dessert, too. But with casual unconcern, he demolished the cake—plus a second piece.

Finally done, he leaned back in his chair and picked up his coffee. For the first time since his food arrived he spoke, smiling almost apologetically. "I haven't eaten since lunch on the plane from Paris yesterday."

"Well, I hope your energy is sufficiently restored to talk business," Jacob said. Picking up the coffee pot, he poured refills for Marina, then Adam.

Ian's eyes flicked around the table, resting briefly on Marina before they moved on. Her neck hairs prickled. Whatever the men had in mind, it *did* involve both her and Adam. Her heart thumped in dread.

Adam regarded the men across the table warily. He hoped their idea would be something he could live with. It involved both him and Marina. He was sure of that. No matter what it entailed, he'd make certain he and Marina kept their distance. Setting his coffee cup down, he lounged in his chair, hooking his arm over the back. The casual facade was a habit he'd developed long ago to conceal uncertainty and discomfort. It worked well.

At the same time, Marina shifted her position, causing her shoulder to come in contact with his hand. An electrical charge crackled between them.

For the first time since they entered the restaurant, their gazes met. The cool, deep blue of her eyes frosted over him. There was nothing there but glittering hostility. Adam's first reaction was desolation. Quickly, he forced that out of his mind. That was how he wanted her to respond, wasn't it?

Ian offered the coffee pot around again, then set it down, his face thoughtful. Both Marina and Adam watched him carefully.

Marina swallowed hard, fighting back the sick feeling in her stomach.

Adam tried to ignore the roaring in his ears.

Everyone at the table sensed the tension. Looking from one to the other, Ian smiled and leaned forward, resting his elbows on the table and steepling his fingers.

"Perhaps, before getting into our proposal, I should tell you about the Foundation. It was set up in the fifties by a number of prominent British Columbia corporations. The purpose of the Foundation is to encourage excellence in the arts and make outstanding art and artists available in all parts of the province." He glanced at Marina and Adam, judging their reaction.

"Every year we select one artist or group for a substantial grant. The terms of this grant require the recipients to spend several months traveling throughout the province and other parts of Canada, performing concerts and offering seminars and workshops." He smiled. "I probably don't need to say that winning the grant is considered most prestigious."

Marina tried hard to concentrate on his words, but her head was pounding too hard. The effect of the aspirin had worn off, and the headache was back worse than ever. Out of the corner of her eye, she could see Adam sitting deathly still, his face impassive.

Ian sat back, and Jacob took over. "This year, the grant is being awarded to the B.C. Conservatory." He beamed across the table at Marina and Adam. "More specifically, it's going to a chamber music group sponsored by the Conservatory, with the condition that the two of you be the featured performers." Marina felt her face go pale. She sensed Adam's sudden rigidity beside her.

Smiling from one to the other, Ian held his hand out across the table. "May I be the first to congratulate you both?"

_____ FOUR _____

An expectant silence hung in the air. Frantically, Marina cast about for an appropriate response, but her mind was frozen. Robot-like, she parroted Adam's words of appreciation and curved her lips upward in an attempt to smile.

The others were rising and she followed their lead. Ian offered his arm, gallantly escorting her toward the door.

"We're delighted with this partnership," he said warmly. "After the remarkable rapport you exhibited last evening, I know it's going to be a memorable year."

Marina swallowed, trying to suppress the nausea welling up. With a wooden smile, she murmured her thanks.

She glanced at Adam. His gaze met hers unflinchingly. His face was inscrutable.

The air in Robert's office was stifling. Marina's head pounded in a steady, pulsating throb as she gathered her thoughts. "Robert, I . . ."

"Well, I see you didn't waste any time getting here."

Both Robert and Marina whirled at the sound of Adam's voice. He stood in the doorway, a small smile curving his lips. His eyes bored into Marina. "I presume you're on the same errand as I am."

Robert's eyes widened, then he stepped forward, his

face bland and friendly. "Come in, Adam. We were just discussing the Foundation grant."

Adam stepped forward, and suddenly the room seemed not just stifling to Marina, but unbearably crowded. She dropped into a chair on the far side of Robert's desk.

Adam sat down and slung his arm over the chair's back, slouching carelessly on the soft velvet upholstery. From her vantage point, Marina watched him. How could he be so casual, when she was tied in knots? Then she saw the small pulse above his left eye. He noticed her gaze and took his heavy glasses out of his shirt pocket. With studied unconcern, he unfolded them and put them on.

Aha! So the cool Mr. Fletcher is not so blasé after all, she thought. The realization brought her a tiny measure of comfort.

Robert had taken his own place and was regarding both of them closely. "Well, now that we're all here, we might as well get this out in the open." He looked from one to the other.

Adam leaned forward. "There's nothing about a Foundation grant in my contract. I have no intention of playing in the group." He sat back and folded his arms across his chest.

Robert slid his chair aside and opened a file drawer in his desk. He rummaged around for a moment, then pulled out a pair of documents. Marina recognized one as the contract she had signed. Without speaking, he shoved it across the desk to her and the other one to Adam.

"If you will look at page four, paragraph two . . ." Robert waited for them to find the place. "I believe it states, 'In addition to teaching responsibilities, the faculty member shall take part in Conservatory-sponsored performance groups as stipulated by the Director.' "

He looked at Adam, his eyes steely. "As director of this school, I must insist that both you and Marina participate in the Foundation program."

Marina opened her mouth to speak, but Robert silenced her with a glance.

, "I must warn you both, this is a major achievement for us. I won't allow prima-donna behavior from either of you."

Adam sat up straight, dropping his arms to the chair arms. "You can't force us to . . ."

"I can, and I will," Robert interrupted, the congeniality gone from his manner. "And please believe, Mr. Fletcher and Ms. Prohaska, if you choose to break your contracts, or to sabotage the grant in any way, I will not hesitate to take legal action."

With that, he rose, his face stern. "And now, folks, I have a great deal of work to do."

Marina sat stunned. This was Robert. Her friend. How could he betray her like this? Adam was on his feet, striding toward the door. Feeling confused and defeated, Marina rose and followed. As she passed Robert, she looked at him, hoping—praying—for some sign of softening. But his mouth was set in a hard line. There would be no help from him.

In a flash of anger, she opened her mouth to speak, then closed it again. He had left her no choice. Like it or not, she and Adam Fletcher were stuck with each other.

The final chords of Ravel's *Introduction and Allegro* fell on Marina's ears with depressing blandness. She looked around at the other performers and saw the same disappointment in every face. Why couldn't they create that spark of excitement the music deserved?

Across from her, Adam sat quietly, his face thoughtful. A few hours after Robert issued his ultimatum, the scene in the hotel lobby had appeared on the evening television newscasts. As a result, the Foundation had nearly withdrawn the grant.

Since then, Marina had been on her best behavior. Considering Adam's subdued manner, it appeared he was making the same effort. But the music just wasn't coming together the way it should.

"Well, people, we seem to have a problem." John Deering, the first violinist, scrutinized the faces around him. "Does anyone have an idea why it's not working?"

Adam maintained his silence, his mind churning. He couldn't say it out loud, but he knew. It was him. Pure and simple. He was holding back. After that unsettling experience at the concert, he was afraid to open himself up again—afraid to risk reviving that magical communion he had felt with Marina. He glanced at her. Although she appeared self-composed and reserved, as usual, something about those ice-blue eyes revealed a hint of the same frustration he was feeling.

"Maybe more rehearsals . . . ?" Annie Taub suggested.

"I don't think that's the problem," John said.

There was a murmur of assent from the rest of the group. Adam shrugged. "What do you suggest, then?"

For a moment there was silence, then Marina spoke quietly. "We may not need more rehearsal, but I don't know what else we can do. Maybe if we spent more time together, got to know each other better . . ."

The thought of more time with her, even in this group, was unendurable. Adam opened his mouth to protest, but John spoke first.

"With the first concert only a few weeks away, we've got to do something. I vote for Sunday afternoon rehearsals."

There was a groan, but the others reluctantly agreed. Adam looked again at Marina, catching her gaze on him. Her eyes were troubled. Had she guessed his problem? He couldn't tell, but he knew he had to get out of there. He stood quickly and picked up his cello, then turned and started for the door.

He couldn't wait to get to his office—away from her, away from the pressure of holding back. Oh, Lord, he had to get a grip on himself. A whole year of this would be more than he could bear.

The moment Adam opened his eyes the next Sunday, he was hit by a familiar sense of foreboding. Rolling to his side, he looked at the clock. Five-thirty. Groaning, he burrowed down into his pillow and tried to sleep again, but a restless sense of urgency refused to allow him to relax.

At last, he threw the blankets back and sat up. A brief wave of dizziness hit him. Today. It would happen today. Thank God it was Sunday, and he could stay at home. He fumbled in the medicine cabinet for his pills. Emptying three of them into the palm of his hand, he tossed them into his mouth and took a swallow of water. Maybe he'd caught it soon enough. Maybe, for once, he'd be able to control it.

He thought about going back to bed—about forcing himself to lie there calmly, practicing the self-hypnotic techniques he'd learned last month in Paris. Then the realization hit him. The chamber group had a rehearsal today.

Lord, what was he going to do? Could he risk it? If he didn't show up, they'd be furious.

But what if . . . ?

No, he'd have to go. With luck, the rehearsal would be over before he had to worry. That was the pattern lately.

He went into the kitchen and put the coffee on, then started some Mozart on the tape player. The ordered precision of Mozart always made him feel in control. Maybe that would help.

By half-past nine, he knew it was hopeless. On days like this, no matter how hard he tried, it was impossible to loosen up. He'd go to the conservatory and practice awhile. It might take away these damnable jitters.

The elegant old building was deserted as he moved through the vaulted hallways. Despite the awkward situation with Marina, he liked it here. The other faculty members were interesting, pleasant people. If they thought he was moody and unpredictable, it was his fault, not theirs. He had to maintain that reputation. It was his cover.

The backstage door of the recital hall was just ahead. It was ajar, and Adam could see that the stage lights were on. He paused, then stepped inside quietly. As he did, the warm, rich sounds of a flute reached his ears.

Oh, God. It was her. She couldn't know he was here. He turned, ready to rush out the door, but something stopped him. She was playing *Syrinx*, a Debussy work for unaccompanied flute. Like *Chansons de la Nuit*, the music was tantalizing, sensual.

Adam found himself trapped by the beauty of it. Of her. Through an opening in the curtain, he could see her profile. Her eyes were closed as she played, and there was a look of exalted joy on her face. Adam stood mesmerized, listening, watching.

She was beautiful. Her hair, honey-blond and shining with golden highlights, was loosely caught up in combs, and it cascaded down her back. Her dark eyebrows arched gracefully—a startling contrast against the fairness of her complexion.

She finished the piece and, unaware of Adam's presence, walked a few steps around the stage, stretching her arms over her head and behind her. He felt a sudden fullness in his groin, as her T-shirt stretched across her breasts. She was slender and graceful. Her movements were fluid, like those of a dancer.

She turned in Adam's direction, and he fell back into the shadows, holding his breath. Had she seen him? But no, she went back to the center of the stage and raised her flute again. Adam moved farther into the wings, nearly stumbling over a chair. If she turned her head, she'd catch sight of him. He sank down, knowing he should leave. But he was powerless. There was a need deep inside. A hunger that made him crave to feast on her beauty—listen to her music—until he had unravelled the tantalizing secret of her.

He waited, his ears strained for the beginning of the next piece. At last it came—the haunting, seductive tones of *Chansons de la Nuit*. Oh, Lord, why hadn't he left? He gripped the neck of his cello, hardly aware of his fingers on its strings.

As it had at the concert, the sound of the flute drew him in. The present receded, and once again he was lost in the experience. Hardly aware of his motions, he positioned himself, ready for his cue. When it came, he began playing. It was as natural—as perfect—as if the full orchestra played in the background.

Marina gave him a startled glance. For a heartbeat, he caught his breath, afraid she'd break off. But she didn't. Instead, the tones of her flute grew bolder, taunting and teasing, sometimes soaring into the darkened auditorium, other times floating down to tangle him in a gossamer web.

All vestiges of Adam's resistance fled, and he gave himself to the music. At last, his desperate hunger found satisfaction. A spiralling joy filled his being. This was what he needed, what he'd been searching for—a spirit that could soar with him. He abandoned himself to the thrill, not thinking, not fearing. This was now. It was forever.

It ended. Silence settled gently around them, allowing a gradual descent from the enraptured heights. Adam threw his head back and inhaled deeply. He felt refreshed, revitalized. The small buzzing in his head barely attracted his notice. It didn't matter now. Nothing mattered except the exhilarating afterglow. He glanced at Marina. She stood motionless, her eyes still closed.

He laid his instrument down and rose. He should leave, he knew, but somehow it no longer seemed so urgent. He'd denied his need to talk with her before, but this time he couldn't. Slowly, he walked onto the stage.

At the sound of his approach, Marina turned. Unsmiling, she regarded him, her eyes questioning. They weren't ice-blue now, he noted, but a rich azure. Her features were soft, vulnerable.

Adam stopped. The buzzing in his head was louder now, but he knew he still had time. He lifted his hand, not knowing exactly what he planned. Marina watched, her gaze shifting with his movement. His fingers itched to touch her face, to trace the delicate lines of her brow, her lips. Unnerved, he stuck his hand into his pocket.

"You're very good," he said softly.

"Thanks." Her voice trembled a little. "You are, too."

There was a beat of silence, then they both spoke at the same time.

"I hope you didn't . . ."

"How did you . . . ?"

Adam gave a shaky laugh. "You first."

Marina smiled in response. It was as if a shaft of sunlight touched her face. "I—you surprised me. I never dreamed you were there."

"I know. I hope you don't mind. I planned to practice before the rehearsal." Now that he was so close to her, Adam wanted to study every tiny detail of her features. He noticed a slight gap between her front teeth, a faint twist to her smile. Rather than marring the classical beauty of her face, they added dimension to it.

"*Chansons de la Nuit* is a wonderful piece. It was a great honor to be the first to perform it."

Her voice pulled him back to the conversation. Her words were polite and a little formal. He hesitated. "I—I wanted to apologize about the concert." He watched her face. A cautious, closed look erased the warmth of seconds before. "I was exhausted," he said. "All I could think of was escaping—finding some peace and quiet."

Marina was quiet for a moment. His nerves tensed.

"I see." She turned away.

"Marina—" Adam couldn't let her reject him. Not now. He stepped toward her and reached out. His heart pounded, and sweat broke out on his face. The buzzing was loud now. Very intense. His hand shook. Oh, God, he had to get out of there.

It took all the willpower he could muster to keep his panic under control. Wheeling, he walked swiftly backstage. Behind the curtains, he broke into a run, dodging the furniture and equipment that littered the area. He *had* to make it to his studio.

In the hallway, he heard the voices of some of the other musicians arriving for rehearsal. He dove around a corner, the racket in his head overwhelming everything else. His studio was just ahead. With a final burst of speed, he gained the door and jammed his key into the lock.

Bursting into the room, he lunged around the door for the sofa. He had a fleeting sensation of softness, of sinking into the plush upholstery.

Then everything went black.

Marina stared after Adam in amazement. What had happened? His apology had thrown her so off-balance that she needed to distance herself for a moment to collect her thoughts. Had he taken that as a rejection?

She was still bemused a few moments later when the others began to straggle in through the front doors.

"Ah, right on time, I see." John Deering gave Marina a big grin as he mounted the steps to the stage. Moving around, he started to arrange the chairs and music stands for the rehearsal. The rest of the musicians straggled in, chatting as they prepared their instruments.

"I came a little early." She glanced backstage, expecting to see Adam at any moment.

At last, everyone was assembled. All except him. John looked at his watch, and then at the other performers. "Has anyone seen Fletcher? He's ten minutes late."

Marina hesitated. For some reason, she was reluctant to mention the earlier encounter.

"Well, if he isn't here in five minutes, I'm leaving," Mel, the bassoon player grumbled. "I'm missing the USC-UW game."

"Oh, I'm sure he'll be here," John said.

They waited, the silence lengthening with each passing minute. Marina looked around the group with discomfort.

"Maybe we should check his office."

The bassoon player looked at his watch. "Nope, not me. I'm heading out." He glanced at the others for confirmation.

"I've got company coming," Annie Taub said. "I wouldn't mind coming in tomorrow evening instead."

There was a murmur of assent.

John considered the matter. "Is that a consensus? If so, we'll meet tomorrow evening." There was a responding chorus of assent. He frowned. "And in the meantime, I'll have a little talk with the unpredictable Mr. Fletcher."

Within moments, everyone had departed. Marina disassembled her flute and tucked it into the maroon velvet lining of its case, then went backstage to turn off the lights. Beside the panel, Adam's cello rested next to the chair where he had sat. Marina's heart thumped in alarm. His Stradavarius instrument was legendary. He wouldn't just leave it around like this. Walking over to it, she leaned down and ran her hand over the smooth varnish.

It gave her a strange feeling. This was a part of Adam—as much a part of him as his arms or legs. She stroked the satiny wood. It was almost like touching him. At the realization, she jerked her hand back, face aflame. What was she thinking?

What should she do now? She couldn't leave the instrument here. Carefully, she lifted it, balancing it on its peg. She'd take it with her and stop by his studio. Maybe he was there. If not, she'd lock it in her own studio and leave him a note.

Tucking her flute under her arm, she picked up the cello and retrieved Adam's bow from the chair. Shaking with nervousness, she started for his studio.

The marble hallway echoed with her footsteps. It was lonely in the building. Spooky. Marina peered over her shoulder as she turned the corner. Could something have happened? Was it possible Adam's absence was more than a fit of temperament?

Down the way, she spied his door. It was ajar. His keys

dangled from the lock. A chill prickled down her spine. What had happened?

Urgency quickened her footsteps. She reached the door shoved it open with her foot. Halting in the doorway, she scanned the room. Everything was tidy, in order. His desk, the bookcase, the grand piano in the corner. Where was Adam?

She stepped inside. His cello case was open on the floor beside the piano. Thank goodness for that. Handling the cello like a rare jewel, she reverently placed it inside. With great care, she closed the case and heaved a sigh of relief. Now, if she just knew where Adam was.

A small sound behind her made her spin around. It was then she finally noticed the sofa, partially obscured by the door. Adam lay there, his clothing disheveled, one arm thrown across his brow.

Marina felt the blood drain from her face. "Adam?" she said. The half-dozen steps it took to cross the room seemed like an eternity. "Adam," she said again.

He gave no sign of hearing. He shifted slightly, and his breathing became heavy and raspy.

Marina hesitated, then moved closer. She leaned over and touched his shoulder.

"Adam, what's wrong?"

She shook him, desperate for a response.

"Wake up. Are you all right?" Tight bands of panic squeezed her chest. "Please, speak to me." Pulling his arm away from his face, she stared at him, willing him to wake up.

Suddenly, his eyes opened. Marina's heart leapt. "Adam, what's happened?"

He mumbled something, and his eyes closed again.

Marina shook him. "Damn it, wake up." She tightened her fingers on his shoulder, refusing to let go, even when he tried to roll away from her. Was he sick? "Adam, do you want a doctor? Should I call an ambulance?"

He stilled. "No. No doctor." It seemed an eternity

before he opened his eyes again and struggled to a sitting position. "I'm fine." His words were slurred and woozy. He dropped his feet heavily to the floor and sat on the sofa, his head in his hands.

"But you're ill."

"No, just tired." He shook his head as if to clear it. "Had to sleep. Just had to sleep." With effort, he smiled at her. "No need to worry. I'm awake now. You can go."

Marina watched him dubiously. Was he really all right? Was it safe to leave him alone?

He stood up and walked unsteadily across the room to his desk. "See, I'm fine. Really." He smiled again.

Marina went slowly to the piano and retrieved her flute. "Well, if you're really sure . . ."

"I'm sure." He leaned against his desk, weaving slightly.

There was no question that he really wanted her to leave. Marina put aside her lingering doubts and walked slowly toward the door. She pulled the keys out of the lock and put them on Adam's desk.

"Next time you decide to take a nap, you'd better take your keys out of the lock." She paused, half hoping for an explanation, but he remained silent. Turning, she started out again. Before she quit the room, she stopped one more time. "And, Adam, I should warn you. John Deering will be in touch. I won't say anything about finding you here, but you'd better have a good excuse for ruining today's rehearsal."

Not waiting for his response, she walked quickly out the door.

FIVE

When Marina arrived at the rescheduled rehearsal the next evening, Adam appeared healthy and at ease. She felt the tense muscles of her shoulders and neck relax. Ever since yesterday's episode, she had worried. To no avail, obviously.

Hurriedly, she found her seat and busied herself with her flute. From the corner of her eye, she saw him take his own seat and begin tuning his instrument. At that moment, he looked up. For an instant, the two locked gazes. Then tentatively, Adam smiled.

Marina's heart thudded. She felt the corners of her mouth move upward in response. A sense of giddy pleasure washed over her.

Don't be silly, Marina. It doesn't mean anything.

Still, a warm glow suffused her. Maybe their conversation yesterday meant friendship was possible between them, after all. The notion stopped her. Yes, friends. That was all she expected. All she wanted.

The other performers were in their places now, and the oboeist played an A for everyone to tune to. There was a cacophony of sound, then the stage quieted.

"Let's start with the Ravel," John said. He glanced around the players. "Ready?"

Adam felt a bead of moisture on his brow. Taking a deep breath, he raised his hand.

"Before we begin, I believe I owe everyone an apology."

Startled faces turned toward him. He kept his eyes away from Marina. "I'm sorry about not showing up yesterday. I—I . . ." He felt his face flush. "I guess all the jet lag from the past few years is catching up with me." He smiled sheepishly. "Or else, this wonderful Vancouver climate is relaxing me *too* much."

An appreciative laugh rippled through the group. "Just before the rehearsal I lay down to rest my eyes for a few minutes, and I guess I must have dropped off." He looked at Marina. Like the others, she had a surprised expression. "Anyway, I wanted to say, it won't happen again."

For a moment, there was silence. Then the voice of Mel, the bassoonist, boomed out.

"Well, I want you to know, the wrong team won because I missed the first half of the game."

There was a burst of laughter and a few other jocular comments followed. Adam felt his tension dissolve. For the first time, they had responded to him. Not just with respect and courtesy, but as a real person.

Was it possible these people could actually become his friends?

The rehearsal lasted far into the evening. It seemed that Adam's words had sparked a spirit of camaraderie within the group. At last, the music burst forth with thrilling vibrancy. Marina could sense the excitement in the others.

Even when they finished, people lingered to talk. Walking out with Annie, Marina noticed Adam ahead of her. He was alone. A sudden impulse to catch up with him hit her.

Giving herself no chance for second thoughts, she turned to Annie. "I'll see you tomorrow. I need to talk to Adam."

Annie grinned mischievously. "Ah, so the feud is over at last."

Marina felt herself blush. "Well, I wouldn't say . . '

With the sound of Annie's laugh echoing in her head, Marina hurried toward Adam's departing figure.

"Adam, do you have a minute?" Now that she was beside him, she felt nervous and shy.

He stopped, then slowly revolved to face her. For an instant, she detected a softening in his features. But before she could be sure, it was gone.

"Adam, I—I . . ." She took a deep breath. "I—just wanted to say thanks for apologizing. It cleared the air." She smiled tentatively. His expression remained sober. "Well, I guess . . ." She began to turn away.

"Don't go." Adam reached out, and for a brief moment Marina's breath caught. Her flesh tingled in anticipation of his touch. Then, to her—was it relief or disappointment?—he drew his hand back and stuck it in his pocket.

Adam wasn't sure what he felt. Surprise, of course, but what was this rush of elation that was singing through him? He gazed at her anxious face and experienced a sudden urge to lean down and brush his lips across hers. The memory of that hasty kiss onstage taunted him. Although his intent at the time had been to erase the pounding need to know her, explore with her the mystical pairing they'd experienced, just the opposite had happened.

Ever since, the memories had tormented him—of her soft lips, the gentle fragrance of her perfume, the sense of joyous abandon that had zinged through him when they touched. So what was he doing now? Why was he letting his guard down?

He heard himself speaking. "I thought I'd stop for a cup of coffee before I go home. Would you like to join me?" He watched her face, praying she'd refuse. He needed to get away from her, be by himself. Reconstruct his defenses.

Marina hesitated. *Don't do it, Marina*, a little voice whispered. She looked at her watch. Ten-fifteen. "Well,

it's a little late, and I have an early seminar tomorrow—"
She looked at Adam's face, and all her resolve departed.
"—but I'm ready for it." She smiled. "Sure. I could use
a cup of coffee, after that marathon rehearsal."

They drove in Adam's car—a bright red Porsche—to
Chollies, a small restaurant a few blocks from the conservatory. Marina was acutely aware of his presence beside
her. A suggestion of the fresh-soap scent that had tantalized her at the faculty meeting hovered in the air, mingled
with the leathery aroma of the upholstery. It was an exhilarating, masculine combination. Marina tried not to notice
the effect it was having on her.

At the restaurant, the waiter—who appeared to be in his
seventies—led them to a quiet booth in the back. Glad to
be away from the unnerving closeness of the car, Marina
slid into the cushioned seat across from Adam. But now
what?

To her relief, the coffee came almost immediately. Adam
reached for the sugar and ladled in three heaping spoons-
ful, then added a large dollop of cream. Marina paused,
her cup halfway to her lips, and watched in fascination.

Looking up, he caught her gaze. "Sweet tooth," he
said, with a sheepish grin.

"I see." She bit back a smile as she sipped her own
coffee, then set her cup on the table. "So, what did you
think of the rehearsal tonight?"

"Fine. I think we're over the hump." Over the rim of
his cup, his eyes met hers. "I feel a little guilty about
making Mel's team lose, though."

Marina laughed. "He'll get over it." She hesitated. Did
she dare ask the question foremost in her mind? Yes. She
had to. "Adam, what was the problem, really?"

His face tightened, and he looked away. "Just what I
said. Accumulated jet lag." His voice was casual. Too
casual. "You do concert tours. You must know about it."

Without waiting for her answer, he signalled the waiter for more coffee.

She watched while he went through the routine of adding sugar and cream again. He took a long swallow and returned the cup to its saucer. Leaning forward, he crossed his arms on the table.

"Now, tell me about yourself, Marina Prohaska. Where did you grow up? How many brothers and sisters do you have? How did you learn to play the flute the way you do?"

Her heart gave a lurch. "Oh, Adam, I—" She glanced at his face. It was warm and inquiring. *Calm down, Marina.* She took a deep breath, avoiding his eyes. "My life isn't very interesting. I grew up in San Francisco. I was orphaned when I was five. I was raised in foster homes." She shrugged. "One of my teachers in school got me started on the flute. She and her husband took me in."

Seeing her tight face, Adam regretted his question. But he had to steer the conversation away from himself. Thinking about yesterday's incident still chilled him. It was a close call. Too close. If he hadn't made it to his studio, if she had found him while . . .

"What about you?"

It took a second for Adam to refocus his thoughts. "Me? Oh—I, uh, I grew up in Montana. My father was a ranger in Glacier National Park." He smiled. "But that's boring. Let's talk about more interesting things, like Vancouver. What do you think of it?"

The switch of subject worked. Marina relaxed visibly, and he, too, was able to let down his guard. Soon, they were engrossed in discussions of the school, their students, the other students in the chamber group. Before either of them realized it, the waiter had pulled the shade on the door and cleared his throat politely.

"I think that's a hint," Adam said.

Marina looked at her watch. "Good heavens, it's nearly midnight."

They hurried out past the waiter, who held the door for them. Just before they reached the car, Adam looked back. The old man was still in the doorway. He gave Adam a knowing wink and went back inside.

For a second, Adam was mystified, then it dawned on him. That waiter thought they were lovers, off for a night of ecstasy. Adam looked at Marina and his need came surging back. A need that must at all costs be denied. It was a wonderful fantasy.

But it would never happen.

Marina drove home with her emotions in a whirl. He was nice. Adam was actually a person she could like. When they talked—even laughed—together, she found her usual reserve crumbling. It was a new, disconcerting experience.

Still pondering the strange, exhilarating evening, she entered her building. As she passed the office, the door opened. Mrs. Reynolds, the very British widow who managed the apartment building stepped out. Her hair was up in rags, and she wore a fuzzy blue bathrobe that must have been twenty years old.

"Oh, Miss Prohaska, thank goodness you're here. There was a gentleman around asking for you this afternoon."

"A man? Did he ask for me by name?"

"Oh, yes. I offered to take a message, but he said he'd stop back another time." Mrs. Reynolds' voice dropped conspiratorially. "I think he must have been a salesman. They're sometimes very cagey, you know." She waited, obviously hoping Marina would volunteer an explanation.

Ignoring the woman's disappointed expression, Marina thanked her and moved toward the stairs.

It wasn't until she was inside her apartment that the old fear washed over her. She leaned against the door, trembling. *Stop it*, she told herself. *That's all done with*. She took a deep breath. It was just some poor salesman trying to make a living. With determination, she straightened her shoulders and thrust her chin out.

But her hands shook as she locked the door, then set the deadbolt.

In the days that followed, the incident faded into memory. Now that Marina and Adam had begun to communicate, it seemed they ran into each other every time they turned around.

They fell into the habit of having lunch together. Little by little, Adam opened up, talking about himself, his music, his childhood.

His young memories were of summers spent hiking and fishing in the mountains with his parents. During the long, solitary winters, the three of them skied and snowshoed and holed up in their tiny, snowbound cabin. Sometimes they didn't see another person for months.

When Adam reached school age his parents sent him to Seattle to live with his aunt and uncle and attend a private school. It was a difficult adjustment for the small boy, one he never made gracefully. Then he began to play the cello, and it became his solace—his only friend.

Not so very different from herself, Marina realized. She suspected that also like her, he had never experienced closeness, had never shared his secrets with another person. Once, with Ramon, Marina had thought it might be possible. But she had been wrong. So terribly, painfully wrong.

Well, with Adam, it would be different. Her instincts said that he would never allow her access to the deep, important things he needed to keep hidden. That suited her. He wouldn't press her for revelations, either. The only problem was the strong physical attraction she felt toward him. But she would keep it in check. It would fade in time.

* * *

The Canadian Thanksgiving holiday came early in October. The week before, Annie Taub caught Marina on the way out of a rehearsal. "We always have a big crowd over for Thanksgiving. If you can stand a mob of kids and the guys watching football, we'd love to have you come, too."

Marina was surprised—and touched. Annie was a warm, friendly person. She seemed determined to include Marina in her family's social activities.

The prospect made Marina nervous. She shook her head. "Annie, it's nice of you to ask, but . . ."

Annie stopped. "But what? Do you have other plans?"

"It's not that," Marina began. "It's just that I won't know anybody. I'm not used to that sort of thing."

Annie considered her thoughtfully. "I can understand that. But we'd really like to have you." The two started walking again. They were nearly at the parking lot when Annie stopped once more. "Ah, I've got it! How about if I invite Adam, too?" She grinned slyly. "The two of you seem to be hitting it off nicely now."

"It's not like that," Marina protested.

Annie just smiled. "I know, I know." She paused. "Don't worry about a thing, Marina. Just be there." Before Marina could refuse, Annie was gone.

The day before Thanksgiving, Adam stopped by Marina's studio, his face glum.

"I hear you got roped into going to Annie's for dinner tomorrow, too."

Marina stifled the impulse to laugh at his obvious dismay. If she hadn't also dreaded the event, she would have.

"Annie's hard to refuse, isn't she?"

Adam frowned. "If you'll give me your address, I'll pick you up." His voice was gruff—almost surly.

Marina's heart leaped. "Are you sure . . . ?" *Calm down*, she told herself sharply. She kept her voice deliberately neutral. "I mean, it's probably out of your way."

Adam looked at her. He felt a warmth suffuse his face. It *was* out of his way. He'd looked the address up in the faculty directory. But it didn't matter. Somehow, having her by his side when he entered that houseful of strangers seemed terribly important—far more important than the occasion merited.

In the brief silence that followed, he had a disturbing thought. Maybe she didn't want to go with him. Although they'd never discussed it, he knew the distance they'd kept in their friendship was no accident. He made for the door. "Never mind. It wasn't really a very good idea," he mumbled. A dark sense of rejection closed around him.

Marina's voice stopped him. "Wait, Adam."

He turned, his heart pounding.

"I'd appreciate a ride." Quickly, she went to her desk. She wrote something on a note pad and tore off the sheet. There was a nervous little smile on her face as she held the paper out. "Here's my address. I'll see you tomorrow."

Without a word, Adam took it and left.

The day was more enjoyable than he had anticipated. The crowd, which included Robert Graves and a few of the other faculty members, as well as some non-musicians, was relaxed and friendly. Children of all ages were everywhere.

Annie's four-year-old twin daughters took Adam in tow. Gravely, they discussed their toys and activities with him. Just as gravely he listened. Finally, with each holding one hand, they led him down the hall to show him the treasures in their room.

As they departed, his gaze caught Marina's. Her heart twinged. He'd confided to her that he didn't know how to act around children, but he was doing just fine. He'd make a wonderful father, if he ever decided to settle down. She felt a strange, empty sense of longing.

The feeling persisted through the rest of the day. Although she tried to busy herself by talking to other people and helping Annie, it seemed that every time she glanced in his direction, he looked up in time to intercept her gaze. At last, he came and sat next to her.

He leaned back on the sofa. His sleeve brushed lightly against her hair and his thigh touched hers. Her pulse began to race. Trying to appear casual, she moved a few inches away. Noticing, Adam carefully shifted himself to avoid contact.

But it was too late for Marina. From then on, she was aware of every movement he made. Her skin tingled with the knowledge of his nearness. Soon, she reminded herself, she'd be safely home and out of his presence.

Adam, too, looked forward to the end of the evening. All day long he had been aware of nothing except Marina. If not for the distraction of Annie's twins, the day would have been pure torture. Driving through the quiet streets to take her home, he felt relief. Soon, he'd be able to leave her at her apartment and escape to his lonely house.

Damn. He should stick to the kind of women he usually dated. Like him, they wanted a good time—sexual release and no commitments. But she wasn't like that. She was—well—vulnerable.

A few times lately, he'd had a glimpse of the warmth and sensitivity hidden behind her carefully-controlled facade. An unfamiliar feeling pulsed through him. It made him want to stop the car and gather her in his arms, protecting her with his strength.

The thought nearly made him laugh. What strength? If she had frailties to conceal, what about him? No, the best thing would be to get her home, and get away.

When they arrived at her apartment building, Marina quickly opened the car door. "Well, thank you for the ride, Adam. It was nice of you to take me."

"I'll walk you to your door," he said brusquely. A faint whiff of her fragrance—fresh and lightly floral—drifted into his nostrils. It was an innocently sensual scent, and it suited her perfectly. Immediately, he felt a fullness in his groin.

Control yourself, Fletcher.

Walking beside her, he kept his hands in his pockets, not daring to touch her, even casually. At the elevator, Marina punched the button, and they stood waiting in silence.

At last the car came lumbering down from an upper floor. The doors slid open, and Marina stepped in. She looked at Adam. Did he intend to go all the way to her apartment with her?

He hesitated for an instant, then moved to her side.

Their gazes clung, and for a hair's-breadth, she recognized the same naked longing she'd glimpsed just once before. "Oh, Adam . . ." she whispered. Before either of them knew it was happening, she was in his arms.

This time, there was no taunting arrogance in his kiss. His lips were gentle and seeking. A wave of need swept over Marina, so intense it drove all other awareness from her mind. The elevator stopped and the doors opened.

Adam drew back. He gazed at her questioningly, his eyes dark and sober. A thrill raced through her, followed immediately by a rush of fear. What was she doing?

"Adam, this is a mistake." Breaking from his embrace, she ran blindly from the elevator. At the door to her apartment, she paused, digging frantically through her purse for the keys.

Stunned by her abrupt departure, he remained motionless. What had he done? Less than an hour ago, he'd promised himself not to let this happen. The elevator doors began to shut automatically. He stuck his arm out to stop them, mobilized into decision. He couldn't leave her like this. He had to explain. Apologize.

"Marina," he called softly, hurrying after her. She looked up, startled at his voice. Tears streaked her face.

"Marina," he said again as he came up to her. A great surge of guilt flooded him.

"It's okay."

She turned back to her purse, pulling out her billfold and her checkbook in an effort to find the keys. Adam watched her fruitless efforts. Finally, he held his hand out. "Would you like me to try?"

Marina hesitated, then jammed the handbag into his waiting grasp. Opening it wide, he reached in to unzip a compartment on one side. The keys were there. Taking them out, he handed the purse back to her. There was only one door key and it fit. He swung the door open and stepped aside. Pulling the keys from the lock, he offered them back to her.

"Thank you." Her words were barely distinguishable. She reached out. Their hands touched. She gasped, and the key ring fell to the floor, its jangle loud as a shot in the quiet building.

They bent to retrieve it at the same time. Their hands touched again, and this time Adam grasped hers. It was cold and stiff. Their eyes met, hers dark with apprehension. But a current flowed between them, drawing them inexorably together. With hands still clasped, they rose, their gazes never wavering.

Adam led her inside and pushed the door closed. He struggled against the urge to wrap his arms around her and kiss the worry away. "We need to talk," he said gently.

"I know," she whispered.

They walked toward the living room. Adam felt her hand begin to relax in his. He guided her to the sofa. They sat at opposite ends, their hands still clasped between them.

"Something's happening to us," Adam said. "It's not in my plans."

"What are we going to do?" she asked. She licked her lips, making them moist and soft looking.

Adam swallowed. "I don't know, Marina. I never

thought . . .'' He realized how ridiculous it was to claim he never thought they would reach this point. It was what he had feared from that very first encounter. It was why he had taken such pains to make her hate him. And now—

She moved then, just a small shifting of position to rid herself of her coat, but her hand tightened on his. Adam felt desire surge hot and heavy through his being. He helped her remove the garment, then shrugged his own off, tossing both coats aside. He reached again for her hand, so small and delicate in his. Her fingers tensed, and he watched her face. Her lips parted, and her eyes softened.

Without conscious volition, he slid across the sofa toward her. Lifting her hand, he brought it to his lips. First he just brushed his mouth across the soft flesh. Then, with his gaze fastened on hers, he turned it over and traced the fine lines of her palm with his tongue. He licked each tiny indentation, laving away the slight saltiness of her skin.

She shivered, her eyes closing. Adam paused, then with a groan, pulled her to him to cover those full, tantalizing lips with his own. The kiss began as a gentle exploration of nibbling and tasting. But it couldn't satisfy the hunger that had built in both of them. Adam thrust his tongue against her lips, and she opened to allow him entry.

''Oh, Marina, how I've waited for this,'' he breathed. She brought her arms up and wrapped them around his neck, her own tongue following as he traced every inch of her mouth. When he withdrew slightly, she whimpered, tangling her fingers in his hair and bringing his mouth back to hers.

Carrying her with him, Adam fell back against the sofa cushions, stretching his legs to bring her body in full contact with his. She responded by moving against him, pressing against the hard, full outline of him.

With his mouth still fused to hers, he raised her slightly to find the soft fullness of her breasts. Her nipples became enlarged and firm as he ran his hand across her blouse, feeling the contours through the fabric.

Impatiently, he pulled her blouse away from the waist-line of her skirt to touch her bare flesh. He slid his hand beneath her bra, and rotated his palm over the nipple, feeling it bead at his touch.

Marina was lost in a haze of sensual delight. Adam seemed to know exactly how to please her. He unbuttoned her blouse, then unsnapped the front opening of her bra. Her breasts sprang free. Abandoning her mouth, he low-ered his head to suckle the erect nipples, first one, then the other. She arched back to allow him better access, gasping as he opened his mouth wide to take in more of the sensitive flesh, while with his thumb he coaxed an exqui-site response from the other nipple.

She felt a surge of tenderness toward him and at the same time, an urgent need to feel his flesh beneath her hands. Fumbling, she unbuttoned his shirt and slid her hand inside. A dense mat of springy hair met her seeking fingers. She found his tiny nipple and caressed it with her thumb in the same way he was touching her. Immediately, it hardened into a firm button. Adam pulled his shirt out of his trousers to give her better access. Then, finding her mouth with his again, he shrugged off his shirt and pulled her tight against him.

Lost in the sensations, Marina barely realized his hands had moved lower on her back, stroking and caressing. All she knew was the intense pleasure he was creating. She moved against him, glorying in the feel of his strong, muscular body beneath her, moving in response to her seeking fingertips.

She was dimly aware that he had unzipped her skirt and was sliding his hands under the waistband.

"Oh, Marina, darling, I want you so much," he whis-pered. His hands continued their magical caresses, moving in easy, rhythmic circles, lower and lower.

Suddenly, the motion slowed. At first she hardly no-ticed, but as his fingers began to explore the ridges crisscrossing her buttocks, the horrifying knowledge of what was happening hit her.

Oh, my God, how could she? The memory of Ramon's disgust hit her like a bucket of ice water. She stiffened.

"Stop it, Adam!" she cried, rolling away from him.

Startled, he sat up. "Marina, what is it? Did I hurt you?"

"No, no. It's not that!" she gasped, her eyes filling with tears. Adam reached for her. "Don't!" she cried, dodging away from his outstretched hands.

She jumped from the sofa and refastened her skirt. Then, keeping her back to him, she went around the room retrieving their clothing. Holding her blouse in front of her, she dumped Adam's shirt and tie beside him on the sofa. Then, with her back to him, she put her bra and blouse back on.

When she turned back again, he was still sitting there with a puzzled expression.

"Please, Adam, leave now." She hugged her arms across her breast, rocking back and forth and crying.

Adam stood up and came over to her, slipping his arms into the sleeves of his shirt. He wanted to touch her, comfort her, but he felt helpless. "Marina, I don't understand what's happening." He waited for her to respond, but she turned away, slapping the tears from her face.

"This shouldn't have happened, Adam. If you knew . . ."

"If I knew what?"

"It doesn't matter." She had stopped crying now, and her voice was low and flat. "Just take my word for it. You don't want me. And . . ." She wheeled to face him. The soft gentleness was gone from her eyes. Now they were once again icy-blue. ". . . and to be honest, I don't want you."

For an instant, Adam was paralyzed. Then a shaft of pain cut through him. He searched her face, half expecting her to burst into laughter. But in his heart he knew she wouldn't. She remained motionless, her eyes hard and determined.

Turning from her, Adam picked up his coat. He started for the door. But before he opened it, he turned back to her. With great deliberation, he smiled and half bowed. Keeping his voice as cool and detached as hers had been, he spoke.

"Thank you, Ms. Prohaska, for a most interesting evening."

With that, he opened the door, stepped out, and closed it ever so gently.

SIX

Marina always kept her thoughts under control. *Always.* But not this time. Over and over, the scene with Adam replayed in her mind. At night she tossed in her bed, the memory of his touch haunting her. If she fell into a fitful sleep, she awakened to the tantalizing sensation of his lips on hers, the hard planes of his body under her fingertips.

It was hell.

The conservatory was no escape. There was no avoiding him.

Marina approached the first rehearsal after Thanksgiving with foreboding. What would she do if he treated her with the bitter sarcasm of their parting? The thought brought a new flood of tears to her eyes. No! She would *not* humiliate herself by letting him see her cry.

As it turned out, the encounter was far worse. It was as if she didn't exist. If Adam had acted angry or hostile she could have handled it. But he did neither. His gaze skimmed over her with cool indifference. Marina felt herself wither under his cold, impersonal regard.

Blinking rapidly, she fixed her attention on the score in front of her and began playing over a solo passage to warm up.

Why couldn't they just get started?

At last, John gave the signal to begin. Marina sat upright, her heart filled with dread. She braced herself for the storm of emotions the sound of Adam's cello was certain to invoke. To her surprise, the first tones washed over her like a soothing balm.

As always, the music stripped away the pain, transporting her to the familiar sanctuary of fluid sound and abstract sensation. Then came blessed forgetfulness. Nothing existed except the power and exhilaration of the music.

In her euphoria, she hardly realized when her gaze fastened on Adam. But one part of her mind registered the expression of serenity and exaltation on his face. His eyes were closed. Marina felt his power surge toward her. As if in a dream, she responded, and they soared together. Then the music ended.

Awareness penetrated with a rude jolt. Adam's face swam before her eyes. Suddenly, her instincts went on full alert. That look on his face, the rapt expression of untrammeled ecstasy—she recognized it. It was how he had looked when he held her in his arms.

Oh, God, how could she stand it?

Halloween arrived a short time later. And with it, the traditional Conservatory masquerade party.

"Marina, are you going with Adam?" Annie asked on the way out of the rehearsal hall a few days before.

Marina looked at her in astonishment. Hadn't she noticed?

"No, I don't believe I'll go."

Annie stopped. "But you've got to. It's going to be a wonderful party." She looked at Marina sternly. "I can see I'm going to have to have a little talk with Adam, too."

"No, don't!" Marina blurted. She felt her face go scarlet. "Annie, Adam and I, we . . ." She paused, hating to go on. But Annie's eyes were full of concern.

Marina sighed. "We decided things were getting too—" she dropped her gaze to her hands, picking at a broken fingernail, "—too involved."

"Oh, Marina," Annie said, her voice disappointed. "I thought . . ."

Marina gave her a sharp look. "Annie, we're both committed to our careers. This year is just an interlude for each of us. There's no point starting something we can't finish."

Annie opened her mouth to speak, but Marina silenced her with a look.

"Please, Annie. I'd rather not discuss it."

To her surprise, Annie didn't pursue the subject.

On Halloween night, Marina was surprised by a knock on her door. Who could that be? Not kids, surely. Her building was full of older tenants, and the surrounding neighborhood consisted mainly of retirees. Marina had chosen the area precisely because of the quiet atmosphere.

Searching her mind for something on hand to give as treats, she went to the door.

"Trick or treat!" A group of half-a-dozen definitely mature witches and goblins leered at her from the hallway. Her heart contracted.

"You've got the wrong place," she gasped, pushing the door shut. Her mind flew to what Mrs. Reynolds had told her that afternoon: The mysterious man had been around again.

There was another knock.

"Better not make the witches mad, dearie," came a suspiciously familiar voice.

She waited a moment, then opened the door a crack. One of the goblins pushed it wider and the whole bunch crowded closer. One of the witches giggled. Marina recognized Annie's lilting laugh. The tension melted out of her. She might as well play along with the game.

"Sorry, kids. You're out of luck here."

"No treats?" She recognized the falsetto voice as Mel's.

From the back, a bent-over wizard pulled a scroll from inside his robe and pushed his way forward. Stepping up to Marina, he unfurled it. In a stentorian voice, he read:

"Hear ye, hear ye. This being All Hallow's Eve, it is hereby proclaimed that all members of the B.C. Conservatory of Music be in attendance at the Halloween gala event.

"Any who refuses to go voluntarily shall attend involuntarily. A select group of personages—" he stopped to indicate the group around him "—shall be appointed to abduct such recalcitrant souls, provide them with costumes, and escort them to said celebration."

With that, he rolled up the parchment and nodded toward the witches. Marina watched in amazement as they pushed their way in and took her by the arms. One followed, carrying a shopping bag. They guided her through the living room into the bedroom, whose door she had unthinkingly left open.

"Now, just a minute . . ." Marina began.

"Now, now, dearie," one of the witches said in a high, cracking voice. "Don't argue. You have to come."

"But I don't want to," Marina protested. "I'm going to work on papers."

"No excuses accepted, dearie." The voice, though disguised through a grotesque rubber mask, had Annie's undeniable inflection.

"Annie, you can't do this . . ."

"They're waiting for us, dearie." Marina detected an unyielding note in the voice.

The witch carrying the bag moved to her bed and emptied the contents out on it. A jangling pile of satin and chiffon spilled out. One of the garments was a brief, form-fitting top covered with brass coins. With the movement, the coins clinked against each other.

"Now, just be a good girl and put your costume on,

or—" the witch gave a loud cackle "—or we'll have to dress you!" The others nodded, agreeing gleefully.

They advanced on Marina. She moved backward. Throwing her hands up in resignation, she gave a little laugh. "Okay, okay, I give." Her mind raced, planning strategy. She'd put in an appearance and immediately take a cab home. "I'll be out as soon as I'm dressed."

"Are you sure we can trust you, dearie?" the crackly-voiced witch said. The three hovered, eyeing Marina speculatively.

She sighed. "You can trust me. Give me ten minutes."

With satisfied chuckles, the others filed out.

"And you can be sure I'll get even one of these days, Annie," Marina called after them. Her only response was an uproarious round of laughter.

The silence was a blessed relief. Now that there was no audience, she examined the costume more carefully. It was a belly-dancer's outfit, complete with jewelry and a wide, heavily ornamented belt. Marina cringed. How could she wear that in public? She started to put the costume back in the bag.

Then curiosity got the better of her.

She'd always loved watching belly dancers. If it weren't for her inhibitions—her heart thudded—and the disgusting scars, she'd have been tempted to try it. Now, in the privacy of her own room, it wouldn't hurt to at least put the costume on.

With trembling hands, she picked up the top, heavy with ornamentation, and slipped her arms in the straps. *Why, this is no more than a fancy brassiere*, she realized, adjusting the cups and hooking the front fasteners. It fit as if it had been made for her. She wiggled her shoulders, and the coins jingled. Interesting.

Standing up, she held her arms out and tried moving her body as she'd seen belly dancers do. Each motion was rewarded with a jingle. Intrigued, she experimented with different motions.

A knock came at the door. "We're waiting, Marina."

"Just a minute." Hurriedly, Marina picked up the pants and stepped into them. They were of a filmy, pale-green fabric. She drew them on and put the belt around her waist, then walked over to the full length mirror on the bathroom door.

She didn't recognize herself. The woman standing there was lovely and exotic looking. Through the sheer pants, her legs were clearly outlined—long and shapely. Marina held her arms above her head and twirled. A burst of jangly sound accompanied the action. Pulling the pins out of her hair, she finger-combed it free to cascade down her back. A wild, reckless feeling swept over her. It would be such fun just to let herself go for one evening.

But could she? What about the scars? Turning, she studied her back in the mirror. The belt rode high, concealing all but one of them. Her pulse quickened. Maybe she could hide that one, too.

On the bed, a mask and a small pile of accessories remained, including several scarves. Marina picked up a gossamer silk confection of deep blue, shot with gold and regarded it thoughtfully. She experimented with different ways of draping it around herself.

Another knock came at the door. "One minute, Marina, then we're coming in."

Oh, Lord, she had to do something. She hurried back to the bed and dug through the jewelry. There were several bangles and a snake arm bracelet—and beneath everything, a filigreed headband. Grabbing it, she arranged the scarf on her head and slipped the headband over it. Perfect. The rich silk flowed down her back like a diaphanous cape. Marina twirled again, and it billowed out gracefully.

"Time's up!" The door burst open.

Marina spun as the three witches crowded in. They stopped in the doorway.

"Oh, Marina, you look beautiful!" It was Annie's voice, undisguised and admiring.

For a second, Marina had the impulse to push them back out the door and tear off the costume. But before she could act, they swept inside and were guiding her toward the dresser.

"Now for the finishing touches," one of the other witches chortled, rubbing her hands together. From somewhere a makeup kit materialized.

Helpless, she allowed herself to be seated.

"Now don't worry, dearie, I'm in the drama department. I'm just going to put a little dab of makeup in the right places and . . ." As she spoke, she began expertly applying eye shadow and eye liner. She dusted Marina's cheeks with blush and outlined her lips in deep red, then filled in with a lighter frost. ". . . perfect!" She stood back and admired her handiwork. "What a striking combination—those deep-blue eyes and that blond hair, with such dark eyebrows and lashes."

The other two gathered around, slipping bracelets on Marina's arms and fastening jewelry around her neck. Marina felt bewildered by it all. But a kernel of excitement grew inside her as she looked at her reflection in the mirror. This wasn't her. It was someone else—a person she had never dared imagine. She fitted the mask on and adjusted it. The last traces of reluctance evaporated.

It would be fun, this Halloween celebration. It didn't even matter if Adam *was* there. Before the time came to reveal who she was, she'd be long gone. Turning to the witches, she smiled.

"Let's go."

Adam knew the instant she walked into the dimly lit ballroom of the Conservatory. From his vantage point on the stage, he stared at the sexy harem girl in the doorway. It was Marina. What made him so certain, he couldn't say. It was almost as if an invisible thread bound the two of them together.

With his eyes following her every move, he played

automatically, improvising his part in the music the hastily assembled dance band was playing. She had hardly set foot in the room, when someone swept her away to the dance floor. Adam felt a surge of jealousy.

Never mind, Fletcher. It's no concern of yours. Insides churning, he dragged his gaze away. It didn't matter. He only had a half-hour left to play. As soon as he was done, he'd get out of here.

The piece ended. He sat back, feeling restless and uncomfortable. Usually, he enjoyed this kind of jam session. It was a refreshing change of pace. But in the last few minutes it had become torture. Jerking down the brief jacket of his toreador costume, he straightened his mask, keeping his gaze deliberately away from the dance floor. It was time for the next tune. He threw himself into it with total concentration.

He'd have been safe if he hadn't caught a sudden flash of swirling gold and blue from the corner of his eye. The sudden, undeniable urge to turn his head took him unawares. Without thinking, he glanced down. At the same moment, Marina looked up. Their gazes collided. His breath stopped. She faltered.

For a heartbeat, the sounds of music and laughter ceased. Nothing existed for Adam except the blue eyes behind the gaudy, bejeweled mask. Then, with visible effort, she tossed her head and smiled up at her partner. Adam stared after them as they spun off into the crowd.

He made it through the rest of the session, but just barely. All he could think of was Marina. It was no good trying to pretend she didn't exist. He had to see her again. Talk to her. Only this time, he'd do it right.

In the lobby, Marina sank into a deep chair and leaned back into the soft velvet upholstery. She felt pleasantly tipsy, but her feet were killing her. For the entire evening, she'd danced with one partner after another, pausing only for brief, refreshing forays to the punch bowl. She'd never had such fun! But now, she needed a few minutes in this secluded corner to rejuvenate herself.

Closing her eyes, she let her mind drift. It was the first time in her life she'd let loose like this. Somehow, the costume had unleashed a bold, uninhibited side of her she'd never known existed. Even the jarring sight of Adam on the stage hadn't dampened it. If anything, she'd found herself excited by the idea he might be watching.

"Marina?"

That punch must be more potent than she thought. The very thought of him sent her imagination off. She'd have sworn she heard him say her name. But, of course, that was impossible. Squeezing her eyes shut tighter, she lounged back, settling into the warmth that suffused her. She wasn't going to let thoughts of him spoil this delightful sense of well-being.

"Marina."

The voice was right at her ear now, and—her eyes flew open—oh, my God, it *was* Adam!

"Marina, are you all right?"

She sat up abruptly, and the elastic holding her mask caught on a button of the upholstery. It jerked the mask sideways, covering her eyes. She clawed at it, trying to right it.

She heard Adam's chuckle, then felt his hands fumbling at it. "Just sit still and let me fix it," he said.

His touch, casual as it was, sent shivers racing up her spine. She froze, hardly breathing, while he untangled the elastic.

"There." Gently, he shifted the mask to allow her to see out the eyeholes.

"Th-thank you, Adam," she said, staring at him. She reached up and felt the mask, staring at him, not knowing what to say. Her gaze flicked over him, from the tight-fitting white stockings covering his shapely calves to the pancake hat perched on his head.

"I was watching you dance," he said.

Marina felt her face color. So he *had* noticed her. A feeling of breathless expectation came over her. What did he want? Why was he here now?

"Will you dance with me?" Soberly, he held his hand out.

Even with his mask obscuring his features, Marina saw the compelling invitation in his eyes. There was no refusing it. She reached toward him. Her fingers touched his. A thrill shot through her. He grasped her hand, assisting her to her feet. Suddenly, Marina felt as if she were floating.

Adam was here, and they were going to dance.

He didn't let go of her hand as they entered the ballroom. The orchestra was playing a slow blues piece that stirred her blood. On the floor, Adam took her into his arms.

At first they moved experimentally, gauging each other. Adam had an easy, natural style that Marina followed effortlessly. The music ended, but he didn't release her.

"You're like a feather in my arms," he murmured, his mouth close to her ear.

"Um-mmm," she responded, not wanting to speak and interrupt the delightful sensations flowing through her. The music started again, this time, something with a steamy Latin beat.

Adam smiled down at her. At the same instant, he spun her off into an intricate series of maneuvers. Marina felt her pulse quicken. It was exciting. Challenging. She threw her head back and a feeling of exhilaration swept over her.

Boldly, she took the initiative. Eyes never leaving his, she began moving back, shaking her shoulders and twisting her body sinuously. The coins on her costume jingled with each motion.

Perfectly still, Adam waited, his mouth curved in a slight smile. With a flirtatious toss of her head, Marina advanced, until her scarf brushed his red-lined cape.

He flicked the cape, revolving slowly in a swirl of satin.

Dipping and turning, Marina moved around him—seductive, elusive. The other dancers shifted away from them, making more space. Only Adam and the heavy, sensuous throb of the music penetrated her consciousness.

He held out his hand. Unable to resist the temptation, Marina felt herself reaching for it. A portent of danger flashed through her mind, but it was gone so quickly she hardly perceived it. Their fingers touched. Now there was no retreat. He drew her to him, and they began a spiral of dizzying turns as the music surged to its climax, finishing with a grand dip, Adam's mouth poised just inches from hers.

A roar of applause exploded around them, accompanied by approving whistles and calls. Startled, Marina broke from Adam's grasp. Immediately, he reached for her hand again.

"Let's get out of here," he said, pulling her through the crowd toward the door. She followed, needing to escape the stifling presence of the others. They reached the outside entrance and Marina hung back, still giddy from the punch and the heady sense of him at her side.

"Where are we going?"

"Out. Walking. Anywhere." He paused, then wheeled to regard her with a long, sober stare. "Get your coat. We need to talk."

Outside, the night was clear and cold. The stars glittered in a jet-black sky. It was a curious, silent walk. Adam, hands in his pockets, wandered along the deserted streets, lost in thought. He seemed almost unaware of Marina. But when she shivered, he opened his cape and drew her inside.

The gesture was unselfconscious. At first, she had the urge to pull free. But the warmth of his body was so delicious she couldn't bring herself to abandon it. He appeared to be barely aware she was still there. Emboldened, she slipped her arm around his waist. They began walking again, and despite everything, her heart sang with the joy of being with him again.

They walked along Georgia Street to Stanley Park, then he turned off on a narrow pathway leading to the water's edge. He guided her to a bench that commanded a sweeping view of the waterfront and the opposite shore.

"I thought we could sit here awhile," he said. There was a surprising gentleness to his words.

"It's beautiful," she said softly, trying not to let herself enjoy his presence so much. It was the kind of place lovers would come to be alone, with the lights reflected in the water and the snow dusted mountains silhouetted against the sky.

But she and Adam weren't lovers. They couldn't be. *What was she thinking of, coming here with him?* Abruptly, Marina dropped her arm from his waist and pushed the cape away. "Adam, we should go back." She jumped up and started for the path, but he caught her arm.

"No, please. I brought you here because I . . ." He drew her back toward the bench. "Oh, hell, Marina, I wanted to say I'm sorry about Thanksgiving. I didn't intend for the day to end that way."

In the darkness, she couldn't see the expression on his face, but she heard the plea in his voice. She wavered, wanting to sink down beside him again, knowing the torture she'd be putting herself through if she succumbed to the temptation.

She felt his hand on her arm.

"You don't need to worry. I won't let it happen again," he said softly.

Marina struggled with herself. It had been insane to give in to the impulse that brought her here. Although Adam blamed himself for what happened between them, she knew she was equally at fault. She knew, too, that she wouldn't have the strength to resist if he kissed her again. Was it fair to expect his willpower to do it all?

She looked at him. He slid over, making room for her.

Well, maybe for a little while. Carefully, she sat down, keeping several inches between them.

Adam made no move to sit closer.

Across the water, a rocket shot into the sky and exploded, followed by another and another. "Look!" she cried in delight. The distant boom of exploding fireworks echoed across the water, as the sky filled with a dazzling array of light and color. She turned to him in surprise. "Why are they shooting off fireworks?"

Down the beach and out of their sight, other people were shouting over each fresh eruption. Adam chuckled. "Maybe these Canadians don't have a Fourth of July."

Just then, a great fountain spewed a flaming geyser of myriad colors. Forgetting herself, Marina seized Adam's hand and clung to it, her eyes on the sky.

Although her childhood had never included the big Fourth of July celebrations most of her friends reminisced about, she had once seen the fireworks over San Francisco Bay from her upstairs window. It had been a magical experience. For a short time, it had allowed her to forget the bleakness of her life. Tonight, the magic claimed her again, and she watched, transported.

When it was over, she turned toward Adam. "Wasn't that . . ." she stopped, realizing the childishness of her reaction. He was watching her, a curious, intent look on his face. Somehow, she knew that all along he had been watching her, not the fireworks. A flush of embarrassment heated her face, as she tried to withdraw her hand from his.

Adam's eyes held hers. He tightened his grip, hauling her toward him. Marina tried to resist, but his gaze mesmerized her. She felt herself leaning closer—closer. Her attention shifted to his lips—full, smiling slightly, rich with promise. She swayed toward him. Suddenly, they were clinging together, their mouths fused.

A rush of joy drove all caution from her mind. His arms closed around her. She slid her hands inside his cape. The muscles of his back tensed beneath her fingers as she explored the firm contours of his body. She felt his tongue probing her lips. Opening to him, she thrilled to his invasion as he tasted and nibbled. She strained closer, allowing her own tongue to engage his, wanting to draw him deeper and deeper.

Their breaths mingled, rasping and quick. Unbuttoning her coat, Adam reached inside it, stroking her in slow, tantalizing circles. Marina nestled closer, gasping with pleasure. His hands moved across her ribs to her stomach. She felt him push her scarf aside, and then his fingers stroked bare flesh. A heavy, languorous pleasure suffused her.

At the same time, an alarm sounded in her head, dulled by the aftereffects of the punch and the pleasure of Adam's closeness. Her hands stilled on his back, and she drew a quick breath.

Immediately, Adam pulled back. He gazed at her, his eyes half closed.

Marina tilted her head back, waiting for the pounding of her heart to subside. "You said you wouldn't do that," she whispered.

He didn't speak for a moment. With one finger, he traced the line of her chin, her lips, her nose, her brow. Marina trembled at the gentleness of his touch.

"I'm sorry. I thought I could control myself." Rising, he offered his hand to help her up. "I think I'd better get you home before I do something we'll both regret."

When she stood beside him, he tucked her coat around her and took her hand. In silence, he led her up the path to the street, and they walked back to the conservatory, neither speaking. The parking lot was empty, except for Adam's car.

When he left her at her door a short while later, he made no attempt to come in, and she didn't issue an invitation. The evening had already strained her willpower to the breaking point. From the way he turned abruptly and headed back to the elevator, she suspected he had the same problem.

If she didn't watch out, this chemistry between them could erupt out of control. And she had no intention of letting that happen. Quietly, she closed the door and locked the deadbolt.

As long as Adam Fletcher stayed on the other side of it, she'd be safe. And she was going to make sure that from now on, that's where he'd be.

SEVEN

Adam bolted upright in bed, listening for the sound that had awakened him. It came again—the faint ring of the telephone from the kitchen. He fumbled for the extension on the bedside stand.

With his hand on the receiver, he hesitated. Three-thirty, the lighted dial of the clock said. Should he answer it or not? It was probably some drunk with a wrong number again—the reason he'd shut the damn thing off in the first place.

Deliberately, he flopped back down and turned on his side, pulling the blankets up to cover his ears. Let the dumb jerk wake someone else up tonight. As if in response, the ringing stopped. He sighed and closed his eyes.

In the distance, the sound started once more. With determination, Adam ignored it. He squeezed his eyes shut tight and concentrated on sleep. Or so he thought. Then he caught himself counting. Six . . . seven . . . eight . . . nine . . .

Hell. Rolling over, he snatched up the receiver.

"Who is this?" Unlike the usual calls, there was no background noise on the other end. "Listen, if this is your idea of a joke, I'm not amused." He was about to hang up, when he heard a faint whimper.

"Hello? Hello?" He sat up and heaved his feet over the edge of the bed, shivering in the cool room. "Who is it?" A small, unintelligible garble met his ear. "Say something. Is anything wrong?"

At last, he heard a voice. "Please . . . Adam . . ."

Lord, it was Marina. A nervous chill ran up his spine.

"Marina—are you all right?"

"Yes . . . all right . . . I—I'm just so scared." Her voice was a whisper.

Icy tendrils of fear threatened to squeeze his breath away. "Are you alone? Did someone break in?"

"No, no. Not that." She gave a shuddering sigh. "Please, just talk to me. Th-then I—I'll be okay."

Adam's thoughts whirled furiously. What had frightened her so? Standing up, he carried the phone with him as he went to the closet and found a pair of jeans. "Marina, stay right there. I'm coming. I'll be there in just a few minutes." As he pulled on the jeans and grabbed a shirt, he kept talking.

"No, no . . . you don't need to . . ." her voice grew faint.

Adam stuck his feet into a pair of old running shoes and leaned down to tie the laces, the phone cradled between his shoulder and his ear. "I'm leaving now, Marina. Don't worry, I'll be there soon." Without waiting for her response, he hung up, grabbed his billfold and keys, and ran for the door.

At the slam of Adam's receiver, Marina's heart thudded. The overwhelming fear that had driven her to call him returned full force. Curling up in a corner of the sofa, she wrapped her arms around her knees and rocked back and forth, staring into space.

That dream. Why had it started again? She shuddered at the memory of it and curled tighter into herself. *His* face, his garlicky breath, swept into her mind, as vividly as if the scene were playing out in reality. The feel of his hands groping and pawing—fumbling to probe the little girl in private places she was supposed to keep hidden. . . .

"Oh-hh-h." The cry escaped her throat, and she fought to suppress it. He'd switch her if she made a sound, even though her buttocks were already raw from the last time. She bit her lip, fighting to remain silent as the memory of the greater pain swept over her. Then, just as she had so long ago, she found the tiny space in her mind that offered blessed escape, and slipped into the velvety, encompassing darkness.

The pounding on her door brought her back. Dazed, she sat up straight, uncurling from her tight, protective cocoon.

"Marina, it's Adam. Are you all right? Open the door. Please." On the other side, the voice sounded low and urgent. Adam's voice.

Marina shook her head. Why was he here? It was the middle of the night. He knocked again, calling to her. This time his voice was louder. Lord, what would the neighbors think?

She stumbled from the sofa to release the deadbolt. Suddenly, she realized all she had on was a filmy white nightgown. She felt naked in it. Opening the door a crack, she whispered, "Just a minute, Adam." She started to close the door again, catching a brief glimpse of his agitated face.

"No. Let me in." Adam pushed the door open far enough to slip inside. Shoving it shut, he paused. She stepped backward, hugging her arms across her chest. His hair was rumpled. He looked like he'd dressed in the dark, with his shirt buttoned only halfway up and his shoes mismatched.

"Marina, are you all right? I came as soon as I could." His worried gaze swept over her, then returned to her face.

For a moment, she was puzzled. Came as soon as he could? What had—? Oh, my God. The dream. She felt the blood drain from her face. A wave of dizziness passed over her. She faltered. Immediately, Adam's strong arms gripped her.

"Easy, Marina, easy. I'm here." He picked her up and carried her to the sofa, speaking in a low, soothing voice.

A great sense of relief came over her at the certainty of his manner and the steady thump of his heartbeat. He laid her on the soft cushions and pulled a chair close. Marina took a deep breath, trying to drive the disquieting memory of the dream from her mind. It was only a shadow now, but the familiar sense of dread still hovered.

"Are you all right?" Adam's face was close to hers, his eyes dark with anxiety.

She tried to smile. Her gaze fell on the telephone receiver, off its cradle on the table beside the sofa. It lay dead and silent, the off-the-hook signal long since discontinued. Dimly, she recalled dialing, trying to talk. But the fear had been so overwhelming it jumbled her thoughts. Oh, Lord, how could she have called him? Now he'd probe, try to discover her ugly secret. She sat up and swung her legs to the floor.

"I'm all right, Adam. Really, I am." Her jaw muscles twitched with trying to keep the smile looking natural. "I'm sorry you . . ."

"Don't, Marina," Adam broke in. "I'm glad I was there when you needed me." Casually, he reached over the arm of the sofa and replaced the receiver. "But I think you owe me an explanation."

He spoke softly, but she heard determination in his voice. Her mind raced for a response. Shakily, she gave a little laugh. "I feel like a fool, Adam. It wasn't necessary to wake you like that." She took a deep, steadying breath, watching his face.

His gaze fastened on her with no responding smile. His very patience made her nervous.

"It was just a dream," she said hastily. "I don't know why it upset me so." She glanced at him, praying he'd stand up, start for the door. But he remained unsmiling, watching her in silence. "You can go now." She'd meant to make it sound strong and forceful. But instead, her voice sounded thin and reedy. She jerked to her feet and walked across the room. With her back to him, she stared out the window into the darkness with unseeing eyes.

Get hold of yourself, she thought frantically. She felt her control teetering. One false move, and she'd lose it entirely.

She heard a rustle, then felt Adam behind her. He touched her shoulder. "You're trembling."

She was. She was shaking like a leaf. A hysterical wave of panic brought tears to her eyes. They overflowed down her cheeks.

With firm but gentle pressure, Adam turned her to face him. He reached out and brushed the tears away. Marina stood frozen, struggling to check her unruly emotions.

"Leave, Adam. Please leave," she pleaded.

"No."

"Please."

"I can't." Resolutely, he guided her toward the sofa. "When you called, you were barely coherent. I need to know what was so terrifying it put you into that state . . ." he paused, ". . . and I think you need to talk about it."

A sob escaped, despite her best efforts.

Immediately, Adam's arms went around her. "It's all right," he whispered into the fragrance of her hair. "It's all right."

Her ability to resist evaporated. With great, heaving sobs, she allowed the tears to flow. All the lonely years, all the effort of keeping her emotions so tightly trussed, dissolved in an uncontrollable flood of salty tears. Adam pressed her head to his chest, murmuring soft, comforting words, stroking her with soothing hands.

Marina buried her face in the fresh-laundered fragrance of his shirt and the crinkly cushion of hair that sprang from the gaps where he'd missed the buttons. The moisture of her tears sharpened and mingled the scents of shirt and shower-soapy flesh. They swirled about her, but her mind recognized them only dimly. More important was the great comfort, the *rightness,* of having him there with her. Gradually the tears slowed, then stopped.

It's time, Marina. Let it out.

I know, I know. But what if he's disgusted? What if he's repelled by the ugliness of it?

It's a chance you'll have to take.

It didn't really matter, she knew. He'd never leave until he knew the whole story. With a deep, quavering sigh, she lifted her head, feeling as she did so that she was leaving a protected haven.

"Feel better?" Adam was looking at her, a slight smile curving his mouth. With a thumb, he rubbed the wetness from her cheeks. It was a gesture so incredibly gentle she almost cried again. She felt cosseted and comforted, the way beloved children are cosseted and comforted. Like *she* had yearned to be cherished when she was a small child.

"Oh, Adam . . ."

"Sh-hh-h. Just sit, now. Soon we'll talk." He urged her down, and like an obedient child, she sat, letting him tuck the afghan from the back of the sofa around her.

It probably wasn't necessary, Adam knew, to tuck her in like that, but he did it as much for his own comfort as for hers. That sheer nightgown was sending his mind off in inappropriate directions.

She appeared calm enough now, but he knew her control was mostly on the surface. What was she hiding? What kind of dream would drive her to the desperation he'd heard on the telephone and witnessed here? Carefully, he sat down beside her.

She watched him, her eyes wide and uncertain. Dark shadows showed her exhaustion, emphasized by her dark, thick lashes and the contrasting ice blue of her irises. He saw fear there. Fear of what?

Reaching out, he touched her arm, feeling her muscles tense. Gently, he kneaded the muscles, feeling the tension gradually disappear. She was like a fragile flower that could be bruised if it weren't handled just right. Shifting closer, he stretched his arm along the back of the sofa, brushing a long strand of honey-colored hair away from her brow. She closed her eyes and leaned her head back.

"What was it, Marina? What frightened you?" He kept his voice soft, not wanting to upset the delicate peace she had achieved.

For a long time, she didn't respond. Adam waited patiently. Finally, she heaved a great sigh and opened her eyes.

"It was the dream." She stopped, and for an instant her eyes clouded with new fear.

"What dream?" Adam felt her determination slipping. "What dream, Marina? Tell me. Let it out."

She closed her eyes again. Her hand crept from beneath the afghan to grasp Adam's. Ah, good. Let her cling to him, if it would make it easier for her.

"It's been coming for years," she said, her voice so faint he could hardly hear it. "Ever since . . ." It faded entirely away.

"Ever since . . . ?" Adam urged.

Marina's eyes flew open, glazed with unreasoning fear. Her hand tightened until he felt her fingernails bite into his skin.

"It's okay, Marina. Take your time." He waited until she relaxed some. "Did something happen that make the dreams come?"

She nodded mutely, her face contorted in pain. "Yes," she whimpered, her voice high-pitched, like a child's. "He said if I told . . ." Tears oozed out from beneath her closed eyelids. ". . . if I told, he'd hurt me."

At first Adam was puzzled. "Hurt you? Who would hurt you?" Then he went cold, as the realization washed over him. "Marina, are you saying what I think you are? Did someone do something to you? A man?"

She nodded again, her gaze avoiding his.

"No, no! Don't turn away from me." Afghan and all, Adam gathered her into his arms. Rocking her, he spoke in soft tones. "When, Marina? When did this happen?"

". . . long time ago," came the muffled reply. She pressed closer to Adam, and he tightened his arms around her. For a moment, he thought she would say no more, but suddenly she started speaking again.

"My mama got sick, and I was only five—too little to help her. I just sat and held her hand. For days, I held her hand." Adam had to lean close to hear the words. "And then, one day, they came and took me away. Mama and I didn't speak English, just Polish. I couldn't understand what they told me.

"Then—" She took a deep breath. "—then I went to live with some people. They didn't like me. I couldn't understand what they said, but I knew they didn't like me. They had a little switch, and they would hit me with it. Finally, someone took me away from there and I went to live in an orphanage.

"I learned English there. And I found out my mother had died." Marina pushed back and looked at Adam. "She'd been dead all those days I sat and held her hand."

Adam's heart twisted at the grief he saw in her face. "Marina, don't, if it's too hard."

She shook her head. "No. I have to finish." Sitting up straighter, she kept talking, not relinquishing her grip on his hand. "I heard about adoption, and for a long time I prayed someone would take me home to be their little girl. But when I finally went to live with someone again, it was another foster home. And there . . ." She swallowed hard. ". . . there was a man. And he . . ."

Now her voice failed, and her breathing became rapid and shallow. She clutched Adam's hand as if it were a lifeline. He patted her arm, feeling helpless. Before she could continue, Marina made several false starts. Adam waited, not daring to interrupt.

"That man would take me up into the attic. He'd make me . . ."

Marina broke off, tears streaming down her face. She tore her hand away from Adam's and wrapped her arms around him, nearly climbing into his lap. "Oh, Adam, I'm so frightened. He said not to tell. He said he'd find me and hurt me, if I did." Fear made her words fall over each other.

"What am I going to do, Adam? I've told you now, and there's been someone coming around. If it's him—" Her voice rose in unreasoning terror. "If it's him—" she repeated.

"Easy, easy, Marina," Adam calmed her. "That was a long time ago. You're safe now." He rocked her as he would a little child, hushing and soothing. Gradually, she quieted, and her breathing grew deep and slow. Some time later, Adam realized she was asleep.

Carefully, he moved her from his lap and rose, stretching to relieve his cramped muscles. He gazed down at her, lying on her side, her face resting on an outflung arm. She looked more serene than he'd ever seen her. Suddenly, he knew it was his presence, here tonight, that had made the difference. A giddy sense of well-being washed over him.

Leaning down, he traced her brow, then the fine, straight line of her nose. She was beautiful. Now her brow was smooth and unlined, and the dark circles that had disturbed him earlier were hidden by the shadow of her lashes.

He gathered her up and carried her into her bedroom, lowering her gently to her bed. He straightened and looked down at her. The afghan had fallen off along the way and now she lay there in that oh, so sheer gown. Adam became aware of a fullness in his groin. But more, he felt an overwhelming tenderness toward the sleeping figure.

Gently, he pulled the blankets up and covered her. He knew he should leave. But what if she woke again, frightened? Just then, she rolled to her side and began moving her hand over the pillow, as if she sought something.

"Adam?" she said sleepily. "Adam?"

His heart contracted. Quickly, he knelt and placed his hand over hers. "I'm here, Marina. Don't worry."

"Mm-m-m," she sighed, smiling, slipping back into a tranquil sleep.

Adam waited until her hand fell open before pulling his away. He gazed at her, jumbled feelings of joy and anxiety battling in his mind. They had crossed a great hurdle tonight. Things would never be the same between them. It was a heady idea that both excited and scared him.

Most of all, though, it made him happy. She needed him. He could no more walk away from her now than he could have ignored the telephone call earlier. If she reached for him in the night, he must be there.

Quietly, he tiptoed into the living room and turned off the light. Returning to the bedroom, he shut the door. By the pale light of the street lamp outside, he sat on the edge of the bed and removed his shoes. Not giving himself a chance to think about it, he quickly shucked his jeans, too.

He drew the blankets back and carefully slid underneath. Marina murmured his name, reaching toward him. Lying stiffly on his back, he moved his hand until their fingers touched. He wanted desperately to hold her, feel her warm body against his, slide his hand beneath that sheer nightgown and touch the soft flesh beneath.

But he knew that would be disastrous. His purpose here tonight was something entirely different. Marina needed him, and as long as that need existed, he'd be there. That was all. He'd made up his mind long ago that he'd never allow himself to become seriously involved with a woman, and he had no intention of letting down on that resolve now.

He'd stay with her tonight, and tomorrow morning he'd get up and go home. That's all it was—all it could ever be.

*   *   *

Awareness came slowly to Adam. He lay half-awake, glorying in the cozy warmth, feeling lazy and pleasantly erotic. He had been dreaming of Marina, and in his dream she slept in his arms, spooned tightly against him. The impression of her breast under his hand, its nipple swollen to a hard nub, was so real it sent him spiralling off into sensuous reveries.

With his eyes still shut, he savored the afterglow of the dream—the sleep-softened seductiveness of her body, the fragrance of her hair. Just the thought of her started his body reacting.

A sigh and a movement jolted him into full wakefulness. It was no dream. Marina *was* there with him, her body pressed close to his. It *was* her breast he was caressing.

He jerked his hand back and rolled away. The events of the past few hours rushed back into his mind. He should have known his baser instincts would win out. Guilt propelled him from the bed into the chilly room. Quickly, he retrieved his jeans from the floor and shoved one leg, then the other into them, berating himself.

How could he have been foolish enough to think he could sleep in her bed without wanting to make love to her? He struggled to zip the jeans, sucking in his stomach to get the tab past the jutting evidence of his lack of control. After all she'd been through, she didn't need the likes of him taking advantage of her vulnerability.

He felt a surge of cold fury at the thought of the abuse she had suffered. Who was the man that had been coming around? *Was* there a connection? Picking up his shoes, Adam tiptoed across the room and sat on the bench in front of her dresser to put them on. If there was, he'd personally confront the bastard and tear him apart. Then he'd . . .

"Adam?"

Adam froze. In the back of his mind, his intention had been to leave a note and slip out the door before she woke.

"Adam . . . you're here? But why . . . ?" Her voice was bewildered.

In the dim light, he saw her looking at him, a puzzled expression on her face. She lay motionless, her hair fanning out on the pillow. There was a sleepy befuddlement about her that sent Adam's pulses racing again. He fought the urge to strip away his clothes and slip back under the blankets. He wanted to gather her close, kiss away the confusion.

With great control, he rose and walked to the side of the bed. Gazing down at her, he tried to smile reassuringly. "I didn't want to leave you. I was afraid you might wake again and be frightened."

At his words, the memory of the night before washed over Marina. Abruptly, she sat up. The blanket started to fall away, and she grabbed it, keeping it tight around her shoulders. How could she have called him? She felt her face flush in embarrassment.

"Adam, I'm sorry," she said. "I don't know why I bothered you." She scrutinized his face with anxious eyes, seeking a sign of the disgust he must feel. When Ramon said he loved her, she'd told him only about the beatings. *That* had been plenty to turn him away. But Adam knew it all now—all the ugly secrets she'd hidden for so long.

Oh, Marina, how could you?

As if he read her thoughts, Adam sat on the edge of the bed and reached for her hand. Holding it loosely, he caressed her palm in slow, soothing thumbstrokes. "Marina, you don't have to be ashamed. It wasn't your fault."

She dropped her eyes, wishing she could lose herself once more in the blissful forgetfulness of sleep. Faint recollections of him holding her, soothing her, hovered at the edge of her mind.

She remembered pressing herself closer to him in the night and felt a deep flush spread over her face, She had needed to feel the warmth and strength of him, the erotic thrill of having him pressed against her. When she woke, it was in a sensual haze. If he'd still been beside her, she knew she'd have tried to seduce him.

The very thought made her cringe. What must he think of her? "Adam, I'm sorry. I—I . . ."

"Look at me, sweet."

She opened her eyes to find his gaze on her face. "I don't want you to regret anything that happened last night." He lifted her hand to his lips and kissed it, then tucked it back beneath the blankets. Standing up, he paused. "I hope you have eggs and bacon in the refrigerator. I'm going to show you that the great Adam Fletcher is not only a world-class cellist, but also a world-class cook."

"Marina, wait up."

Marina paused on her way down the hall from her woodwind master class. Annie caught up with her, breathless.

"Let me buy you a cup of coffee," she said, falling in beside Marina. "I thought you might want to room together on the tour."

Marina hadn't even thought of room arrangements for the chamber group's first tour, which was only a few days away.

"I guess we should make some plans, shouldn't we?" She gave Annie a sideways frown. "I have a few other things to discuss with you, too. Like the great Halloween kidnap caper." Stopping, she faced Annie, hands on her hips.

Annie had the grace to look sheepish. "Aw, come on, Marina. You had a wonderful time." She took Marina's arm and steered her toward the faculty lounge. "We looked for you to take you home, but you'd already left," she said, lifting her eyebrows knowingly. "Several people said they saw you go with Adam."

Marina felt her face redden. "It wasn't like that," she said as they entered the lounge. Inside, Adam was at the coffeepot, pouring himself a cup.

"Ah, ladies, good morning." He lifted the coffee pot.

"May I do the honors?" Although the question was directed at both of them, his eyes were on Marina.

A little shiver of pleasure chased up her spine.

"Well, ah—"

"Sure, you can," Annie said quickly. She went to the cupboard for some cups.

"Is everything all right?" Adam asked in a low voice.

She hadn't seen him since Saturday, when he'd cooked a monstrous breakfast and they'd dawdled over it until well into the afternoon, although he'd called several times.

"I told you, Adam, I'm fine." She kept her voice low, too, glancing at Annie. Finding only one clean mug in the cupboard, Annie was washing another at the sink. "I don't want you to worry about me," Marina whispered urgently. "It was very nice of you . . ."

"Here we are," Annie said cheerfully, coming up from behind. She set the mugs on the counter for Adam to fill. Glancing from him to Marina, she hesitated. "I'm not interrupting anything, am I?"

"Oh, no," Marina said quickly.

"Of course not," Adam agreed. "We were just saying how much we're looking forward to the tour." Picking up his coffee, he motioned the women ahead of him to a group of easy chairs on the other side of the room. A few seconds later, two more members of the chamber group wandered in and joined them.

With all the discussion about the week's rehearsals in preparation for the tour, there was no further opportunity for Marina and Adam to talk—to Marina's relief. That incident had been humiliating enough as it was. She was going to make every effort to forget it ever happened.

As they left, Adam hung back to walk with her. Just outside the door, he said, "I'll pick you up for the evening rehearsals this week."

"That's not necessary, Adam," Marina protested. "I'm perfectly capable of taking care of myself."

Stopping, he gave her a hard look. "I'll be by at quarter

of seven." Giving her no opportunity to respond, he turned on his heel and hurried toward his office.

A week later, the chamber group arrived in Victoria for the opening tour of the Foundation series. They would go from there to several other communities on Vancouver Island. The initial concert would be held at the venerable old Empress Hotel that evening.

Everyone was keyed up. On the ferry, Marina had tried to enjoy the spectacular scenery of the Gulf islands, but her mind refused to focus on anything except the performance. She hardly glimpsed Adam. He prowled the decks like a restless lion. When they returned to the bus, he went directly to a seat at the rear, hardly speaking as he passed Marina.

"I wonder what's got his goat," Annie commented.

Marina didn't respond. Throughout the day, he'd acted remote, uncommunicative. Had she done something to upset him? When he'd left after dropping her off the evening before, he'd been polite and friendly, as usual.

At the hotel, there was a flurry of activity as the musicians received their keys and room assignments. John Deering rounded everyone up for a brief meeting. "You're on your own for a few hours, but be back here at three for rehearsal," he said.

Marina watched Adam. He seemed fidgety and more restless than ever. As soon as the meeting was finished, he hurried toward the elevators. What was bothering him? Marina started after him, but he had already stepped into an elevator and the door was closing behind him. It must be pre-concert jitters.

Still . . . The worry nagged at her. Since *that* night, he'd been hovering around her like some kind of guardian angel. Maybe she'd better find him—get things straightened out. Picking up her suitcase, she headed for the elevator.

"Wait up, Marina."

At the sound of Annie's voice, Marina swung around. The other woman came puffing up, lugging the largest garment bag Marina had ever seen.

"Let's get this stuff to the room, then go to lunch."

Marina hesitated. "I'd love to, Annie, but I want to find Adam. He's been acting so unfriendly."

Annie laughed. "You're overreacting, Marina. He's just like the rest of us—nervous about tonight's performance." Shifting her garment bag to the other hand, she hoisted it. "Come on. Let's go to our room and get settled. He'll probably beat us to the coffee shop. You can see him there."

But Adam didn't show up in the coffee shop. Marina kept glancing at the doorway, waiting for him to put in an appearance. Had he gone to eat somewhere else? Was he sick? Her mind uneasy, Marina paid for her lunch and turned to Annie.

"You go ahead with the others. I'm going to find Adam."

Annie began to protest, but Marina held firm. "I'll see you at rehearsal."

All morning long Adam had felt restless and twitchy. He was always on edge just before an important concert, but today was worse than usual. The ferry ride had been almost unbearable, cooped up on the vessel with nowhere to go for privacy. When Marina had come to sit beside him in the passenger cabin, it was all he could do to keep from snapping at her.

It wasn't until they'd nearly reached the hotel that the buzzing started. Suddenly, the significance of his irritability hit him. He should have known. It had been nearly six weeks since the last time—longer than usual. Lord, why couldn't it have happened a few days ago? A sensation of near panic seized him. He had to get to his room, away from all these people.

Impatiently, he waited for his key, then stood at the

edge of the group while John Deering gave his briefing. The buzzing grew louder—not critical yet, but he knew he didn't have any time to waste.

He saw Marina start toward him. Quickly, he broke away and headed for the elevators. He'd make excuses to her later. He had to get out of here now. Away from her. Away from all the others.

The elevator was old and slow, and the ride to his room on the fourth floor seemed endless. The car was crowded, stopping at every level on the way up. His head throbbed with anxiety, the persistent drone increasing in intensity. Each time the door opened, he had to control the urge to bolt.

At last, the elevator reached his floor. He hastened out and down the corridor. Hurrying past each room, he glanced at the numbers on the door. Ah, here it was! The key rattled as he stabbed at the lock. His head felt like it would explode. Finally, the door swung open and he staggered inside.

He kicked the door shut and fell across the bed. Thank God! He closed his eyes. No need to fight it now. He lay there, waiting.

His mind floated free, bits of scattered thoughts congealing, then evaporating in the prescient waves of sensation. Suddenly, he tensed. The whirring in his head grew and expanded, driving away all else. His body stiffened, anticipating the final onslaught. At last, suddenly and completely, the overwhelming darkness descended.

Marina waited until the others had left, then hurried to the elevators. She'd heard the desk clerk tell Adam he would be in room 422. Impatiently, she stabbed at the call button. It seemed an eon before the car arrived and the doors rumbled open.

Inside, she hesitated, her finger poised over the panel of buttons. Would Adam be upset if she came barging in on him? Maybe he was one of those musicians who needed complete isolation before a concert.

No, there had to be something else. If it was something to do with her, she had to know, clear the air before the concert. Straightening her shoulders, she jabbed at the button for the fourth floor.

At Adam's door, she stood for a moment trying to quiet her pounding heart. It was silly to be so nervous. Raising her hand, she knocked softly, then waited.

There was no response. She knocked again, harder. Nothing. A pang of disappointment washed over her. Where could he be? Slowly, she turned and started back down the corridor, thinking.

"Can I be of assistance, ma'am?"

Marina looked up to see a maid standing outside an open door a few rooms away. "Oh, no, but thank you. I guess he's not there." Then a thought hit her. What if Adam was sick? He hadn't looked well when he left. It wouldn't hurt to check. Just in case . . .

"Actually," Marina gave an embarrassed laugh, "I left my key inside, and my husband . . ." She hesitated. "Do you think you could let me in my room?"

"Why certainly, ma'am."

To Marina's relief, the maid went unhesitatingly to the door and unlocked it, holding it open slightly. With her hand on the knob, Marina smiled at her. "Thanks so much. I really appreciate this."

"Always glad to help a guest. It's part of the Empress policy, you know." Briskly, the maid hurried back to her cart.

Marina waited for a moment to get her courage up. Maybe she should just forget the whole thing. Adam would be at the rehearsal. She could talk to him then.

With a sigh, she began to close the door. Just before it latched, she paused. But what harm would it do just to take a quick look—make sure he *wasn't* in there? He'd never know. Not giving herself time to change her mind again, she shoved the door open and slipped inside, closing it quietly behind her.

There was a short corridor before entering the room proper. Marina could see Adam's suitcase on the floor near the window, but a wall hid the rest of the room. She almost turned around and left then, but something propelled her further.

Slowly, she walked to the end of the corridor and peered around the corner.

Adam lay face down on the bed.

EIGHT

Marina stood there, staring at Adam's still form. A giddy wave of relief swept over her. He was taking a nap. That was all.

She started to tiptoe out, but the sudden realization that he still wore his jacket pulled her back. That was strange. The room was quite warm, but he hadn't even taken the jacket off. As she looked at him, his eyes opened slightly. They were glazed and out of focus. Her heart constricted. This was more than an ordinary nap.

Moving closer, she reached out and touched his shoulder. There was no response.

"Adam, wake up." She spoke softly.

He blinked, but gave no sign of real awareness. She nudged him, gently at first, then harder. The tempo of his breathing continued, labored and irregular. Her mind flashed back to that other time, when she had found him in his studio.

"Adam, can you hear me?" She shook him. "Adam? Adam?" No matter how loudly she called or how hard she shook, he failed to respond. What was wrong with him? What should she do?

Driving back a rush of panic, she tried to think what to do. He needed help. A doctor. Maybe there was a hotel physician. Yes, that was it. Hurrying to the phone, she punched the number for the desk. Her hands shook so hard she could barely hit the buttons.

"A doctor, please. Room 422." Anxiously, she looked at Adam. "Hurry. *Please*." Disconnected thoughts raced through her mind as she hung up. She walked from one side of the room to the other, then back again. Was it a stroke? A heart attack? What if he died? Oh, God, how could she stand it?

It seemed hours before there was a quiet tap at the door. She ran to open it. A dapper little man carrying a black physician's bag stood there.

"I'm Dr. Hughes. Where's the patient?"

"In there, doctor."

Quickly, the doctor walked to the bed. Adam's eyes fluttered open as the doctor rolled him to his back and unbuttoned his shirt, then took out his stethoscope and began to listen to his heart.

Adam groaned and raised one arm to push the doctor's hands away.

Marina stood by the bed watching anxiously. "What's wrong with him?"

"I don't know yet." The doctor leaned closer while he palpitated Adam's chest and stomach.

"Go 'way," Adam muttered. He plucked at the offending hands ineffectually. "Don't need you."

The doctor leaned forward, sniffing. "Has he been drinking?"

"I don't think so." Marina had rarely seen Adam take a drink. And never in daytime. "No, I'm sure not. He has a performance this evening." She leaned forward, bending over the doctor's back.

"Marina—go," Adam mumbled, his voice slurred.

The doctor paused and turned to her. "Is that you?"

Marina nodded.

"Perhaps you'd better wait in the hallway. You appear to be upsetting him."

Her first impulse was to refuse. She opened her mouth, but the doctor spoke first.

"Please, ma'am. I'll keep you fully informed."

Marina glanced at Adam hoping for some sign, but he had closed his eyes again. "All right," she said softly. Reluctantly, she turned to leave.

Outside, she paced the corridor her mind whirling. What was wrong with Adam? Why didn't he want her there? At last, she perched on a chair in the lounge near the elevator, staring at Adam's door.

Fifteen minutes later, the doctor came out. Marina sprang to her feet and hurried to him.

"Is he all right?"

The doctor smiled and walked briskly toward her. "He's fine. Nothing to be alarmed about."

Marina felt the tenseness drain out of her. "But what was wrong with him?" She watched the doctor's face.

His smile turned polite and professional. "You'll have to talk to him. I can't discuss a patient's condition with anyone else."

"Couldn't you just give me some indication——?"

"I'm sorry." The doctor's smile was sympathetic, but his voice remained firm.

Marina turned from him, her mind racing. Would Adam talk to her? Somehow, she doubted it. But——she threw her shoulders back in resolution——she was going to give it a try.

"Thank you, doctor." Her voice was brisk now. "I'll do as you suggested." She started toward Adam's door.

"Ma'am——" The doctor's voice halted her. "Mr. Fletcher asked me to tell you that he'd like to rest undisturbed, but he'll be at the rehearsal this afternoon." There was a note of apology in his tone.

Marina gave him a hard look.

The doctor shook his head, evading her eyes. "I'm sorry, but I'm bound by professional ethics." He glanced at his watch. "And now, I really must be off." He held his hand out. "You can take my word for it. There's nothing to worry about. Mr. Fletcher is in excellent health."

Swallowing back her frustration, Marina shook his hand. "Well, anyway, thank you for coming, doctor. At least you've put my mind at rest." As he turned to go, she stuck her hand in her pocket and watched him walk down the corridor. He was hiding something. She was certain of it.

And so was Adam.

Slowly, she turned toward the elevators. Someday soon she was going to get to the bottom of this. She'd revealed her darkest secret to Adam. If he had something to hide, he owed it to her to be honest, too.

Shortly before three o'clock Marina went to the ballroom for the rehearsal. Most of the other musicians were already there.

"Marina, you missed a wonderful tour," Annie greeted her with characteristic ebullience.

She babbled on, and Marina made automatic responses. But her attention was on the doorway. Would Adam get there?

At last, she saw him walking through the lobby, carrying his cello. Annie was in mid-sentence, but Marina interrupted. "Excuse me, there's Adam. I need to talk to him." She left Annie standing there, a surprised expression on her face, and started in Adam's direction.

Without a glance her way, he began to uncase his cello. She reached him just as he started for his chair.

"Adam, wait a minute . . ."

"All right, everybody, take your places." John Deering had moved to the front of the room and stood there waiting for the group to settle down.

"I'll talk to you later," Adam muttered. Quickly, he moved past Marina to his seat.

She watched as he situated himself, her eyes alert for a

sign of the symptoms she saw earlier. He seemed pe fectly normal.

"Marina, are you ready?"

She wheeled at John's voice, embarrassed to find herself the only one not in her place. "Why—sure." Quickly, she moved to her seat and busied herself arranging her music on the stand. Immediately after, John took his own seat and the rehearsal began.

It went without a hitch. Adam's playing was perfect—if possible, surpassing his usual performance. At every opportunity, Marina stole a glance at him, seeking some sign of illness, but he appeared perfectly normal.

When they finished, Adam sat for a moment. The aftereffects of the—episode, as he preferred to think of it—were still with him. He felt logy and unwound. From the corner of his eye, he saw Marina headed in his direction, a determined look on her face. What could he tell her? She wouldn't let him put her off again. Not after finding him like that. Mustering his courage, he rose to face her.

"Marina—I was just coming to get you." His face felt frozen in its tight smile. How could he disarm her? He struggled to appear casual, motioning toward his instrument. "Let me put this away. Then—" he looked at his watch. It was nearly five-thirty. "—let's go for dinner." He'd make sure they ate with the others.

She stared at him, her eyes worried. "Do you feel all right, Adam? The doctor said . . ."

"I'm fine." Busying himself with his cello, Adam avoided her gaze. He felt damn guilty. Her concern wasn't just curiosity—she really cared. He owed her some kind of explanation. But what?

He thought for a moment. A headache. That would do it.

Fastening the case, he straightened. "Uh, Marina . . ."

Her eyes sharpened. "Yes?"

Adam took a deep breath. "I don't want you to worry about this afternoon. You see, I get these—headaches."

"Headaches?" He noted surprise in her expression.

"Since I was a child. Migraines. They come on fast and hard, and the only thing I can do is sleep them off."

"I see." She smiled then, and he could see the lines of tension in her face relax. "Oh, Adam, I'm so relieved. You can't imagine the awful things that were going through my mind."

He felt his own nervousness fade. A tiny trace of guilt nagged at him, but he forced his mind away from it.

George Russell's voice from across the way saved him from responding. "You two coming for dinner?"

Adam looked at Marina, and she nodded. There was no shadow of worry on her face now, no lingering doubt. Adam felt almost giddy relief. Suddenly, he was excited at the prospect of having dinner with her—with all of them. The worst was behind him. At least a month of worry-free time was ahead.

He was going to make the most of it.

The concert went wonderfully well. From her vantage point in the center of the ensemble, Marina maintained a wary observation of Adam, alert to any sudden change that might signal a problem. But he was in perfect form. The whole group was in perfect form.

Afterward, Robert Graves appeared backstage with Ian Campbell and Jacob West at his side. All wore broad smiles. Robert stepped forward and clapped his hands for silence.

The easygoing chatter ceased. Hurriedly the musicians closed their instrument cases and turned their attention to the newcomers.

"I want to introduce Ian Campbell and Jacob West, of the B.C. Arts Foundation. They flew over with me this afternoon to attend tonight's premiere," Robert said. He glanced around the group, his pride obvious. "I wanted to tell you all how pleased we are. Tonight's performance surpassed our fondest hopes."

Ian stepped forward. "I'd like a word, too, Robert." His gaze fastened on Marina, then shifted to Adam. A mischievous smile danced around his mouth. "After our somewhat—ah—*inauspicious* beginning, I must admit we had a few reservations about this program."

There was a scattering of chuckles, and Marina felt her face redden. She glanced at Adam. He smiled uncomfortably and looked away.

Ian waited for the noise to die down and continued. "But—I'm delighted to say our confidence in your abilities and your professionalism has been handsomely rewarded. The Foundation is very proud of all of you, and we look forward to the continuing season, and the possibility of a more permanent arrangement in the future." He smiled warmly. "Thanks, folks, you've done a terrific job."

His words were met with a burst of applause from the members of the ensemble. Marina looked again at Adam. This time, he was smiling in her direction, clapping along with the rest. Adam came over to her.

"Do I dare ask you to come to the reception with me?" He rubbed his face and grinned slyly.

For an instant, Marina didn't realize what he was referring to. Then, the vision of her livid handprint emblazoned on his cheek burst into her mind. To her amazement, she felt not embarrassment, but a nearly uncontrollable urge to giggle.

"Well?" Adam watched her, his head tilted to the side.

She sighed. "Now why did you have to bring that up?"

He gazed at her, face sober, eyes twinkling. "I believe that was the inauspicious beginning our friend from the Foundation was referring to."

Marina shook her head. "Oh, Adam, I can't believe I did that." She gave a rueful laugh.

His deep chuckle joined hers. "It was a little stunning for me, too." He took her hands and wheeled her around so they were facing each other. The amusement in his eyes faded. Marina felt the smile leave her face.

"We've come a long way since then, haven't we?" Adam said softly. His coffee-brown gaze was warm and tender.

Her pulse began to pound. She darted a look around. All the others had left.

"Adam, we should go. . . ."

"In a minute." Gently he pulled her closer. "I've regretted my bad behavior that evening. I want to apologize for it. . . ."

His face was so close now that his features were blurred. Marina wanted to step back, but the will had deserted her. "It's okay, Adam. I forgave you long ago," she said faintly.

He paid no attention.

". . . and to give you a proper kiss of congratulations. . . ." He brought his hands up to cradle her face, tilting it until their lips were only a fraction of an inch apart.

Marina caught her breath, waiting. His lips touched hers, and she closed her eyes, unable to resist the sensations that rioted through her body. His mouth explored hers gently. She allowed the textured silkiness of his tongue to part her lips, savoring his taste and feel.

That's enough, Adam. Step back before it's too late.

But Adam knew it was already too late. He gathered her to him, deepening the kiss.

Marina slipped her arms around him, threading her fingers in his hair to draw him closer. His scent of soap and bow resin wafted into her nostrils like a dizzying balm. In the silence that surrounded them, she heard the rasp of their breathing. A longing started deep inside her, heavy and urgent.

Adam had intended it to be no more than a gentle kiss. But the moment he touched her, his control left him. She was so soft, so delicate. Holding her in his arms seemed so right, so natural. It made him feel whole.

"Oh, Marina," he whispered. Every time they made music together, he dreamed of holding her like this.

She moaned softly, letting her head fall back to allow him access to the silken flesh of her throat and neck. He felt her shudder as he licked the sensitive area beneath her ear. He had a strong urge to draw the skin into his mouth and suckle, leaving his mark. No, he couldn't do that to her. The evidence would be there for all to see, and this was something very private, very personal between them.

"Hey, you two, don't you know the reception's already started?" At the sound of Annie's voice, the spell shattered. She stood in the doorway, squinting in the dim light.

Marina jumped back, and Adam quickly turned.

"We'll be right there, Annie," Marina said. Adam detected a breathless quality in her tone.

"Oh, my, I interrupted something." Annie began to back out, her voice contrite.

"It's okay," Adam muttered. "We were on our way, anyhow." Keeping his back to her, he busied himself with fastening his cello case. He looked down. His cutaway, with its impeccably tailored trousers, concealed nothing. The evidence of his response to Marina was all too apparent.

He glanced at her. She was pulling at her dress and smoothing her hair back. Her eyes met his, then dropped to his crotch.

The corners of her mouth twitched. "Uh—Adam, maybe you'd better . . ."

"I know, I know." He shrugged, smiling. "It's what you do to me." He tucked a honey-colored strand of hair back in place behind her ear. "I'd say you could use a little repair work, too."

Her lips, devoid of lipstick and still swollen from his kiss, looked soft and tempting. He felt the tightness in his loins begin again, and sucked in his breath. "Maybe if you'll take yourself off to freshen up, I'll be able to get my body parts under control again," he said softly.

Marina looked at him with a slow smile that nearly did him in. Before he could act, she picked up her flute case and gave her hair a final pat. "I'll meet you in the lobby in ten minutes." Not giving him a chance to respond, she scampered out the door.

Adam watched her go with mixed relief and regret. She was getting under his skin in a way no woman ever had. If he wasn't careful, he'd lose control completely, and that would do neither of them any good.

He took a deep breath and picked up his cello. In the relaxed, almost euphoric state that always followed his episodes, he'd let down his guard. But he couldn't let himself slip again. It was too risky. They would be friends. That's the only thing that could work. He walked thoughtfully through the silent room. That way, at least, he'd never have to confess his awful secret.

And he'd never have to face either her pity or her disgust.

A week later, the chamber ensemble returned to Vancouver. As the bus rolled off the ferry at Tsawwassen for the last brief leg of the trip, Marina settled against the reclining seat and studied Adam's profile. As he had every day on the road, he shared her seat.

This was a strange relationship they'd developed. He stirred sensual feelings in her she'd never experienced before. Whenever he was near, she could hardly concentrate on anything else. For the first time in her life, she found herself fantasizing over the physical pleasures they could experience together—a subject that had always filled her with paralyzing terror.

She affected him in the same way, she was certain. Little signs, like the tenderness in his face when he looked at her, or the way his eyes followed her in a crowd, spoke with quiet eloquence. But since that evening backstage, he had made no move to touch her or to take their relationship further than friendship.

That puzzled Marina. But at the same time she felt relief. She had a very successful career, one that had taken many years of dedicated work to create. Music was her life. Her need for personal relationships was fulfilled by wonderful friends scattered around the world. Her life was very complete. Very satisfying. Introducing a foreign element, such as a love entanglement, would upset its delicate balance.

Adam turned his head and smiled. His eyes were gentle, with the special light that appeared only when he looked at her.

"You're awfully quiet. What are you thinking about?"

Lazily, Marina stretched, catching the high seat back in her hands. "Oh, I don't know. How good it's going to be to get home, how much fun it's been."

"It has, hasn't it? I had no idea Vancouver Island was so big, or so beautiful." He leaned back in his seat, his gaze far-off. For a time they rode in silence. Then Marina spoke up.

"What's putting that pensive look on your face?" Strange how comfortable she felt with him now. A week ago, she'd never have dared ask such a question.

Adam smiled. "Just daydreaming, I guess. Remembering what that teacher in Duncan said about skiing on the island—how you can see all the way to the west coast from the top of Mt. Washington. It must be like skiing on the top of the world." He sighed, eyes remote, a small smile playing around his mouth.

Marina settled back. The thought of skiing with him, standing by his side on top of a mountain, sharing wth him the beauty, the intense pleasure of flying down the slopes, brought with it a pang of nostalgia. She hadn't skied for several years, not since Alison and Sam died.

Alison Kyle, a music teacher in the grade school Marina

attended, had seen the child's talent and had taken her from the orphanage when she was eleven. Everything Marina became, she owed to Alison and her husband, Sam. They had given her a loving home, flute lessons, taught her to ski and swim. From a frightened, uncertain child, they'd transformed her into a strong, self-confident woman. Then they'd died in a plane crash her first year of college.

Quickly, Marina pushed the memory from her mind. The pain of their loss was still so intense she couldn't bear to think of it. That's the way it was with deep personal relationships. When something happened to end them, it hurt too much.

"Marina, it's time to go." Adam's voice jolted her out of her reverie.

She'd been so lost in her thoughts, the bus had stopped and the others had begun to stir without her noticing. With an apologetic glance at him, she fumbled for her purse and other belongings. He waited until she found everything, and they left the bus together.

"Well, I guess I'll see you tomorrow." Marina picked up her suitcase. Adam still had to wait for his cello to be unloaded. To her surprise, the thought of leaving alone, of going back to her quiet apartment held no appeal. Somehow, the solitude she had always treasured seemed lonely now.

Don't try to fool yourself, Marina, you don't want to leave Adam.

Instead of joining the crowd gathered around the bus, he remained at her side. "Wait for me. I'm coming with you."

Marina's heart leaped. Immediately, she caught herself. "There's no need, Adam. I can manage alone."

"Don't argue, Marina. I'm going to make sure your mysterious caller hasn't paid a visit while we were gone." He gazed at her, and once more the warmth of his eyes wrapped her in pleasure. "Please," he said softly. "Stay here. I'll be right back."

She watched him walk away. If she were smart, she'd ignore his instructions and get away from him as quickly as possible. But it was as if her feet were bolted to the ground. Adam cared about her, and he was looking after her. No man had ever treated her that way. It made her uncomfortable, but at the same time she loved it.

Suddenly, a startling fact struck her. Not only did she love the way he treated her, but she loved him as well. A sinking sensation caught her in the pit of her stomach.

All the defenses she had worked so diligently to build were crumbling. And in the process, she was leaving herself vulnerable. Adam had become so much a part of her life that she couldn't bear to turn him away.

God, what was she going to do?

NINE

Christmas was coming. The season started early in December, when faculty and students gathered to decorate the grand old Conservatory building. With contagious high spirits, they draped fragrant cedar garlands and hung over-sized evergreen wreaths. Amid exuberant snatches of Christmas carols and great draughts of pungent mulled cider, they decorated the fifteen-foot Douglas fir in the lobby with twinkling white lights, lacy Victorian bows, miniature musical instruments, and sparkling crystal icicles. Afterward, a group of students formed an impromptu band, and everyone danced in the cavernous marble hallway until midnight.

A week or so later, carolers started to roam the corridors during the noon hour, and the sweetness of traditional songs rang out from every nook and cranny. The energy and excitement of the season vibrated in the air as everyone made plans for their own celebrations.

Marina hated it.

Since Alison and Sam had died, Christmas had been a lonely time for her. For a few years, she'd accepted the invitations of friends, but she found her loneliness even greater being in the midst of their love and warmth. It was a family time. She had no family. She preferred to spend the day helping with meals for the homeless or some other charitable effort.

Since the tour, she and Adam had seen each other nearly every day. He frequently picked her up on his way to the Conservatory and delivered her home at the end of the day. As often as not, he'd remain for dinner, chatting with her from a safe distance as she moved around her tiny kitchen. They never seemed to run out of things to say. Afterward, they'd both squeeze into the narrow space to wash the dishes and tidy up.

It was all very domestic. Also very chaste. Since the kiss they had shared backstage after the concert, both had maintained a careful distance.

Twice they went skiing at Grouse Mountain, just across the Lion's Gate Bridge on the north shore. Nervous at first, Marina quickly found her skill returning. Adam was a superb skier. By the end of the second day, they had skied every part of the mountain, taking turns leading the way, keeping close together.

Afterward, Adam took her to where he lived, in West Vancouver. It was a large, sprawling house high on a rocky promontory with a sweeping view of Burrard Inlet and the city. He leased it from a professor on sabbatical in Europe.

They walked into the living room and Marina immediately moved to the wide picture window. She stood there for a moment, taking in the broad sweep of water, mountains, and city. "If I had this view, I'd spend all my time looking at it," she said softly.

She hadn't heard Adam's footsteps behind her on the deep, sumptuous carpet. She turned, and her movement caught both of them unawares. Adam tried to dodge out of the way at the same time as she tried to pull back. Off balance, they both reached out.

Marina found her face buried in his chest, the fresh, outdoorsy fragrance of wind and snow and sunshine swirling in her nostrils. Her cheek rested on the slick nylon of his parka. His heart pounded a thumping tattoo beneath her ear. For a long, luxurious moment, she didn't move. It had been so long since he'd held her, she'd nearly forgotten how good it felt.

Then, slowly, she lifted her head. Adam gazed down at her, his eyes soft and full of tenderness. His arms tightened around her. Mesmerized, Marina waited, watching his mouth move toward hers. Her breath caught, and with all senses at full alert, she closed her eyes in anticipation.

But the kiss never came. Instead, Adam set her back gently, his hands remaining on her arms to steady her.

"You okay?" He regarded her with that gentle look that always made her insides melt.

She swallowed, trying to keep the disappointment out of her face. "I'm fine." She felt her lips tremble as she returned his smile. "But, Adam . . ."

Immediately, his face grew wary, and he dropped his hands.

Let it go, Marina. Don't ask questions you don't want to hear the answers to. She hesitated a moment, then gave in to the inner urging. "Never mind. It wasn't important."

A wave of relief washed over Adam. How could he have answered the question he knew must be in her mind? By now, she had to realize he was making a deliberate effort to keep her at arm's length. With effort, he pulled his mind away from the disturbing thoughts.

"Well, I know something that *is* important. Dinner." He reached over and tugged at the zipper of her parka teasingly. "How about getting out of that and keeping me company in the kitchen. Tonight, Chef Adam is going to show you he not only knows how to cook breakfast, but the world's finest dinner, as well."

By the time they finished eating, things were back to normal. Well, *nearly* normal. They talked and laughed, making little jokes about events of the day, incidents at school—the usual lighthearted chit-chat. But Adam detected a faint shadow in Marina's eye, a look of puzzlement as she watched him, thinking he was unaware.

Afterward, they took their coffee to the living room. Adam built a fire in the fireplace and put a Bartók string quartet on the stereo. He relaxed against the soft upholstery of the sofa, sipping his coffee, enjoying the music, watching Marina.

Instead of joining him, she wandered around the room, coffee mug in hand, looking at the collection of small primitive pieces that complemented the simple elegance of the furnishings. Adam regarded her thoughtfully. Her face was still flushed from the sting of snow and the chill wind from the day's skiing. She looked youthful and carefree.

He had to admire her gutsiness. For someone who hadn't skied in ten years, she wasn't afraid to tackle anything. True, on the first trip they'd stuck to the intermediate hills so she could get the feel of the new-style equipment. But today, knowing he usually skied the expert slopes, she'd insisted that they tackle the toughest runs on the mountain.

At first, he'd taken it easy, but soon he saw that she could keep up. Her nerve never deserted her, even when she took a bone jarring fall that sent her head over heels. She dusted herself off and aimed her skis down the fall line. He didn't catch up with her until they reached the bottom.

He smiled, remembering. A thought began to form in his mind. With the Christmas holiday so near, maybe they could . . .

No. The timing wasn't right. He couldn't take the risk. Firmly, he rejected the notion.

Marina's voice jarred him back to the present. "Your landlord must be a world traveler."

Adam started. "What? Oh—oh, yes. He's an anthropologist." Abruptly, he set his mug on the coffee table and stood up. "He and his wife have been collecting artifacts for over thirty years." Moving to where Marina stood in front of the mantel, Adam watched her run her hand over a cribbage board carved from a walrus tusk. "That's my favorite."

Standing next to her, he watched her face as she touched the surface of the ivory, feeling the contours of the carved walrus head at the end, the tiny details of the hunts etched along the sides.

In the dim lighting of the room, her long, dark lashes cast feathery shadows on her cheeks. The straight line of her nose might have been sculpted by one of the artists that created the artifacts she was looking at. Her lips were slightly parted as she concentrated on the piece. A surge of desire caught Adam so suddenly he could scarcely control the impulse to reach for her.

No. He'd promised himself.

"Do you play?"

It took a moment for Marina's words to sink in. He looked up to see her gazing at him, her eyes questioning.

"Why—sure." The clear blue of her eyes made his breath catch. With trembling hands, he picked up the ivory board, pretending to study it while he collected himself. "Would you like to try a game?"

"Sure," she said softly. A small smile played about her lips. "But watch out. I'm a pro."

All during the dozen or more games, the thought of a ski vacation with her nagged Adam. Mentally, he counted the weeks between the start of the tour and Christmas. Five and a half. The longest he'd ever gone was six. If something happened while they were together, would he be able to fob it off as another headache?

No, better let well enough alone. He fished his glasses out of his pocket and put them on.

"Adam, it's your turn." She was looking at him with that puzzlement in her eyes again. Her two cards were in the crib and he still held all six of his.

Quickly, he selected a king and a nine and added them to the crib, then grinned at her. "This time I've got you, my friend."

"You think so?" She laid down a five.

Adam glanced at the up card. It was a five, too. He

covered hers with a jack. "Fifteen for two," he said, pegging his points with a flourish.

Marina looked at him with a sneaky smile. She laid down another jack. Nobs. "Twenty-five—for two." Delicately, she pegged her points and looked at Adam with a question in her eye.

"It's a go," he said, sighing. She added a second five and pegged one more. He put down his other jack, and she covered it with another five.

"Fifteen for two," she said softly.

"I'll be damned," Adam muttered. "A perfect hand." He looked at the board, mentally counting. Although he had a head start on her, she was going to win. Again. Pulling a woeful face, he tossed the rest of his cards in. "Okay, okay, I concede."

"Poor thing," Marina said solicitously. She reached over and patted his hand. He could see the twinkle in her eye. "I told you I was a pro." Gathering the cards, she laid the deck on the table and looked at her watch. "Much as I hate to quit while I'm ahead, it's time to go home." She stood up and picked up the coffee mugs. With a superior smile, she started toward the kitchen. "Any time you feel like getting trounced again, just let me know."

Scowling as fiercely as he was able, Adam picked up the ivory board and took it across the room to the mantel. "It was luck. Pure luck."

"Well, we'll see," Marina said pausing at the doorway. Then she disappeared around the corner.

Adam broke down and chuckled. There was nothing he'd enjoy more than taking her on again.

The cribbage game gave only a brief respite to his distracting thoughts. On the way to her apartment, the notion of a ski vacation wouldn't leave his head. As they drove down the quiet city streets, festive with Christmas decorations, his mind roved free, indulging his fantasy. In his reverie, he heard the whisper of snow beneath their skis and felt her presence beside him at the top of a mountain. The sky stretched out, vivid blue against the brilliant white of the snow and the . . .

"Watch out, Adam!"

Just in time, Adam jerked the wheel to avoid straying across the centerline. Lord, he needed to keep his wits about him or he'd kill them both. He glanced at Marina. She was watching him with concern in her eyes.

"Are you all right?" He heard worry in her voice. "You aren't getting one of those headaches, are you?"

A nerve began to tic in Adam's throat. He kept his eyes straight ahead. "No, I was just daydreaming." There was a red light ahead. It gave him a chance to look at her. He smiled disarmingly. "Really, Marina, the headaches are nothing to worry about. They don't happen that often— less than once a month."

"Oh." She fell silent, and he could almost hear her mind working. The light changed. When they started moving again, she spoke. "Then they're predictable? You can tell when one's coming?"

Adam felt the smile on his face stiffen.

"Well, sort of." He took a deep breath. "Just leave it alone, Marina. They're nothing to worry about."

He reached over and punched the radio on. The sounds of a Haydn symphony filled the car. He let the uncomplicated tones wash over him, distancing him from the troublesome thoughts he knew were in Marina's head. They weren't far from her apartment now. If he could just get her home before the music was over, he'd avoid more questions.

He should have known she wouldn't be so easily distracted. From the corner of his eye, he saw her reach for the radio. Immediately, the camouflaging sound ceased. The silence seemed heavy and ominous.

"Adam . . . ?"

He felt a strangling wave of panic rise in his chest. Desperately, he cast about for something—anything—as a distraction. Her apartment was just ahead. He slowed the car and pulled up to the curb. Wrenching the key from the ignition, he turned to her and blurted the first thing that came into his mind.

"Are you going anywhere for Christmas?"

There was a surprised silence. Then, in the light from the streetlamp, he saw her face grow wary.

"Well, I . . ." she paused, a look of confusion replacing the wariness. "I don't think so. Why?"

You've done it now, Fletcher.

He swallowed. She was waiting. "I don't have any plans either," he heard himself say. "Why don't we spend a week or so skiing?"

"Skiing?" Marina gazed at him, her eyes searching his face. "I don't know . . . ," she said, looking away.

She didn't like the idea. He was off the hook. Adam waited for the relief to come, but instead an irrational pang of disappointment swept over him. Arrogant fool. What right did he have to assume she'd jump at the chance to go off with him? Jamming the keys in his pocket, he reached for the door handle.

"That's okay. It was just a thought." He opened the door and started to get out.

"Adam."

He wanted to turn at the sound of her voice behind him. But he needed to free himself from her presence. Just for a moment, while he recovered his control.

It was crazy, overreacting like this.

A chill wind had come up since the afternoon, bringing with it a few flakes of snow. It was bracing. The sting of the snow on his face hurt just enough to get his mind away from the pain inside. He heard Marina's door slam. When he got around the car, she stood on the curb, waiting for him.

"It's cold," she said, smiling through chattering teeth. She had a long wool scarf over her head, the ends tossed back over her shoulders. Snow glistened on it and on her eyelashes.

Adam fought the impulse to pull her close and warm her with his body heat.

"We'd better get you inside, so you don't freeze." He tried to keep his manner light and casual. Neither spoke as they walked toward the building.

Inside, Marina made no protest when Adam escorted her to her apartment. By now, it had become routine for him to make sure everything was all right.

But tonight, there was a strain between them that hadn't been there for weeks. Adam waited only long enough for her to get the lights turned on and take a quick turn through the rooms.

"Well, I guess I'd better go, if I'm going to beat the snow."

"Just a minute." Marina dropped her scarf and parka on the sofa and followed him to the door.

He stopped, hand on the knob.

"Your idea about going skiing, it caught me by surprise."

Adam felt another twinge of pain, deep inside. He fought to keep the polite smile on his face. "It doesn't matter, Marina. I thought it might be fun."

"It would be. I'd like to go."

For a second, Adam just stood there and stared at her. Then a great surge of joy bolted through him.

"Well," he said. He smiled, then felt his lips stretch as the smile grew wider and wider. "Well, well." He laughed in delight. All at once, the whole evening took a new turn. They had plans to make. Things to talk about.

Marina laughed, too. "Shall I make some coffee?"

"That would be nice." Adam followed her back into the apartment, unzipping his jacket as he went. He threw it on the sofa beside her things and perched on the stool in front of the breakfast bar. "I thought Mount Washington might be fun. Ever since the tour, I've been thinking about it."

Marina measured the coffee and poured the water into the hopper. "Me, too."

Adam noticed a lilt to her voice that hadn't been there earlier. *She's excited*, he thought. A tremor of pleasure passed through him. Suddenly, the whole idea of Christmas took on a new aspect—a breathless quality he hadn't felt since he was a kid.

As they drank their coffee and made their plans, his anticipation kept growing. By the time he finally left, he felt like a kid waiting for Santa Claus. Marina's sparkling eyes told him she felt the same way. This would be a Christmas to remember.

It wasn't until he was back in his car, driving through the snow across the Lion's Gate Bridge, that he began to come down to the reality of the situation.

He couldn't possibly spend a week with Marina, twenty-four hours a day, without falling in love with her. How was he going to handle *that?*

A shiver of excitement raced up Marina's spine as she pulled into Adam's driveway. In an hour, she and Adam would be on the Nanaimo ferry, off to Mount Washington for a glorious ten days of skiing. For the past week, her mood had alternated between excitement and dread at the prospect. Now, two days before Christmas, the time had finally come.

The door was ajar, and without knocking she pushed it open.

"Adam, I'm here," she called. There was no answer. She walked in and stopped. The house seemed quiet. Too quiet. An uneasy feeling prickled the base of her neck.

"Anybody home?" Her voice hung in the still air.

She had a fleeting impulse to turn and run, but it died almost before she was aware of it. Adam must be home. His car was in the driveway. Anxiety drove her forward, through the living room and the dining room. In the kitchen, the dishwasher drying light was on. But where could Adam be?

She started down the hallway toward the bedrooms,

peering in each one as she passed. Everything was in perfect order. Adam's cello and computer sat undisturbed in the study. Now there was just one door left, and it was half-open. Adam's bedroom.

She held her breath as she moved down the narrow Persian carpet toward it. Suddenly, she stopped. What was that sound? It was faint and rhythmic, not a snore, exactly, but a breathy rasp. All at once it dawned on her. It had to be Adam—with one of those headaches.

Her step quickened. She didn't know whether to laugh or cry. "Adam," she called, hurrying into the room. He lay across the bed, his clothing in disarray. A backpack was propped against an easy chair near the door. A heap of clothing littered the floor near the bed.

She went over and sat beside him. "Adam, it's me, Marina," she said, speaking loudly. He made no response. *Don't worry, he's all right*, she told herself. Still, anxiety tightened her chest.

Take it easy, Marina. He'll wake up soon. Don't make a fool of yourself by overreacting.

As if her thoughts transmitted themselves to him, he rolled to his side and his eyes flickered open. Unfocused, they had a look of dazed confusion.

"Adam, I'm here." Marina leaned closer, bringing her face into his field of vision. She watched him struggle to fix his gaze on her. He lifted his hand, and she grasped it. "Are you all right?" she asked.

Adam groaned, clinging to her. Gently, she stroked his hand.

"Is it a headache? Can I get you some medicine?"

With a great heave, Adam pushed himself up, then fell back again. " 'S okay," he mumbled. "Jus' takes . . . time." He lay for a moment, his eyes closed.

Marina watched him, alert to any sign of a problem. Obviously, their ski trip was off, at least for now. A pang of disappointment flickered through her. Guiltily, she forced it from her consciousness.

His grip tightened, and he struggled to sit up. She touched his shoulder with a restraining hand. "Just rest, Adam. Wait until you feel better."

Impatiently, he brushed her hand aside. "No problem now."

He *did* look better. His eyes had lost their dazed look, and he seemed more awake. Hesitantly, Marina sat back and watched as he sat up and slid his legs over the side of the bed. Pulling away from her, he sat for a moment with his elbows on his knees, resting his head in his hands. Marina hovered beside him.

"Adam, why don't you go back to bed. Rest for today. We can leave tomorrow."

His head jerked up. "No!" he said sharply. Although he appeared tired, he seemed alert now. "I'm fine. Just give me a few minutes to get these things together, and we can go." As if to show her the truth of his statement, he rose to his feet. Weaving slightly, he started picking the clothes up off the floor.

Marina jumped up. "Sit down. I'll do that." Nudging him aside, she took the clothing from his hands and put it in the backpack. He stood there, watching. "Just sit," she said sternly. Then she softened a little. "You can tell me where you want things." To her surprise, he didn't object. Good. Once she got the packing off his mind, she'd get tough about waiting until tomorrow.

It only took a few minutes for her to get everything shipshape. "Anything else?" she said, stuffing the final pair of jeans into the pack.

He rose. "No, I got everything ready before this damn—uh, headache—hit. Let's go." He smiled, and she could see it was an effort.

She took a deep breath. "Adam, I think we should talk about that." Moving closer, she planted herself squarely in front of him. "I think we should wait until tomorrow. That way . . ."

His jaw tightened, and his eyes sparked with determination. "I'm fine now. We can go." He started around her to get the backpack.

"But you're not well . . ."

He stopped, then moved back toward her. Heaving a sigh, he planted his hands on her shoulders. "Marina, I've been dealing with this for years. I know what to expect. You don't have to worry about me."

His smile was benign, but she felt steel in his grip. Picking up the backpack, he started for the door. "Coming?" Not waiting for her response, he continued out and down the hallway.

She stood there. It appeared that Mr. Adam Fletcher was not to be easily dissuaded. She'd better stick with him, if for no other reason than to protect him from himself.

"There!" Marina jammed the last can of soup into the bulging cupboard and shut the door. "I think we're safe from starvation for at least a month. Maybe two."

Adam grinned at her from behind the stack of empty boxes in his arms. "Better too much than too little."

She groaned. "Honestly, Adam, if I'd known we had to pack in a quarter of a mile through the snow, we'd have gotten along without most of this stuff, especially the soft drinks and wine. And the canned stew and chili." She flopped into a kitchen chair and propped her elbows on the table. "And the *ice cream*."

He had the good grace to look sheepish. "Aw c'mon, Marina. We're on vacation." Before she could say any more, he ducked out the door, headed for the storage room to dispose of the boxes.

Marina watched him go. There was no sign now of the disabling headache. Still, she couldn't help but worry. He'd seemed so disoriented, so out of it.

Pushing the nagging thoughts to the back of her mind, she kicked off her snowboots. Wiggling her toes inside the bright red ski socks, she stood up. Adam was fine. The energy and vitality he'd displayed during his trips back and forth from the car couldn't have been manufactured to fool her. She wandered out of the kitchen, examining her surroundings.

The condo wasn't sumptuous, but it was definitely comfortable. An eating bar separated the kitchen from a large common room that was obviously the center of operations. A game table sat in front of a wide, paned window. Nearby, a long bookcase housed several shelves of paperbacks and a stereo system. A collection of tapes and records occupied two more shelves.

Marina moved toward it. Under her feet, the fawn-colored carpet was thick and deep-piled. The furnishings were in muted earth tones. Immediately, she felt a sense of warmth and relaxation.

One entire wall was taken up with a massive stone fireplace. In front of it, a long sectional sofa curved invitingly. For an instant, the vision of flames dancing and herself and Adam nestled together flashed into her mind.

No, Marina! Don't torment yourself!

Quickly, she grabbed a record from the shelf. It was an old Sinatra album. *For Lovers Only*. She jammed it back on the shelf.

"Marina?"

She jumped and whirled. Adam stood in the kitchen. As she turned, he spotted her.

"There you are." With a smile, he started toward her. He looked strong and virile. That unruly lock of hair had fallen across his forehead again, and Marina's fingers itched to smooth it back.

She swallowed. Despite her best efforts, her mind swerved back to the scene before the fireplace. Oh, Lord, had she made a terrible mistake coming here alone with him? Would she be able to stand the torture of having him so near, but so inaccessible?

Adam paused before he reached her side. Backlit by the fading light from outdoors, Marina appeared silvery and mysterious. Her features looked soft and delicate, and her hair, disheveled after its confinement under her fluffy mohair ski hat, formed a pale nimbus around her face. His breath caught. She was a fragile dream-lady. He felt a sudden, powerful urge to take her in his arms.

What had he done, bringing her here alone like this? Was all their time together going to require a struggle to control himself?

"Adam?" Her voice held a note of alarm. "Are you all right?"

She took a step in his direction, and that small motion was enough to arrest his disturbing thoughts. He was strong and well disciplined. He'd be damned if he was going to let anything spoil this vacation.

"Of course, I'm all right." He felt proud of the calmness in his voice. "We'd better get the rest of this stuff stashed—" He nodded toward the hallway, "—or we'll be falling all over it for the rest of the day." He picked up a couple of suitcases and started down the hall toward the bedrooms.

The first held two sets of stacked bunk beds and two dressers. There was barely enough space to turn around. Striding by it quickly, Adam opened the door to the other room, obviously the master bedroom. It was spacious and comfortable. A huge, king-size bed occupied most of one wall, while louvered doors along the other side hid a closet and built-in dresser.

Adam carried Marina's suitcase in and laid it on the bed. Behind him, he heard the intake of breath as she stopped in the doorway.

"There you are, madame. All the comforts of home." With a sweep of his arm, he motioned around the room. As he turned, he saw a confused expression on her face. Suddenly, he was seized with the fantasy of lying naked in that large, comfortable expanse, with her in his arms. A fullness began in his groin.

"Adam, I can't sleep here. I'd get lost in that bed."

Her words only served to ignite his desire. Desperately, he fought back the tantalizing sensations he felt.

"You take this room. The other will be fine for me."

Adam inhaled slowly, willing his unruly emotions back under control. "Nonsense, Marina . . ." he began.

But she was having none of it. She marched in and hauled her suitcase off the bed, starting for the doorway. Adam couldn't let her do that. If he slept there alone, he didn't think he'd be able to resist his need for her beside him. He made a grab for her suitcase, and for a moment the two of them engaged in a polite tug of war.

"Really, Adam. I mean it."

She had a determined set to her jaw, and he knew he was on the verge of losing the battle. This was ridiculous.

Desperately, he cast about for a way to stop her. He fished in his pocket for a quarter. "Okay, we'll flip a coin." He held up the coin and showed her both sides. "You call."

Marina didn't say anything—just stood there with that stubborn look on her face.

Adam shrugged. "Okay, I'll call. Tails." He sent the coin spinning high into the air, and reached out to catch it. But it glanced off his hand toward Marina.

She jumped back, and the coin fell to the floor. With a startled glance at Adam, she dropped to her knees to retrieve it.

Instinctively, Adam reached for it, too. Their hands collided, and she jerked hers back. Suddenly, Adam knew the source of her reluctance. She wanted the same thing he did.

Slowly, he moved his hand away from the coin, hardly daring to look down. Her eyes dropped, and his gaze followed.

The coin on the floor showed heads.

TEN

Marina woke the next morning just as the first rays of sunlight colored the dawn sky. From down the hall, she heard the faint rattle of pots and pans in the kitchen. Adam was already up. He must not have tossed and turned all night, as she had.

Every time she began to drift off, the tantalizing thought of him just beyond the thin wall had sent waves of longing through her. She had strained her ears for the slightest sound, only too aware of the emptiness of her too-large bed.

When she entered the kitchen, he was breaking eggs into the frying pan. The fragrances of bacon and fresh-brewed coffee filled the air. Her stomach growled.

"Well, it's about time, sleepyhead." Spatula in hand, he turned from the stove at her arrival. His hair was still damp from the shower. He took a mug down and poured a cup of coffee for her. "Here. Wake up with this while the eggs cook."

Not waiting for her to respond, he plunked the coffee on the breakfast bar and turned back to the stove, whistling a jaunty snatch of the Bach C minor Fugue.

Marina climbed up on the stool and sipped her coffee. How could he be so disgustingly chipper first thing in the morning? She watched him toss a couple of slices of bread into the toaster and slam the lever down, then swing back around to turn the eggs. Places were already set at the bar, and the plates sat on the counter beside the stove. Efficiently, he served each with eggs and bacon, then snatched the toast out, buttered it and added it to the plates.

"Your breakfast, ma'am." With a devastating smile, he put one heaped-up plate in front of her and seated himself across the way. He picked up his fork. "Well, dig in."

Marina laughed. "Lord, Adam, are you always like this in the morning?" Shaking her head, she regarded him dubiously while he dipped his toast in the egg yolk and took a big bite.

Washing it down with a swallow of coffee, he grinned. "Think you can stand it for nine more days? I like to get up and at it." He took a bite of bacon. "It must carry over from when I was a kid. My dad and I used to be on the stream at dawn to fish the morning rise, then Mom would cook our catch for breakfast."

Thoughtfully, Marina spread raspberry jam on her toast. "It must have been nice, having parents to do things with, knowing you belonged to someone."

The playfulness went out of Adam's eye. "It was. I hated it when they sent me away to school. All I could think of was getting back—to them, to the peace of the mountains." His eyes had a far-off look. "I've always thought . . ."

Marina stopped eating, ears sharply attuned. A dozen questions leapt to her lips, but she pushed them back waiting for him to go on. "You've always thought . . . what, Adam?"

At her voice, he started. "Wha—? Oh, nothing." With visible effort, he smiled. "Just silly childhood dreams. They don't mean anything."

"But, Adam . . ."

"Come on, slowpoke, there's a foot of powder out there waiting for us." The lighthearted glint was back in his eye. He polished off the last of his egg, then leaned back in his seat with a look of contentment. "Ah, that was good."

Marina hurried to eat her last few bites. She felt his eyes on her, restless, eager, impatient to be on their way. His energy and enthusiasm transmitted themselves to her, and by the time she was done, she was as excited as he to get out on the slopes.

Getting him to finish what he'd started to say would have to wait until later.

Adam was aware of Marina's presence every moment of the day. On the ski lift, his flesh tingled at the casual contact of their shoulders and thighs, even through his heavy ski clothes. On the slopes, he couldn't take his eyes off her graceful figure as she shot down the runs. When they talked, it took all his willpower to keep from brushing a flake of snow from her eyelash or tracing the line of her lips as she laughed in exhilaration at the bottom of the hill.

Damn. He'd been doing fine until the argument over the bedrooms. All night long, he'd lain rigid in the narrow bunk bed, trying not to think of her in the next room. And then that conversation at breakfast. If he hadn't caught himself, he'd have blurted out those ridiculous fantasies he'd kept so carefully hidden since he was a teen.

Now, he waited in the lodge for her to return from the ladies' room so they could eat lunch. With Christmas so near, there were few people around. Even so, the building was decorated for the season. A large fir tree stood in the entry hall, adorned with glittery snowflakes and foil icicles. Evergreen branches and big red bows gave a festive touch to the windowsills and doors.

Adam felt a sharp pang of nostalgia for the cozy ranger cabin of his childhood. Although there were only the three of them in that isolated spot, his mother always filled the house with aromatic evergreen boughs and lovingly-crafted

Christmas decorations. For weeks, the spicy scents of Christmas baking filled the air. It was an exciting, happy season, and the very thought brought back a boyish sense of delight and anticipation.

"Ready?" Marina said, coming up beside him. He'd been so lost in his thoughts, he hadn't noticed her coming.

She'd taken off her ski hat, and her hair fell over her shoulders, softly curling. Adam turned an unwary gaze on her, still caught up in memories. With stunning suddenness, the sight of her—face ruddy from the outdoor chill, framed by a honey-gold cloud—hit him. He drew a sharp breath, fighting back the urge to bury his fingers in the silkiness of her hair and taste the sweetness of her smiling lips.

Forcing a responding smile, he stuck his hands in his pockets.

"You bet. I'm starved."

They ate in the cafeteria, carrying trays of chili and sandwiches to the rough wood tables where they could look out across the valley. But Adam's mind wasn't on the scenery. All during lunch, his thoughts kept returning to those childhood times. It had been years since he'd paid any attention to the holiday season. Usually, he was on the road and Christmas Day was spent in a hotel room, relaxing between appearances.

But this year, things were different. An idea began to take form in his head. He and Marina could have their own little celebration. In his mind, he could almost smell the piney scent of the tree and visualize it in front of the cabin's large picture window.

Marina was chattering on about the excellent snow and the magnificent view from the top of the upper chair. Impulsively, Adam set his mug of coffee down and leaned forward, forearms on the table. "Marina, let's get a Christmas tree."

She stopped midsentence. "What did you say?"

Adam chuckled. "How about a Christmas tree? Here we are, in a Christmas-card setting. We should get into the spirit of it."

For an instant, Marina thought he was joking. But one look at the eagerness on his face told her otherwise. She felt a knot begin in the pit of her stomach.

"Oh, Adam, I didn't think . . ." she paused, searching for words. She struggled to hide her dismay.

". . . I'd go for something like that?" Adam grinned. "I'm really a sentimental fool. Being here brings back all my warm, cuddly childhood memories. Mom and Dad used to . . ." He stopped abruptly. "Oh, God, I'm sorry. I wasn't thinking, Marina."

Marina stared at his face. His eyes reflected concern and self-reproach. Immediately, she felt guilty. He'd been so enthusiastic, just like a kid. It was a side of him she hadn't seen before—a side she suddenly realized she wanted to know better. As for her, she was grown now. Those sad childhood years couldn't touch her any longer. It was time to cast them out of her life and start anew.

Mentally squaring her shoulders, she looked him in the eye and smiled.

"I think a Christmas tree would be a wonderful idea."

"There. That should do it."

Stretching precariously, Adam placed an aluminum-foil angel on top of the eight-foot Noble fir standing in front of the picture window. Climbing down from the kitchen stool, he stepped back and viewed his handiwork.

"Not bad, if I say so myself."

Marina couldn't help but smile at his obvious satisfaction. All afternoon and evening he'd been caught up in making plans for their celebration, infecting her with his excitement.

First, there had been the madcap shopping trip to Courtenay, where they'd stopped at the first Christmas tree lot they found.

Adam had insisted on buying the tallest, most perfect tree on the premises.

Next, he'd hauled her to a nearby variety store, where they bought the last of the lights and several boxes of foil icicles. Loaded down, they made a final stop at a grocery store, where Adam loaded the cart with frozen cookie dough and packaged cake mixes.

"We'll make our own Christmas cookies," he'd insisted, tossing in every variety of sprinkles on the shelf.

Marina followed, hurrying to match his long strides. "Adam, remember we have to carry all this stuff," she reminded him laughingly.

"Don't worry about a thing," he said with a breezy wave of his arm. "I've got it all under control."

Marina just shrugged. It would have done no good to object, anyway.

As soon as they got back—him carrying the tree, her staggering along behind with two grocery bags full of supplies—he set her to work cutting snowflakes out of paper towels and twisting aluminum foil into stars. He set up the tree and put the lights on.

Now they were finished. The tree stood there in twinkling splendor. The fragrance of cinnamon and cloves emanated from the kitchen, mingled with the woodsy scent of the tree. The music of Christmas carols played softly in the background. Adam went over and turned the overhead lights off, plunging the room into darkness, leaving only the tiny points of brilliance on the tree.

Marina stood quietly, taking it all in. "It's beautiful," she murmured. Sensing his presence behind her, she turned. "Oh, Adam, it's beautiful." Unexpectedly, her eyes filled with tears.

"Aw, now, Marina." With clumsy gentleness, he rubbed a tear away with his thumb. Another immediately took its place, then another and another. "Don't cry. There's nothing to be upset about," he murmured, attempting vainly to staunch the flow.

Marina tried to smile, but the tears just kept coming. "I'm not upset, Adam," she sobbed. "I'm happy. I've never felt like this before."

Before either of them quite realized what was happening, Adam's arms were around her and he was kissing the salty moisture from her cheeks.

He wanted her. With an intensity he'd never felt before, his body clamored for the release he'd denied it. He felt her unresisting form melt into his, her breasts thrusting against his chest.

Even as he fought the temptation, his lips sought hers, finding them open and moist, inviting his tongue to plunge deeply into the recesses of her mouth.

Snatches of rational thought flitted through his mind. *Adam, get yourself under control. Don't spoil it.* He moaned, seeking to drown out the unwelcome reminders. He slid his hands under her sweater, impatient to feel her burgeoning breasts with his sensitive fingertips. In response, she burrowed her arms beneath his shirt, running her hands over his taut flesh in slow, wide circles.

"Yes, Marina. Touch me," he whispered, moving slowly against her.

Don't, Adam, the sane part of him cautioned. *It isn't right. It will cause both of you more pain.* The notion might have stopped him, but at that point, Marina found his nipple. She rubbed the heel of her hand over it, sending excruciating sensations through his body. He stiffened, and all sensible thought fled his mind.

"Ah-h, Marina," he breathed, burying his face in her hair. He stumbled backward, seeking the sofa. He needed to stretch out and feel her beside him, where he could love her slowly and thoroughly. At the motion, she stiffened and pulled back.

Adam froze. "Marina?" A part of him rejected the idea of stopping now, but another part acknowledged the prudence of her action.

He lifted his head and gazed into her eyes. They were heavy-lidded, and in the dim light, soft with emotion.

"Marina?" he whispered again.

Instead of moving from him, she remained in the cradle of his arms, her eyes searching his face. Did she see his disappointment? His relief? He steeled himself, ready for her to turn away.

"Adam, I—"

"It's all right, Marina. I understand," he whispered, touching her cheek with gentle fingertips.

She caught his hand and brought his fingertips to her lips. For an instant, her eyes clouded, then her face gentled in a shy, hesitant smile.

"Adam, I—I want to make love with you."

At first he stared at her, not sure he'd understood her words.

She kept her smile, but he saw that her lips trembled. "Do I have to ask you twice?" So low he could hardly hear it, her voice betrayed her uncertainty.

"Oh no, Marina. No, no," he whispered, gathering her close. He kissed her once, then again. She melted against him, burying her face in his shoulder.

"I'm so nervous, Adam. I'm not experienced, except for . . ." He felt her shudder.

"Sh-hh-h. Don't think about that. This is us, and it will be wonderful. I'll be gentle—you'll see." In his arms, he felt the tension ease out of her.

"I want to please you," she said hesitantly, her words muffled.

Taking her head between his hands, he tipped her face up and looked deep into her eyes. "You couldn't help but please me. I—" he caught himself just as the word love began to form on his lips. The voices he had tried so hard to ignore now came back, full force. But it didn't matter.

She wanted him. Needed him. He didn't know where this would take them, but he had to answer the gnawing hunger that had plagued him since the first moment he laid eyes on her.

Bending down, he captured her lips with his. They were soft, and they tasted sweet. Oh, so sweet. He felt a great surge of tenderness, coupled with a sense of joyous elation. With a sigh, she wrapped her arms around his neck. The gesture was trusting, almost childlike. For an instant, Adam hesitated. She was so vulnerable. He would be gentle, but what if he frightened her—hurt her?

Marina drew back, her eyes soft and questioning. "Adam? Is there something wrong?"

Resolve replaced his uncertainty. Quickly he kissed her. "Oh, no, love." Not taking his mouth from hers, he shifted his position to slide his arm behind her knees and lift her up into his arms. Slowly, he began to walk down the hall to her bedroom.

A prickle of nervousness shuddered up Marina's spine as he carried her inside. Gently, ever so gently, he laid her on the bed, pulling the pillow from under the bedspread to cushion her head. The light from the hallway slanted in, casting the room in half-shadow.

She shivered in mingled excitement and apprehension, her gaze fastened on his face. She loved him. Trusted him. He'd understand if . . . No. She wouldn't allow the ugly specters of her past to intrude. Not now, not when she'd finally found the strength to banish them.

As if he sensed the conflict she was experiencing, Adam hesitated.

"Marina, are you positive?" The tender, caring look on his face reassured her.

"Yes—oh, Adam, I do want you," she whispered.

The bed gave, as he sat on the edge. "Ah, Marina," he sighed. Placing one hand on either side of her, he leaned forward to brush his lips across hers.

She closed her eyes, willing all thought from her mind, allowing the feel and taste and texture of him to permeate her senses. "Mm-mmm," she sighed, savoring his touch, wanting more.

He shifted, stretching out on the bed, his upper body pressing her into the soft mattress. A deep, heavy torpor began to build inside her. His hand came into contact with her bare flesh, and she moaned.

"It's all right, love," he said softly. Carefully, he maneuvered her sweater up and over her head. Then his mouth was on hers again, warm and gentle, moving over her lips, her jaw, down her neck.

She felt his hands fumble at the catch of her bra. It fell free, and she felt her nipples harden in the chill of the air. He touched her then, capturing her breast in his hand, kneading it gently, allowing the nipple to burgeon and swell under the heat of his palm.

Waves of sensation washed over her. Hesitantly, she placed her hand on his chest, sliding it between the buttons of his shirt. Her fingers encountered the soft mat of hair on his chest, and she began to pull back.

"No, don't stop," Adam whispered, gasping with pleasure. With fumbling fingers, he unbuttoned the buttons and opened his shirt to her. Shyly, she explored the firm, muscular flesh.

Adam moaned, the sound coming from deep in his throat. Tearing his mouth from hers, he brushed his lips down the sensitive curve of her neck, drawing the silken skin into his mouth, leaving a trail of moisture in its wake. Her small whimpers of pleasure only served to heighten his excitement.

He dipped his mouth lower still, seeking the turgid tip of her breast, laving it with his tongue.

Marina felt a fiery heat begin deep in her center. It radiated through her body. Adam slid his knee between hers, and she felt his erection straining against her abdomen. Responding involuntarily, she shifted to bring her body in closer contact. His hand left her breast and migrated downward, toward the waistband of her jeans. Slowly, gently, he slid his fingers beneath the band and inside.

His fingers paused as they encountered the puckered ridges of her scars. Marina gasped. Suddenly, her languorous warmth was pierced by panicky chill. Instinctively, she shoved herself back, away from the memories that were trying to force through the barriers of her mind.

"No!" she cried. "Adam, I can't do it!"

Adam's body stilled, but instead of allowing her to push away, he held her to him tightly.

"Easy, easy, Marina," he whispered. He moved his hand from the offending scars and rubbed her back in slow, soothing strokes. "I don't want to rush you." With infinite gentleness, he kissed her, teasing the tremble from her lips with caressing nibbles. "It's all right," he murmured. "We can stop if you want to."

Gradually, her fear quieted. Adam felt her body relax as his calming ministrations took effect. With effort, he controlled his own desire. He didn't dare allow himself to follow his instincts. One false move could bring back all the horror of her past.

"Adam, I'm sorry." In the dim light, he could see the distress in her eyes. "For a minute I just . . ."

He kissed the words from her lips. "Don't worry. If you want to stop, we will."

For a long moment, she was silent. He sensed a battle raging within her. His arms tightened in a protective circle. Damn the person who did this to her. Damn all of them who allowed it to go on.

"Adam . . . ?" Her voice was tiny, so low he could barely hear her.

"Yes, Marina." He brushed a strand of hair away from her brow and leaned close to hear her words.

"You won't hurt me too much, will you?"

Adam's heart gave a lurch. "Hurt you? Oh, my darling, I'll try not to hurt you at all." His desire, quelled for a moment, came raging back, so strong he felt his body begin to shiver. With infinite restraint, he kissed her, gently at first, then as she responded, with greater urgency.

With startling suddenness, her body took fire. Beneath his lips, hers opened; her tongue meeting his, tasting, exploring the sensitive surfaces, pulling it deeper into the warm, sweet darkness.

With a groan, Adam rolled to his back, taking her with him. He felt her hard nipples against his bare chest, and the slow, back and forth motions she made as she rubbed them over his sensitized flesh nearly drove him mad.

He slid his hand between their bodies to the fastening on her jeans. She lifted so he could unzip the zipper. With both hands, he nudged the jeans down, then her panties. To his amazement, he felt her hand at his belt, fumbling with the buckle. Rolling to his side again, he started to help her undo it.

"No, let me," she said. Sitting up, she used both hands to unfasten the belt, then the zipper. When her fingers came into contact with the hard bulge of flesh, barely restrained by the fabric, she hesitated.

Adam held his breath. Would she lose her nerve?

But no. She pushed the jeans down until he could kick them free and returned to his briefs. Adam struggled to a sitting position, maneuvering to help her remove them.

At last, they were both free of their clothes. As if she only then realized what she had done, Marina gave a small gasp and raised her eyes to his face.

He smiled, feasting upon her beauty. Her hair, escaped from its usual confinement, tumbled over her back and shoulders in a soft, tangled mass. "You're beautiful," he whispered.

Her lips curved in a small, tremulous response. Kneeling, he raised her to face him. She was perfect. Exquisite. His gaze traveled from the smooth, classic planes of her face, over her breasts, past her narrow waist and the gentle roundness of her hips to the honey-dark triangle at the apex of her thighs. She watched, eyes anxious.

He ran his finger over her lips, then brushed a strand of hair from where it had fallen over her forehead.

"Beautiful," he whispered again.

Her face relaxed then. Tentatively, she reached toward him, her fingers traveling down the line of his cheek and across his jaw. Her touch was butterfly delicate, fragile and sweet. Adam caught his breath, struggling to control the ripples of sensation her leisurely investigation created. Slowly, she explored his body—his neck, chest . . .

As her fingers journeyed lower, Adam remained perfectly still. If he allowed himself to move now, he'd be out of control. He clenched his teeth, trying not to tremble as the delicate tracery moved closer . . . closer. He closed his eyes, waiting, scarcely daring to breathe.

Her fingers stopped. *No, no . . . not now.* He opened his eyes to find her looking at him, uncertainty in her face.

"Yes, yes—go on," he breathed. He threw his head back, every muscle crying out. At last, she touched him. She ran her fingers over and around the rigid, thrusting flesh, sheathing him gently. It was all he could stand.

"Oh, God, Marina. You're driving me mad."

She jerked her hand back. "Adam, I'm sorry . . ."

"No, no. It's wonderful." Laughing softly, he gathered her to him. "But it's enough to make me crazy." He kissed her. To his joy, she responded with a passion that matched what she had built in him.

Now there was no more hesitation. Adam's fingers found her open and waiting. Her legs spread readily at his touch, and he poised himself above her. To his surprise, she grasped him, arching her back, guiding him toward her welcoming warmth.

Every thread of Marina's awareness was concentrated on the heated core at her center. It was an emptiness that demanded to be satisfied. Heedless of the tiny flickers of apprehension, she shifted her body to accept him. She felt him probing, positioning himself for the thrust that would fill her aching void. Involuntarily, she tensed against the inevitable pain.

Adam froze. "Are you all right? Am I hurting you?"

"No, no. Don't stop," she insisted breathlessly. Responding, he pressed against her, gently but firmly. A terrifying flash of memory took command of her mind. Marina gasped.

"Easy, love. Just relax."

At the soothing rumble of Adam's voice, the memory retreated. She felt his lips on hers, heard his tender words of reassurance.

"Are you ready?"

"Yes," she whispered. "Please . . ."

Slowly, carefully, he eased himself into her tight, moist sheath. The restraint took all his willpower.

Marina felt him spreading her, sliding inside, filling her emptiness. Then, he stopped.

"Are you all right?"

Marina couldn't say anything. To her amazement, there was no pain. Instead, she felt a thrilling sensation of completeness.

"Oh, Adam, it's wonderful," she whispered.

"Ah, good," he murmured. Supporting himself on his elbows, he held her face between his two hands, gazing into her eyes. He moved slowly outward, then in again. "How's that?"

It only took that slight stimulation to cause Marina's momentary satisfaction to transform itself to a whole new kind of need. Pleasure and excitement mingled, and she thrust herself up to meet his movements.

Adam tried to restrain himself from the hard urgency her motions created in him.

"Easy, Marina, I don't want to hurt you."

"Oh, God, Adam. You won't hurt me." She pulled his lips down, kissing him recklessly, wanting to feel his power unleashing itself into her.

At that, Adam abandoned his constraint. With deep, forceful thrusts, he filled her, moving slowly at first, then faster and faster.

Marina felt her excitement spiraling, carrying her toward a realm she'd never known before. Unleashed, Adam's power was more thrilling than anything she'd ever known. Like a giant swell of music, they rose to the crest together.

"Oh, Adam, Adam . . ." she cried.

"Yes, darling, let it go," he gasped. He plunged into her, deeply, finally. His body stiffened, then relaxed, then stiffened again.

At the same time, everything exploded for Marina, and she found herself engulfed in a throbbing, pulsating, ecstatic wave of sensation. It was like nothing she had ever experienced before.

Afterward, they lay exhausted. Adam began to roll away, but she stopped him.

"No, don't," she murmured.

"But, I'm too heavy . . ."

"It feels good." Her voice was drowsy and satisfied.

Adam felt his eyes closing, too.

For the first time in his life, he felt complete. The realization came over him as he drifted off to sleep.

He woke later with a start. It was midnight, and the room was chilly. Marina still slept, her body soft and warm in his arms. Careful, so as not to wake her, he disengaged himself from her and pulled back the blankets, tucking them back around her. She murmured his name as he did so, and he leaned down and pressed his lips to the tip of her head, which was all that was visible in the tangle of covers.

Silently, he tiptoed into the other bedroom. His bathrobe hung in the closet. He put it on before he went out to the common room.

The Christmas tree stood as they'd left it, its lights reflecting on the snow outside. Fine flakes were filtering down, and Adam could see that nearly an inch had been deposited since he and Marina had left the room. The fire had burned down. Not even an ember remained.

Adam sat down on the sofa. He had to think—make some decisions. This thing with Marina was taking exactly the course he'd determined it would not. Only six months remained of their stay at the Conservatory, and then what? What about their separate careers? Marina wasn't the kind of woman to take a love affair lightly.

In his heart, he knew he was skirting the real problem. He loved her. No matter how hard he tried to delude himself, he knew he'd never be able to walk away from her, as he had the other women in his life. And that meant . . .

He shuddered. No. He couldn't tell her. She'd probably say it didn't matter, but he knew it would be a lie. The first seizure would send her running.

The knowledge ripped through him like the slice of a knife. Oh, God, why? Why hadn't he played it safe, stuck to his usual kind of woman—the kind who, like him, wanted nothing more than a brief, passionate affair. There were plenty of those around, and nobody got hurt.

But now he was going to hurt Marina, and that was the last thing he wanted to do.

He owed her honesty, at least. Tomorrow he *would* tell her. No matter how difficult it would be, she was entitled to know. He closed his eyes tightly against the pain that swept through him at the idea. He'd steel himself to her pity and disgust and confess the whole, ugly secret. That would put a stop to any escalation of what had begun tonight.

Give them a few days, and they'd be able to get back to the comfortable, friendly relationship they'd enjoyed before. They'd have a wonderful holiday, and once they got back to Vancouver, they'd go their separate ways.

He closed his eyes, willing away the pain the thought created. At least Marina would be all right now. She'd broken through the trauma of her childhood at last, and she'd be able to function like a normal woman.

Adam smiled grimly. Yes, he'd done a wonderful job of helping her overcome her problems—so she could enjoy a relationship with another man.

Good work, Fletcher.

He rose and pulled the plug on the Christmas tree lights, then turned off the tape deck.

For the rest of your life you can take comfort in that.

ELEVEN

Feeling guilty and miserable, Adam started down the hallway toward his own bedroom. The thought of Marina sleeping peacefully, expecting him to be there when she awoke, tormented him. What a mess he'd made of things.

He turned into the room and was about to pull the blankets down to climb into bed when he remembered his pill. Usually he took it right after dinner, but tonight he'd completely forgotten.

The bottle of pills was in the pocket of his jeans, which were . . .

Oh, Lord. They were in Marina's bedroom. His stomach tightened. If he went in to search, he might wake her.

He started for her room, and paused outside. How stupid of him to carry them in his pocket, at least while he was here at the cabin. But long ago he'd developed the habit of keeping them on his person. He couldn't risk being caught without them. Could he take the chance of waiting until morning? The memory of that Paris nightmare swam before his eyes. No. He'd have to get them.

He was on his hands and knees, feeling around for the jeans, when she woke up.

"Who's there?" In the darkness, her voice was sharp with fright. "Is that you, Adam?"

Adam's heart plummeted. "It's all right, Marina. I was just looking for my clothes." Beneath his hand, he felt the stiff denim he was searching for. He fumbled for the pocket. Ah, good. The unmistakable bulge of the small bottle of pills met his searching fingers. Quickly, he took it out and opened it, shaking a pill out and tossing it back in his throat.

He'd just gotten it down, when Marina turned on the light beside the bed.

"Couldn't you wait until morning to tidy up?" Blinking in the sudden brightness, she smiled. Her eyes were soft as she gazed at him, and her hair fell over her bare shoulders in sensual disarray.

Adam caught his breath, willing his truant body not to react. But it was no good. He felt the heat rising in his loins, and desire began to pound through him. Despite himself, he returned her smile, wanting nothing more than to tear the blankets back and bury himself in her warm, welcoming body.

"I hoped I wouldn't wake you," he said. His voice felt gravelly with tightness. Although he tried to keep his eyes away from her face, they were drawn there as if by some magnetic force. Awareness crackled between them like silent static.

For a moment, neither spoke, then Marina lifted the blankets in invitation. "It's cold out there. Why don't you come back to bed?" Her face sobered as blatant desire sparked in her eyes.

Adam looked away, then cleared his throat. *Say it, Fletcher. Don't give yourself a chance to change your mind.* He took a deep breath. "Marina, I think it would be better if—ah—I sleep in the other room tonight." Silence met his words. He didn't dare look up to see her reaction. At last, he heard the rustle of the blankets.

"I see." Her voice was quiet. Hurt.

A flood of guilt washed over him. He glanced up, but she had rolled on her side and her back was to him. *Go,*

Adam. She'll get over it. Don't let yourself weaken. Full of resolve, he got to his feet. He walked over to the bed and stood beside it, looking down at her.

"I shouldn't have let this happen, Marina. It wasn't fair to you." She lay there, rigid and unmoving. Adam's heart wrenched. Oh, Lord, he couldn't just walk away from her like this. He sat on the edge of the bed, laying his hand on her shoulder. Through the blankets, he felt a convulsive movement. She was crying.

A great surge of love for her made his throat ache. "Aw, Marina, don't cry. Please." He rubbed her back, wanting to bring comfort, fearful of the effect touching her would have on him. But he couldn't leave her now. Gently, he tugged her toward him. He needed to see her face.

With a muffled cry, she resisted. "Don't worry, Adam. I'm fine." She burrowed deeper in the blankets.

For a moment he sat there irresolute. He had to explain. Had to make her understand it wasn't her fault. But how could he, without confessing the reason for his action?

Beneath his hand, her back stiffened. "I'm sorry I disappointed you. Now, go away."

Lord, he couldn't let her think that.

"Marina, it's not you. Believe me. Please, believe me." He leaned down, pulling the blanket away from her head and burying his face in her hair. It was silken beneath his cheek and carried a light floral scent. Her scent. He felt a dangerous surge of emotion.

She froze at the contact, then seemed to wilt. Despairing sobs racked her body.

The last of Adam's self-discipline evaporated. Awkwardly, he pulled her toward him, but the blankets got in the way. With an oath, he tore them away from her. She made a frantic grab, but he slid in beside her and took her in his arms.

"Sh-hh. Don't cry, Marina love," he murmured. Rolling her to face him, he held her close, whispering endearments.

She struggled, but it was futile. Adam brushed the hair back from her face and kissed the tears from her cheeks. They were salty and warm. The taste of them—of her—ignited his senses once more. With a feeling of desperation, he made one last attempt to distance himself from her, at least mentally. But it was too late.

Somehow, his lips were on hers, nibbling, tasting, coaxing a response from her. At first she was unyielding, then she, too, took fire. Her lips softened and parted in invitation to his tongue. Under his caressess, her body lost its rigidity. With small whimpers, she made room for his hands to slip between their bodies, touching her breasts, her abdomen, sliding between her legs to the warm, waiting moistness.

Adam could stand it no longer. With a groan, he rolled away from her and tore the belt of his robe loose, shrugging his arms out of one sleeve, then the other. He flung the robe to the floor and pulled the blankets up to protect them from the coldness of the room.

When he came back to her, she was ready for him. It took only the slightest nudge, and her legs opened to receive him. He buried himself in her, deep, deeper. Oh, the beauty of it. The ecstasy of their slow, undulant rhythm.

"Marina, darling, darling . . ." With strong, powerful strokes, he moved faster and faster. Wrapping her legs around his back, she countered his movements, striving against him to make their joining complete.

"Oh, yes, Adam," she cried.

Adam felt her body convulse against his. It drove him over the brink, into a shattering explosion of pulsing light and sensation. He clasped her to him, burying his face in her neck.

"Oh, God, Marina, I love you," he gasped, then collapsed, exhausted. His surrender was complete.

Marina awoke to the feel of Adam's lips nuzzling her neck. She opened her eyes slowly, then shut them tight against the sunlight streaming through the window. It bounced off the glittering new snow, filling the room with eye-dazzling brilliance.

"Merry Christmas, love." Adam's voice was low and sexy.

She rolled over and tried opening her eyes again. He was propped on his elbow, gazing at her. The blankets had fallen from his bare shoulders, and she could see the dark thatch on his chest. It was incredibly sexy, especially when she realized that she, too, had nothing on. She felt her face heat up.

"Adam, I—" she began, but her words were cut off by his kiss. Instantly, a fierce flame ignited deep inside her. "Oh, Adam," she sighed, succumbing to the sensations created by his hands exploring her body.

Later, she felt Adam stir. Lazily, she opened her eyes. He sat on the edge of the bed, a mischievous smile playing across his face.

"It's time for a shower?"

Marina yawned. "You go first. I'll stay here." She burrowed down into the warm covers and closed her eyes again.

"Oh, no, you don't." Adam tugged the blankets away, capturing her hand and pulling her toward him. "I believe you missed my point." He grinned. "I need someone to wash my back."

"Oh, you," she laughed, trying to extricate her hand. "We wouldn't both fit."

"Let's try," Adam said.

Her hand remained locked in his, and the expression in his eyes made her want to melt. Tantalizing erotic images played in her mind. Soap-slippery bodies, hot, hot water, the tight, steamy cubicle—

Her mouth went dry. As if she had no will of her own, she followed him.

Afterward, Adam held out one of the huge, fluffy bath

sheets from the cupboard. "Come here and let me dry you, you wicked wanton."

The deep rumble of his voice sent shivers up Marina's spine. She tried to control her reaction, while he rubbed and patted her, lifting her arms, one by one, to stroke the moisture away, capturing a droplet from each nipple with his tongue before he gently covered each breast with the towel, massaging away the moisture. Marina felt the heat begin to build in her groin. She could see that the ministrations were having their effect on Adam, too. She shivered in delight. When he was done with her, she'd—

"Turn around, love. Let me do your back now."

Obediently, Marina turned, lifting her hair to provide him access to the full length of her spine. Flesh tingling, she gave herself over to the sybaritic pleasure of the rough towel in Adam's hands. He worked his way downward, and suddenly, he paused.

Puzzled, Marina waited. She felt the gentle touch of his fingertips on her buttocks.

"Oh, my darling," he whispered. "Is this what . . . ?"

The scars. How could she have forgotten? With choking panic, she jerked away, snatching the towel from his hands to wrap it around herself. "Don't look, Adam. They're ugly. Dirty." She backed away from him.

"No, no, Marina, don't think that." Adam reached for her again, gathering her into his arms. She tried to resist, but he refused to allow her to pull away. Rocking her gently, he held her, rubbing his hands up and down her back across the shaggy texture of the towel. "It's over, Marina. That's all in the past."

Gradually, Marina's panic ebbed and she succumbed to the healing magic of Adam's reassuring words. It was true. The past was behind her. She was no longer a frightened child. She was a strong, confident, successful woman. The scars were ugly reminders, but that's all they were. If Adam loved her in spite of them, they didn't matter any more.

Slowly, she eased back from his tight embrace and looked into his face. His eyes were tender and full of concern. Marina smiled, feeling her lips tremble with the effort.

"Oh, Adam," she said softly, "I do love you."

Adam gazed at her gravely, then lifted his hand to her cheek. "Marina, you're so beautiful, and you make me so very happy." He leaned down and kissed her with exquisite gentleness.

They finished in subdued silence, the earlier, light-hearted banter out of place now. At last, Marina picked up the blow dryer and turned it on.

"Let me," Adam said, gently taking it from her hands. While she sat, he played the stream of warm air over her long hair, running his fingers through it until it became soft and silken. Then he brushed it.

When he was finished, Marina picked up her combs to catch it back, but he stopped her.

"No, leave it down," he said, his voice husky. "It's too beautiful to bind up," he whispered, burying his face in it.

Desire leapt between them. "Adam, it's nearly noon," Marina laughed, as he led her back to the bed.

"Do you have—" he kissed her lips, "—an appointment—" then nibbled at her jawline, "—with someone?" He ran his tongue across the sensitive flesh just above her collarbone.

Moaning, Marina lifted her chin to give him better access. "I just thought . . ." she gasped, as he moved down to her breast.

"Don't think," he whispered. "Just let me love you." When at last they arose, she scolded him laughingly when he tried to help her dress. "At this rate, we won't get out of here all day." Scooting him out the door, she closed it firmly, then went to the dresser. In the top drawer was a gaily wrapped parcel—an exquisite antique cribbage board she'd found in an out-of-the way shop on the Vancouver waterfront. She'd bought it for Adam.

When she reached the common room, he was already there, and had plugged in the Christmas tree lights and started a fire in the fireplace. The fragrance of brewing coffee filled the air. When he went into the kitchen, Marina hurried over to place her gift under the tree. There was already another package there, awkwardly wrapped and tied with a simple shoelace bow.

"Aha! I see Santa Claus didn't miss us," Adam said, plunking steaming mugs on the coffee table.

He opened the cribbage board first. Marina watched his face, her heart pounding. He examined it carefully, then put it on the table and came over to her. Leaning down, he kissed her. It was a gentle, lingering kiss. "Thank you, Marina. I love it." His voice had a roughness to it, and he looked away quickly, clearing his throat loudly.

His gift to her was the tape of *Chansons de la Nuit* from the premiere performance, which he had obtained through hard-fought negotiations with the Musician's Union, he told her.

"It's the only one, Marina. I wanted you to have it."

With tears in her eyes, Marina put the music on, and they sat close together on the sofa to listen to it. Then, with the lush tones as a backdrop, Adam loved her, bringing to life the seduction which had taken place on stage that night.

And so the days passed. They skied, and when they finished skiing they made love—or listened to music or played cribbage. Their lovemaking was rapturous, tender, playful, seductive, and they found endless ways of pleasing each other.

When frightening memories of Marina's past pushed their way into her consciousness, Adam was always there, patiently helping her through them, until one by one they were laid to rest. At last, Marina felt whole, a complete person. And she loved Adam more than life itself.

But it had to end.

Now they were leaving. Marina swept up the last of the needles from the Christmas tree and tossed them into the trash bag that stood by the door.

"Ready?" Adam came over to her and put his arm around her shoulders, pulling her close.

Marina slipped her arm around his waist. "I guess so." She couldn't keep the sadness out of her voice. "It's too bad . . ."

"Sh-hh," Adam said. He leaned down, stopping her words with his lips.

Marina felt herself melting into his embrace. The last ten days had been filled with such joy that she couldn't imagine how she'd lived before. She tilted her face upward, her heart wrenching at the thought of leaving this cozy cabin, where they had discovered such peace and contentment.

With heartrending gentleness, Adam brushed his mouth across hers, putting her away from him before the kiss could deepen. Hands on her shoulders, he gazed at her, his eyes sober. It was as if he were fixing her face in his memory.

Marina tried to swallow, but the lump in her throat made it impossible. Through a blur of tears, she attempted a watery smile. "I hate to leave here."

Adam regarded her with a deep, searching look. With his thumb he rubbed the tears from her cheeks. "Me, too. But—" Suddenly, he clutched her to him, burying his face in her hair. "Oh, Marina, I love you so much," he whispered. "Whatever happens, remember that. *Always* remember that."

A chill of foreboding ran up Marina's spine. "What do you mean, Adam?"

Not answering, he dropped his arms and turned quickly, kneeling to slip his arms into the straps of his backpack.

Keeping his eyes averted, he shrugged the pack on and rose.

"Adam, what do you mean?" Marina stepped in front of him, but by now his face was calm and contained.

"Just what I said." He smiled, then glanced at his watch. "If we don't hurry, we'll miss the ferry." He started for the door, leaving her to follow. By the time she caught up with him, he was standing there with the keys in his hand, ready to lock up the cabin.

With a final glance backward, Marina picked up her suitcase and started slowly down the trail to the road. The foreboding she had felt before closed down on her like a dark cloud. He was hiding something, and it had to do with them. A knot began to form in her gut. Whatever it was, she wouldn't let it take him away from her now.

During the trip home, Adam was quiet. Marina's efforts to make conversation either drew no response, or terse, abrupt answers.

As they neared his house, he broke the silence he had maintained since they left the ferry.

"Marina, I'll unload my things here, then I'll follow you home in my car."

She felt a pang of disappointment. "Don't be silly, Adam. Leave your car. I'll bring you home tomorrow." She glanced at him, beside her in the passenger seat.

"No!" The word shot out harshly. Avoiding her gaze, he tempered his response. "I won't be staying the night."

His driveway was just ahead, and Marina pulled the car into it. Switching off the ignition, she turned to him. "Now, Adam, suppose you tell me what this is all about."

For a moment, he sat there, not speaking. Marina watched him, searching his face for some hint of what it was that had so changed him. He was acting like the Adam of old—gruff, uncommunicative.

"We've got to talk, Marina," he said at last. He sighed,

then opened the door. "It'll just take a minute to unload my things, then I'll be ready to go."

He stayed close behind her all the way home. When they arrived, he was, as usual, cautious and protective, insisting on entering the apartment first to make sure all was in order.

At last, everything was inside and put away. "I'll make some coffee," Marina said, starting for the kitchen.

Adam laid his hand on her arm. "No. I've got to talk to you. Now."

The tension in his body communicated itself to her, as he guided her toward the sofa. The foreboding she had felt earlier increased until it screamed in her head. Something was terribly wrong.

Gently, he urged her down to the soft cushions. Her gaze followed him as he moved to the other end and perched on the arm.

"Adam, what is it?" Her throat closed with dread. "Why have you changed so? Have I done something?"

For a moment the steely look in his eyes softened. "No, no, Marina, you haven't done anything. Please, don't ever think that." He closed his eyes briefly, and a look of pain came over his face. "It's me. I haven't been honest with you."

He was married. The last remnants of hope died in her. "So, you're married." Her voice was flat.

He shook his head. "No, it's not that. I—"

A tiny flame of hope rekindled. "Then what are you worried about? If there's a problem, let me help you." Tears sprang to Marina's eyes, and she started to rise. "I love you, Adam, and you love me. There's nothing we can't handle, if we're together."

"Stay there!" It was nearly a shout. "You can't help. Nobody can." His face worked with the effort to get the words out. "I lied about the headaches. I've never had a migraine in my life."

"Then what . . . ?"

He paused, then the words shot out. "I have epilepsy." Jumping up, he strode over and stood in front of her. "Fits. Seizures." His voice rose. "I fall down on the ground and my body convulses." He leaned closer, his face barely inches from hers. "I froth at the mouth, Marina. Sometimes I lose bladder control. I'm repulsive. Disgusting." He spat the words at her, and Marina flinched backward, speechless with shock. She shook her head slowly, her eyes wide.

Abruptly, Adam jerked upright and stood in front of her, legs apart, hands on his hips. "So now you know my ugly secret." He gave a short bark of a laugh. "And you've reacted as I knew you would."

The words had barely begun to make sense to her, when he spun and grabbed his coat. He started for the door, but before he got there, his steps slowed and he turned. There was a look of despair on his face.

"I'm sorry, Marina. I never should have allowed myself to give in to my selfish desires." His voice broke. "I hope you can forgive me," he said, his words barely audible. With one last look, he pivoted swiftly and jerked the door open.

The motion jolted her back to life. She leaped to her feet.

"Adam, wait!" she cried, tearing to the door. Hands slippery with desperation, she fumbled with the knob and finally got it open. "Adam, it doesn't matter," she called, running toward the elevator. With her heart pounding, she watched the light move to the second floor, then the first.

She turned and rushed to the stairway, making a mad dash down the three flights to the lobby. Stumbling in her haste, she dodged around a couple entering the door and ran outside the building to where Adam's car had been parked.

But she was too late. Just as she reached the curb, she saw him turn the corner at the end of the street.

"Adam, come back!"

The words died on her lips as she stood there, heedless of the frigid temperatue or the fine flakes of snow that caught on her eyelashes and hair. It was no use.

Adam was gone.

Somehow, Marina made it through that night and the next day. He couldn't mean it. Not after what they had shared, the love they felt for each other. She picked up the phone and dialed his number. He answered, but when he heard her voice, he hung up. Later, he turned on his answering machine. Gradually, her despair turned to determination.

She didn't know a thing about epilepsy. If she ever intended to convince him it wasn't important to her, she'd better know what she was up against. Rather than mope around the house, she'd find out.

She dove into her task with fanatical energy. From the telephone book, she discovered an organization called Epilepsy, B.C., and she spent most of the afternoon at the office, perusing the collection of books and articles. When she left, she took with her a mountain of information to read when she got home.

She found that epilepsy was caused by uncontrolled electrical discharges in the brain, that it sometimes could be controlled with medication. Adam had said his "headaches" only came on every four to six weeks. Did that mean his epilepsy was under control? She also found that seizures ranged from brief periods of disorientation to full-body convulsions and were sometimes preceded by auras, which could give varying periods of warning before an attack began.

By the time she had waded through all the information, it was past midnight. Her head was buzzing. She had a lot to think about. Not that it mattered. Nothing she had found out made the slightest difference in the way she felt about Adam.

With a hopeful heart, she gathered up the materials and

put them away. First thing tomorrow, she'd call him, and she wouldn't let up until he agreed to talk to her face-to-face. Just let him try to walk away from her. Once she put her mind to something, there was no stopping her.

If Adam didn't know that already, he'd find out.

When the phone rang at eight o'clock the next morning, Adam was groggy with sleep. After spending the whole previous day and evening tensed for Marina's call, he'd begun to relax. Maybe she was convinced he meant what he said. Now, not fully alert, he reached for the receiver.

"Fletcher here."

"Adam, this is Marina."

At the sound of her voice, he came immediately awake, his senses reeling. Then he caught himself. He should have known.

"Are you there?"

"Yes, I'm here." Sitting upright, he flung his legs over the edge of the bed. "Marina, I'm not going to talk to you, so don't waste your time calling again." He started to hang up.

"Adam!"

The sharpness of her voice stopped him. Not saying anything, he stared at the receiver, then slowly lifted it to his ear again.

"You had your say, now I insist on having mine. I'm coming over."

"Don't—" Adam began, but it was no use. The line was dead.

With a sigh, he replaced the receiver in its cradle. What should he do now? She'd had that determined sound in her voice.

Well, he wouldn't be here. He'd go skiing. To Grouse Mountain.

Quickly, he got ready. He didn't bother with breakfast. The important thing was to be gone before she arrived. It took only a few minutes to put the ski rack on his car and get his skis loaded. Then he was off. It was just twenty past eight.

As soon as she'd hung up, Marina realized her mistake. She'd given him plenty of time to clear out before she arrived. Without question, he'd take full advantage of the opportunity.

She'd turned off the Lion's Gate Bridge to the Upper Levels Highway and was nearing his turnoff when she spotted him coming the other direction. She'd know that red Porsche anywhere. And it had skis on it.

Marina's heart thudded. Grouse Mountain. That had to be where he was headed. From her rearview mirror, she watched him disappear in the traffic. Had he seen her? Not likely. Her car was an older Canadian model. It looked like hundreds of others on the highway.

Pulling to the side of the road, she thought for a moment. If she could just get him alone on a chairlift he'd be a captive audience. Yes, that's what she'd do. She'd go back home and get her ski gear, then she'd follow him to the mountain.

It was nearly eleven when she arrived at the parking lot. Sure enough, there was Adam's car, parked close to the gondola station. Hurriedly, she put her boots on and took her skis off the rack. There was no telling where she'd find him on the mountain, but she wouldn't quit until she did.

By the time she reached the top, it was snowing lightly. Good. Although it would make it harder to spot Adam, he wouldn't be as likely to notice her and take evasive action. Not that he would anyway, probably. She was wearing an old ski jacket he hadn't seen before, and with her goggles on, it would be hard for him to recognize her.

Adam stuck to the expert slopes, both for the challenge, which would use up the nervous energy that was making him jumpy, and to avoid any chance encounters with people he didn't want to see. Marina didn't worry him too much. He'd made a clean getaway. She wouldn't be likely to guess where he'd gone.

As the day progressed, he found himself relaxing more. The slopes were nearly empty, and the snow was light and powdery—just the way he liked it. He'd take one more run, then go back to the lodge for lunch.

Marina spotted him from the lift line when he was still far up the mountain. Her heart lurched. There was no mistaking the red stripes on his black jacket and his red ski cap. Quickly, she got out of line and stood off to the side, waiting for him to arrive.

He came closer, first traversing the slope, then pointing his skis down the fall line and heading straight toward her. For a heart-stopping moment, she thought he saw her, but his gaze flitted casually over her as he took his place in the line. Moving forward behind the other skiers, he took his goggles off and knocked the snow from them.

Casually, Marina got in line behind him. It was snowing harder now. Visibility was diminishing. Looking ahead of Adam, Marina counted the others waiting their turn. There were five of them. Would Adam be paired with the skier in front of him? Anxiously, Marina watched the first couple take their place and settle back in the chair as the attendant positioned it under them. She held her breath, watching to see what would happen for the next one.

Only one person got on. Marina let her breath out. Immediately, the next two skiers shoved themselves forward into position. Marina watched them smile at each other as they waited, then go swinging off, sitting so close together their thighs touched. Keeping her head averted, Marina pulled her hood forward to hide her face.

Adam moved into place. The chair was beginning to round the turn. It was now or never. For an instant, Marina felt her courage falter. *Go, idiot!* With a glance at the approaching chair, she scrambled up beside Adam. Her heart pounded so hard, she almost felt faint.

It was only seconds, but it seemed like an eternity

before the chair arrived and she felt herself sliding onto the seat. The next thing she knew, her skis were swinging free, and they were on their way up the mountain.

Adam settled back, hunching down into the collar of his jacket. Damn. He'd hoped to make the twenty-minute ride by himself. Making polite conversation was at the top of his list of things he didn't intend to do today. With determination, he kept far to his side of the chair, taking care not to look toward his companion.

He concentrated on emptying his mind of everything except the quiet serenity around him and the feel of the icy snowflakes hitting the skin of his face. It was no good. The memory of Marina beside him, of her snuggling against him and turning her cold lips for his kiss wouldn't leave his mind.

He felt the curious glance of his companion. Carefully, he kept his gaze averted. There was something familiar about the way the other skis looked. They were tidily together, their tips straight ahead. That was the way Marina sat on the chair.

His heart twisted. Lord, couldn't he see *anything* without being reminded of her? He looked away, but without even realizing it, he found himself glancing again at those skis.

Oh, Lord! They *were* hers. There was that M-shaped gouge from the time they stopped in the middle of the slope to kiss, and their skis got tangled up. Adam felt the air go out of him. For an instant, irrational panic seized his mind and he gathered himself to jump off the chair. Then reason returned and the impulse faded.

"Adam . . ."

Her voice was low and urgent. He tried to shut it out, but despite his efforts it fell on his ears with aching familiarity. Unable to help himself, he half-turned toward her, his eyes hungry for the sight of her face. She had thrown back her hood and pushed her goggles down to dangle around her neck. Now she regarded him with that heart-stopping blue gaze, the flakes of snow clinging to her eyelashes, touching her flesh and melting to tiny droplets.

Adam stared at her, taking in the graceful curve of her cheek, the soft fullness of her lips. For a fleeting instant, the urge to lick away the glistening drops, devour her with his passion, nearly overwhelmed him.

"You can't run away now, Adam."

The brutal truth of the words jerked him back to ugly reality.

"You shouldn't be here, Marina. I told you there's nothing to say."

That unsettling stare homed in on him, seeking out his eyes behind his clear goggles.

"That's not true, and you know it. You've made your speech, that's all." She brushed a snowflake—or was it a tear?—from her eye. Her chin rose. "Or are you the only one that counts in this relationship?"

She hit home with that one. Guilt surged over Adam, heavy and hard. He tried to look away, but her gaze locked on his, refusing to yield.

"I love you, you fool. It doesn't matter to me that you have epilepsy. You've gotten along with it all your life. And very well, I might say." Her eyes softened. "Adam, please. We love each other."

He felt his conviction waver. Maybe it would work. Maybe . . . His hands tingled to reach for her, to gather her in his arms and kiss away the worry in her face. He stared at her, irresolute. Could he risk it?

"I can live with it, too. Let me show you—"

Abruptly, the memory of that sunny afternoon in Paris flashed through his mind, the feel of the curb digging into his back, the horror on the faces of the onlookers, the fear and disgust in Lili's eyes. No. Nothing could make him go through that again. Nothing.

"No!" he shouted.

Marina recoiled.

"God, Marina, you don't know what you're asking. I've been through it. I've lived with it."

A spark of anger flickered in her eye. "And what does that make you? Some sort of noble, self-sacrificing hero? Sure, Adam. It's truly heroic of you to protect poor little Marina from the gruesomeness of your seizures."

He reached for her then, wanting to grip her shoulder, make her understand. But she shook him off.

"Why didn't you think of that before? Why did you let me fall in love with you?" Her eyes filled with furious tears. "You're not fair. And I won't let you get away with it."

Adam was cornered by her logic. The words cut close, unleashing the load of guilt and frustration that had been his constant companion for the past week. With no rational response, he lashed out with caustic virulence.

"You think not? Well, lady, you're only one-half of this pair, and the other half says it's over. Done. Finished." Not giving himself a chance to see her reaction, he yanked his hood up and deliberately turned away.

But not soon enough. Marina had seen the uncertainty on his face. She stared at his back, fighting the pain. Somehow, she had to make him understand.

Ahead the towers of the landing appeared, barely visible in the falling snow. Only moments were left to make her case. She thought for a second, then slid as close as she could to him.

"I love you, Adam. I've been reading about epilepsy and learning. I want to talk to you, find out what I'm going to need to become accustomed to, because I won't let you go."

It was time to get ready to debark, and she slid back over to her side. Stiffly, Adam turned, arranging his skis and poles. In silence, they waited until they reached the landing.

Adam was out of the chair like a missile, shooting down the ramp. Marina was right behind him.

"Wait for me, Adam," she shouted.

But he didn't even stop to adjust his poles, just turned his skis down the fall line and started over the moguls on the steep face.

Marina paused just long enough to slip her goggles in place, then she followed. The moguls were icy and treacherous. Adam was below her, diving around the hummocks with total disregard for the danger. Marina felt a stab of fear. She had to catch up with him or he'd kill himself trying to outrun her.

Not daring to think what she was doing, Marina pointed her skis downhill and took off. With her heart in her throat, she let her skis run out. Her intention was to reach Adam and make him slow down, but from the moment she hit the first mogul she was out of control.

There was no checking her speed. The pitch of the slope was almost vertical, and if she tried to turn now she'd surely catch a tip in the tight gutters between the mounds. Gripping her poles, she concentrated on keeping her tips up as she came off the tops and became airbound. Adam was just ahead.

"Track!" Marina screamed, and then he was behind her. Everything was a blur, and she was conscious only of paralyzing fear. She was nearly at the bottom now, and her strength was failing. She took a deep breath, and set her muscles for the for the final icy hump. She hit it hard and fast, then took off.

Without the steep slope and the unending moguls, she sailed through the air in an exhilarating rush. She tensed for the landing, and to her amazement, hit the powder in perfect control. She was down. Thank God. But where was Adam?

Resting on her poles, willing her shaky knees to relax, she turned and squinted toward the face. He was just coming off it. But he wasn't slowing.

"Adam!" she called. He went past her in a swish of

snow, and she took off behind him. "Damn it, Adam, stop!"

But he didn't. She'd had a moment to rest and gather her strength, but he must be exhausted. In front of her, she saw him falter, then recover himself. The slope turned just ahead, necking down to a narrow, steep section. When Adam hit it, Marina was only fifty feet behind him.

"For God's sake, Adam, slow down."

Just as he started into the gully, he glanced back toward her. The motion was only a slight one, but it was enough to throw him off balance.

Behind him, Marina saw it happen.

He started into a turn, then the edge of his right ski caught. With flailing arms, he tried to right himself, and the heel of his left ski hit a rut. It threw him sideways. He slammed into the hard-packed snow, his body windmilling down, down, off the trail, toward the tree looming in his path.

Oh, God, no . . . Marina heard a scream of horror, and realized it was her own voice.

He must have seen it coming, because he tried to cover his head with his arms. But nothing could stop the inevitable. Headfirst, he crashed into the tree and rebounded, sliding a few feet more, and then lay motionless.

Still as death.

TWELVE

Marina held his limp hand in hers through the endless ambulance trip to Lion's Gate Hospital. *Wake up, Adam*, she prayed, staring at his face, willing the flutter of an eyelid, a twitch of his mouth, a hint of color to erase the terrifying pallor. Should she tell the attendants about his epilepsy?

In the background, their voices were calm and efficient as they monitored his vital signs.

"Blood pressure . . ." "Heartbeat . . ." Despite her worry, Marina felt relieved. They didn't seem overly concerned. When Adam regained consciousness, he could decide whether—

"Oh-oh!"

Marina barely heard the exclamation. Adam's hand had suddenly gripped hers.

"It's a seizure!"

His face contorted, then his back arched and his entire body went rigid. She felt her bones compress painfully as his hand squeezed tighter and tighter. Then, abruptly, her hand was flung away as his body began to convulse.

Before she could react, one of the attendants shoved her aside. In helpless panic, Marina watched as he loosened Adam's jacket and unbound the tight straps of the stretcher.

"What are you doing?" Marina cried. "He'll fall."

The attendant glanced at her. "It's okay, ma'am. We don't want him to break any bones." Then he turned back to Adam.

Helpless, Marina watched the seizure wrack his body. Sick horror engulfed her. Was he going to die? It would be her fault.

Please God, make it stop, she prayed.

But the spasms went on and on—for an eternity, it seemed. Then, as abruptly as it had begun, the paroxysm stopped. Immediately, the attendants began checking heart, blood pressure, pulse, lifting his eyelids to shine a bright beam of light into his eyes.

"Is he all right?" Marina's throat was tight with fear.

The attendant with the light smiled reassuringly. "Don't worry. These things look a lot worse than they really are." He pulled the stethoscope away from his ears and let it dangle around his neck. "Has he had seizures before?"

Marina's heart jolted. What should she say? The man was watching her, waiting for her response. It was Adam's secret. She couldn't betray him.

You have to, Marina. Adam's life could be at stake.

And it was *her* fault. Oh, God, why had she pursued him? Why hadn't she just—

"Ma'am?"

Forgive me, Adam. She took a deep breath, then looked away from the questioning gaze.

"He has epilepsy."

She waited for a reaction, but to her surprise, the attendant said nothing. He was busy writing when she dared glance in his direction again.

"Adam . . . Adam. Open your eyes." The masculine voice came from a great distance. "Come on, Adam. You can do it."

It was a friendly voice. And persuasive. For some reason, Adam had to try. But it was such an effort. And his head hurt.

There was a murmur of strange voices, an unfamiliar stir around him. And a smell—not unpleasant, but institutional. He forced his eyes open a slit. A shaft of pain shot through his head. Oh, God, the light. Quickly, he closed them again.

"Good, Adam. Now, try again."

Adam wanted to ignore the quiet tones and slip back into the void. But they persisted, like a fly buzzing around his head.

"Just one more time, Adam."

"Go 'way," he muttered, lifting his hand to slap it away. He felt a tug at the back of his wrist.

"Careful, Adam. There's a tube in there."

Tube?

The notion was so surprising that Adam opened his eyes to look. Again that blast of pain hit him, but he tried hard not to notice it. Where was he, anyway?

"You've had an accident, Adam. You're at Lion's Gate Hospital. I'm Dr. Layton."

Adam tried to concentrate on the words.

"Accident? When?" he croaked.

"Ah, good. You understand me. Five days ago. At Grouse Mountain."

"Oh." Adam closed his eyes again, letting the information penetrate the fuzzy edges of his brain. Five days. He'd been here five days.

A worrisome notion niggled in the dark recesses of his consciousness. Something important. What was it?

"Are you awake, Adam?"

His pills. He needed his pills.

"My pills. Need my pills." Although he spoke very clearly, the words came out slurred. What was the matter with him, anyway?

"Easy, Adam. We found the pills. We're trying a different medication now."

Alarmed, Adam struggled through the haze to force his eyes open again. "Different? Why?" The room spun and his head pounded. Gradually, he brought his gaze to focus on the doctor beside his bed. He was pleasant looking and he appeared very young. "Why?"

Dr. Layton appeared uncomfortable. "Adam, you've had several seizures. We've been trying to bring them under control."

Seizures. Now, he remembered. "But, can't—"

Dr. Layton bent closer. "Adam, listen carefully. We've been in touch with your doctor in New York. I know your seizures have been under control. But you hit your head in the accident, and now . . ."

Adam never knew what the rest of the sentence was. A familiar buzzing began in his brain and, with only a split second's warning, the darkness descended.

Marina arrived shortly after noon. Just before she reached Adam's room, Dr. Layton stopped her in the hallway. Since Adam's arrival, she'd spent many hours at his bedside each day. The doctor, finding that Adam had no immediate family, had kept her updated on Adam's progress.

"Marina, wait."

She whirled, her heart pounding. "Is he all right?" She searched the youthful doctor's face.

He hesitated before he spoke. "Adam has regained consciousness."

Joy leaped into Marina's heart.

"Thank God," she said softly. She smiled at the doctor, but something in his face made the smile falter. "What is it?" she whispered.

"He's had another seizure."

The words hit her like a blast of icy water.

Sudden tears filled her eyes. "They're getting worse, aren't they?"

Dr. Layton's features were gentle and sympathetic. He nodded his head. "I'm afraid we don't have the resources here to give him the treatment he needs. We're transferring him to the neurological unit at Vancouver General Hospital."

Marina felt her face pale. "What will they do?"

The doctor avoided her eyes. "In some cases surgery is indicated."

It was as if he'd punched her in the solar plexus. Brain surgery. It could mean . . .

"He's a musician, doctor. An outstanding artist. Could the surgery . . . ?" The words refused to come.

"I don't know. It depends on where in his brain the damage is located." His voice was quiet. "In some cases, the risk is too great. Surgery isn't an option."

"And then?" A suffocating sense of dread began to close over her.

"They'll do the best they can with medication."

Marina followed the ambulance that took Adam to Vancouver General Hospital. The closer she got to the sprawling medical complex, the more terrified she became. What if they couldn't perform surgery? Would they be able to control his seizures? Would the operation affect his memory? His ability to read? To talk?

To perform?

She'd heard of people suffering all those things from brain surgery.

Oh, Adam, can you ever forgive me?

The thought refused to leave her as she hurried through the maze of hallways to the neurology reception area. The middle-aged nurse at the desk looked up at Marina's approach. She had a stern, forbidding face.

"Could you tell me what room Adam Fletcher is in?"

"Just a moment." The woman brought the information up on her computer monitor and turned back to Marina. "Are you immediate family?"

The question caught Marina off-guard. "No—"

"Then you can't see him. He's in serious condition, and only immediate family is allowed in." The nurse turned back to her papers.

Marina hesitated. She *had* to see Adam. "Ma'am?"

"Yes?"

"He has no immediate family. I'm his—fiancée." She concentrated on keeping her face calm and composed. *It's only a little lie.*

The woman regarded Marina intently for a few seconds, then her features softened. "Take a seat in the waiting room. I'll see what I can do."

Adam was awake when Marina finally got to his room, lying on his back, staring at the ceiling. He didn't turn at her entrance. She stood in the doorway, her stomach in a tight knot of apprehension.

"Adam?"

At the sound of her voice, he turned his head slightly. Even with that small movement, he grimaced in pain.

He looked so helpless there in his hospital gown, with tubes in his arms and his face pale and slack from the drugs. Marina's heart twisted. Somehow, seeing him conscious was even worse than it had been earlier. He gazed at her, his face uncomprehending.

Marina tried to smile. "It's me, Marina," she said softly.

For a moment he appeared puzzled, then recognition passed over his face. Recognition and a flash of gladness.

"Marina?" It was only a croak.

The knot in her stomach unwound a little. "Don't try to talk, Adam. I'll just sit here." Carefully, she pulled a chair up next to the bed. His hand lay palm up on the coverlet beside her, and she covered it with her own. Weakly, he gripped it.

"They want to operate on my brain."

His words were slurred and faint, but beneath the soporific effect of the drugs, Marina heard a note of fear.

"Sh-h. It's all right." Her own terror surged forth with sickening intensity. *Don't, Marina. You have to stay strong.* Taking a deep breath, she battled back the paralyzing sensations. With the control came a new sense of resolve.

It was her fault he was here. No matter what, she'd always be there by his side.

*　　*　　*

The next day when she arrived, the doctor was just leaving Adam's room. He spotted her down the hallway and swerved to intercept her.

"Ah, you must be the fiancée—Marina, isn't it?" At her surprised look, he smiled. "I'm Dr. Johns. Adam has been asking for you."

The doctor's manner appeared relaxed and unperturbed. With wary optimism, Marina shook the hand he offered.

"Is he better, then?"

Dr. Johns paused. "Well, I'd say he's holding his own. We've loaded him up with medication to reduce the seizures, so he's still not very alert. We'll start testing today to see if he's a candidate for surgery."

The dread that had been her constant companion for the past days returned full force. "About the surgery, doctor—" Marina studied his face, "—what about Adam's music? His concert career?"

The expression on the doctor's face became sober. "That's why we do all the tests beforehand. We need to make sure no vital centers will be affected. If we decide surgery is an option for Adam, it'll be because we know that the seizure activity is localized in a part of the brain that can be removed without seriously impairing his ability to function."

He hesitated before he went on. "But you must understand, if the activity center is near a part of his brain that controls his musical ability, there could be some ill effects."

As he spoke, Marina's guilt welled up in an agonizing ache behind her breastbone. She felt tears rush to her eyes. "And this is all because of the accident." The words slipped out almost without her realizing she had spoken.

Dr. Johns fell silent, gazing at her thoughtfully. "The accident?" Rubbing his jaw, he considered for a moment. "Well, surely that didn't help matters, but the epilepsy problem was there already. Based on what we know, it might eventually have come to this anyway. If surgery is indicated, Adam's likelihood of remaining seizure-free for the rest of his life is better than seventy percent.'' He smiled. ''That's what you should focus on. You and Adam.''

''You mean he could be cured?'' It was too good to be true.

With a smile, Dr. Johns nodded. ''That's a real possibility.'' He looked at his watch. ''And now, I need to get to my other patients.'' He held out his hand. ''I'm glad we've met, Marina. And think about what I've said. I have a feeling Adam's going to need your support through this, more than he realizes.''

And then, with a brief, reassuring squeeze of her hand, he was gone.

The specter of the surgery haunted Adam. Through the endless procedures—the EEG's, the brain scans, the 24-hour monitoring of his brain function, Marina's frequent visits were oases of quiet enjoyment.

Now, he lay in his bed, watching the rain fall outside his window. Tantalizing snatches of memory chased through his mind—a Christmas tree, Marina in his arms, a deep, contented sense of happiness. He wasn't sure whether they were fact or fantasy, but he basked in the pleasure they brought him.

''Hi, lazybones.''

It was Marina. As usual, his heart lurched at the sight of her. She came to the bed and leaned down to kiss him. Reaching up, he pulled the pins out of her carefully caught back hair. It fell in a fragrant cloud around his head, and he tangled his fingers in it, deepening the kiss. For a moment, Marina responded fully, then she pulled back.

''Don't let Dr. Johns catch you doing that.''

''I just wanted you to know I'm glad to see you,'' Adam said, smiling as she gathered the pins and hastily raked her fingers through the tangled strands. He lay there, feeling shamefully sybaritic. Suddenly, his mind jumped ahead. It was after the surgery, he was seizure-free, and . . .

Stop it, Adam. He had deliberately schooled himself not

to think that way. Maybe the tests would show he wasn't a candidate for surgery. Then he'd have to live with the way things were now, and that life couldn't include Marina. It probably would mean an end to his performing career.

"What is it, Adam?" Marina gazed at him, her eyes anxious.

"Nothing." Adam cast about for something to take his mind away from such troubling thoughts. "I just . . ."

"Well, Adam, I see you've got company."

Both Adam and Marina jumped guiltily at the sound of Dr. Johns' voice.

"Oh, doctor, I didn't expect you at this hour. I'll leave." Marina picked up her purse and started toward the door.

"Wait, Marina. Adam may want you to hear this."

The smile of welcome froze on Adam's face. He glanced at Marina. She was tense, like a cat about to spring.

"I have the results of your evaluation, Adam." The doctor's face was serious. "Since you and Marina plan to marry, she should be in on this, too."

Marry? For a second, Adam had an absurd impulse to laugh. Then he caught sight of Marina's face. It was embarrassed and full of guilt. He wished he could climb out of bed and take her in his arms. "If she wants to stay, it's all right." She might as well. He had no secrets from her. Not any longer.

Dr. Johns glanced from one to the other. Then he began.

"First, some of the findings. We discovered an arterial narrowing due to scarring from past seizures. At the moment, it isn't causing any problem, but in two to three years it will. That means that eventually, surgery will be mandatory.

"Also, I don't think we'll be able to find a combination of drugs that will give you adequate control, even to the extent that you had it before, without leaving you badly sedated. If the seizures continue as they are at present, there will be additional scarring that will lead to a decline in your mental abilities.''

He paused. "Any questions so far?"

"Keep talking," Adam said, his voice strained. Somehow, Marina's hand was in his, and he clung to it as if it was an anchor for his very life.

"Good. Now, the language dominance test revealed that the left hemisphere of your brain is the center of speech function. That's good news, since the problem area is in the right hemisphere. You're lucky, too, that the focus of activity is localized, rather than scattered throughout the brain." Dr. Johns shuffled through a sheaf of papers he held in his hand.

In the absolute silence, Adam could hear his heart pounding. He cast a quick glance at Marina, who remained immobile, her concentration totally focused on the doctor.

He cleared his throat and looked up from the papers. "I guess that's all. Our conclusion is that you're an excellent candidate for the operation."

The air escaped from Adam's chest with a whoosh. Marina's hand relaxed in his. Adam drew a deep breath. "I . . ."

"You don't need to make your decision right now. Talk it over together and . . ."

The doctor's voice disappeared under the onslaught of ominous buzzing in Adam's head. *Not now, please not now*, he thought, struggling fiercely to resist the sensation. But it was no use. The room dissolved in a wave of darkness.

The operation took place three days later.

In the waiting room, Marina paced restlessly. She glanced at her watch. Nearly four hours had passed since they'd wheeled him into surgery. It seemed such a long time. Had something gone wrong?

Dr. Johns had explained the process to her—how Adam would be conscious through the surgery, the delicate probes and wires that would be inserted into his brain to identify the exact location of the seizure area and avoid damage to vital centers, the painstaking process of removing brain tissue, bit by tiny bit.

Oh, Adam, I'm so frightened! She buried her face in her hands, struggling to contain the terrifying thoughts that kept breaking through. It *would* go well. It had to. And for the rest of his life, Adam would be free of seizures.

Thank goodness her apartment was large. There would be plenty of room for both of them. While Adam was recuperating, they'd . . .

"Marina?"

She whirled, her heart pounding. Dr. Johns had entered the room, still in scrub clothes. He was smiling.

"Dr. Johns! Is he . . . ?" The words stuck in her throat.

"He's doing very well." Dr. Johns pulled the cap off his head and ran his fingers through his hair. "The scarring was more extensive than we expected, but we were able to remove all of it."

"Then he's—cured?" Marina searched the doctor's face, not daring to give release to the elation that tore through her.

"Possibly," he said. "But until there's been time to heal, we won't know for sure. Tomorrow, we'll start conducting tests to see if the surgery caused any deficits."

Deficits. Marina's elation evaporated. "You don't think . . ." She searched his face. "Dr. Johns, is there something you aren't telling me?"

"Relax, Marina. The tests are routine. I don't anticipate any problems at all." His smile broadened. "And now, if you promise not to stay more than five minutes, I'll let you see Adam."

Although she'd been prepared for it, the sight of Adam, with his head swathed in bandages and all the tubes and wires attached to his body, still shocked her. She paused in the doorway, collecting herself before she entered the room. He sensed her presence.

"Marina?"

"I'm here, Adam." She hurried to the bed and leaned above him so he wouldn't have to turn his head. "How do you feel?"

"Well, I have one hell of a headache." Adam tried to smile, then winced. "And wait until you see me without the bandages. They shaved all my hair off."

Marina thought with regret of the dark, unruly tangle she so loved to run her fingers through. With effort, she kept her voice light. "Oh, it'll grow back." She patted him on the hand. "I'll get you a wig."

With surprising agility, Adam turned his hand to grasp hers. He made a sound resembling a snort. "Thanks." Then his grip relaxed, and he drifted into sleep.

Marina felt a light touch on her shoulder and turned. A nurse stood behind her. "Miss Prohaska, it's time to go."

"I'll be back later," Marina said softly to Adam's sleeping form. "Get well, my darling."

As she hurried through the corridors, her steps felt light and her heart surged with new hope. The guilt, which for weeks had weighed on her like an oppressive miasma, began to fade. The operation was over. Adam was on his way to a new life—a normal life.

And she was determined to share it with him.

Seven days later, Adam sat beside her as she drove toward her apartment, his heart full of elation. A new, exciting life lay ahead of him. It would be a month or more before he could move home and go back to work, but that didn't matter. He needed time to practice—and to adjust to living without the constant worry of seizures.

He felt reborn. The future was full of promise. Although Dr. Johns had warned him that they couldn't be sure of a cure for several months, Adam *knew* he was cured. Life now had infinite potential. Even—he looked over at Marina, who, feeling his gaze, took her eyes from the road briefly and smiled at him—even marriage, perhaps.

In her apartment, he sank gratefully into an easy chair. The effort of getting from the car inside had left him weak and trembling, even with her shoulder to lean on. He wouldn't admit that to her, of course, but . . .

"You're exhausted, aren't you?" she said.

Bingo. Why had he thought he could fool her?

Her eyes were watchful, following his every move with concern. "Let me help you into your bedroom, so you can lie down."

"No, no, I'm fine," Adam said, waving her away. "Just let me rest here awhile."

Marina stood in front of him, hands on her hips. "Adam, let's get something straight right now. Dr. Johns said you should go right to bed and stay there for a few days. I intend to see his orders followed."

Adam had to smile at the determination in her face. "Aw, Marina, I've been in bed for weeks. Now I want to sit up."

She gave him a stern look, and he grinned sheepishly.

"Just for a little while. Please?"

For a moment she stared at him, then relented. "Well, okay." She bent to pick up his suitcase and fastened him with a stern look. "But I don't want you passing out, or doing anything that's going to scare me half to death, you hear?"

"You bet, boss!" With a little salute, Adam settled back into the comfortable cushions. He smiled, his thoughts moving ahead to the days to come.

Tomorrow he'd get back to his cello, which was sitting across the room. It would be difficult at first, he knew, as weak as he was. But without the constant fear of seizures, he could handle anything. For the first time in his life, he felt he had things under control.

It was a heady sensation. He still had no idea how the accident had happened, and Marina had little to say about it. But it didn't matter. Because of it, he was cured. Anything was worth that.

*   *   *

That night Marina woke with a start. She stared uncomprehending at the unfamiliar shadows around her, then remembered. This was the spare room. Adam was in her bed. Relieved, she began to settle back beneath the covers. Suddenly, she came to her senses. What had wakened her? Had Adam cried out?

Alarmed, she jumped from the bed. Without pausing to put on her robe, she hurried into the hallway. At his door, she paused and listened. Everything was quiet. Slowly she pushed the door open and went inside.

By the dim light filtering through the gauzy curtain, she could see his still form beneath the blankets. His eyes were open.

"Adam, are you all right?" she whispered.

"Marina?" There was surprise in his voice. "What are you doing here?"

She went over and turned on the bedlamp. Adam squinted in the sudden brightness. "Is everything okay?" she asked anxiously. "I thought you called for me." She leaned over him, smoothing the blankets, adjusting his pillow. His hair had begun to grow back, and there was a slight fuzz around the livid scar that circled nearly half his head. Her heart contracted at the sight.

Smiling, Adam grabbed her hand. "Now, now, mother hen. I had a dream, that's all." His gaze caught hers, and his eyes sparkled. "It was an erotic dream," he whispered wickedly.

Beneath the teasing, Marina detected an undercurrent of invitation. She tried to pull her hand away, but not before her body betrayed her by responding.

"Adam, it's too soon for that sort of thing."

"No, it's not—if we're careful. I asked Dr. Johns." His eyes no longer teased, they hungered. With a steady pressure on her hand, he pulled her down until their lips were only inches apart. "I've dreamed of loving you from the moment you walked into my room."

The desire was naked on his face. Marina felt her will to resist abandon her. "Oh, Adam, why do you tempt me so?" she whispered. "I don't want to hurt you—" He brought his hand to the back of her head and pulled her lips to his. Then he wrapped his arms around her, drawing her close.

"You won't, love. I promise." He laughed softly, nuzzling her face to find her lips.

The kiss was gentle and tender. But beneath it, Marina could feel the great effort he exerted to maintain control of his instinctive needs. That fact was even clearer as he moved to bring their bodies into closer contact. Through the blankets, she could feel the hard thrust of his desire.

Eyes half-closed, he gazed up at her, a lazy smile playing around his mouth. He slid his hands over the glossy satin of her gown, and moved against her. She gasped, as his hand roamed down her leg and bunched the gown, pulling it up so he could stroke the silky flesh of her thigh.

"I'll just lie here and let you have your way with me," he murmured, claiming her lips again.

His searching fingers crept higher, and Marina struggled against the delicious sensations creating such havoc in her mind. "Adam, don't. You're making it impossible for me to think."

"Don't think, Marina. Just let yourself go." With that, he slipped both hands beneath her gown and ran them up her body, lifting the gown to expose more and more of her bare flesh.

She gasped as he reached her breasts. He covered them with his hands, rubbing in slow circles, the taut nipples pressing against his palms.

"Want me to stop, Marina?" he whispered. He shifted her, so he could take a nipple in his mouth and tease it with his tongue.

The last vestiges of her control left her. "Oh, Adam," she breathed. Pushing away from him, she shrugged the gown off and let it slither to the floor beside the bed. Then she pulled the blankets away. Beneath them, Adam was nude. She'd known he would be.

For a moment, she gazed at him. He lay there, shivering slightly, his eyes heavy with passion. Then she ran her hand over his chest, across his stomach, down his abdomen. He sucked in his breath.

"Oh, God, Marina. I can't stand this."

She laughed, and sat back. "Remember, you said you wanted me to have my way with you. This is my way." She rubbed her hand across his abdomen, so low she felt the soft mat of hair beneath her palm. Leaning over, she nuzzled his chest, finding his tiny nipple, running her tongue over and around it.

Adam groaned.

"Am I hurting you?" she asked innocently, lifting her head and allowing her hand to encircle him loosely.

"Don't stop," he moaned. He reached for her, but she eluded his grasp.

"You're being impatient, Adam," she said as calmly as she could manage. With delicious shivers chasing up and down her spine, she resumed her casual exploration of his body, nibbling, rubbing, pausing at every center of sensation to taste and caress. Adam groaned with pleasure.

"Lord, Marina, you're driving me crazy," he cried finally.

Her own excitement spiraled out of control.

"Ah, yes," she breathed.

Throwing her leg across his thighs, she mounted him. She rode him deeply and hard, her passion overflowing. The peak, when it came, hit them simultaneously. With an ecstatic cry, Adam thrust upward. Marina met the thrust strongly, burying him deep, deep in her welcoming warmth. The world exploded in a myriad of shuddering sensations, more powerful than anything she had ever experienced before.

Afterward, they lay together, still entwined, his hand on her hip, hers on his chest.

"See, I told you it wouldn't hurt me," he whispered.

"That's because I did all the work," she whispered back.

He chuckled. "I appreciated that. I'll make it up to you when I'm stronger." He yawned. "But right now, I'm ready for sleep." With that, he drew her closer, fitting her to the contours of his body.

Marina felt drowsiness slip over her, and happiness. They were together again, and she loved him. Could there be any greater joy?

Adam was still sleeping when she tiptoed out of the room to get ready to go to the Conservatory the next morning. By now, everyone knew of his accident and the surgery. All day long well-wishers stopped by her studio to leave cards and offerings of food or other gifts for her to take to him. With his shaved head, Adam had so far refused to allow anyone but Marina to see him.

Between that, and half a dozen calls from him, she was frazzled by the time she reached home. She pulled up outside her building and began unloading the gifts, and also the groceries she'd stopped for on her way. Darn. She'd have to make two trips.

She hurried to the elevator and fumbled to punch the button. One of the packages fell to the floor. A man sitting in one of the chairs in the vestibule hurried over to pick it up.

"I believe you dropped this." His smile was friendly and pleasant.

"Oh, thank you," Marina crooked an elbow. "Can you just put it there?" He tucked it in, then moved back to his seat.

The elevator came and she stepped in, her mind moving ahead in anticipation of seeing Adam. When she reached her floor, he opened the door while she was fumbling for her keys.

"Ah, it must be somebody's birthday." He dodged one

way, then another, in search of a way around the gifts to kiss her.

"Mm-m," Marina murmured, lifting her chin as he gave up and nuzzled her neck. "They're all for you. Here, take this one, so it doesn't fall again."

She followed Adam inside and dumped the rest of the packages on the sofa.

He sat down next to the pile and picked one up thoughtfully. "For me, you say?" He shook it, while Marina put her purse away and hung up her coat.

"There are more in the car, but I'll get them later," she said, sinking into the easy chair opposite him. She smiled. He was busy examining each gaily wrapped package, hefting it, guessing the contents. "Well, why don't you open them?" she said.

He drew back, a shocked look on his face. "My dear lady, don't you know there's a technique to opening gifts?" He picked up a large, flat square. "Half the challenge is guessing what's inside, then . . ."

A knock at the door interrupted him.

"Were you expecting anyone?" Marina stood up.

"No, were you?"

She shook her head, then shrugged her shoulders, starting for the door. "Must be someone from the Conservatory. I told them you weren't ready for visitors, but maybe—" Standing on tiptoe, she peered through the peephole.

It was the man who had helped her with the package. Marina paused. Why would he come here?

He knocked again. Suddenly, she felt nervous. As quietly as possible, she fastened the security chain, then opened the door a crack.

"Yes?"

He smiled, and stepped back slightly. "Are you Marina Prohaska?"

Marina hesitated. "Who are you?"

He smiled, and through the slit of the door, handed her

some identification and a business card. "Miss Prohaska, my name is Jeffrey Tompkins. I'm a private detective." He nodded at the items he'd handed her. "The identification shows that I'm registered with the State of Massachusetts."

Hands trembling, Marina took a quick look at the picture I.D. card. It *looked* official. She handed it back, keeping the business card. What did he want with her? She took a deep breath, pushing back her nervousness.

"Yes, Mr. Tompkins?" Her voice betrayed her by shaking.

"Uh, I wonder if I could come in. I have something of rather great importance to discuss with you, and standing here in the hallway—well, it . . ."

Marina hesitated, then unchained the door. "I'm very busy, Mr. Tompkins. I hope this won't take long."

She stood aside to let him in.

He paused in the doorway. "Miss Prohaska, if you'd rather I come another time, when you aren't so busy . . . ?"

For a second, Marina was tempted to let him go. But he'd just come back again. She shook her head. "No, we'll get it over with now."

"Ah, good."

He followed her into the living room, where Adam still sat on the sofa, looking puzzled.

"Adam, Mr. Tompkins is a private detective." Marina could see Adam was puzzled—and, like her, apprehensive.

He cast a glance at her, then held out his hand to the detective. "You'll pardon me if I don't stand, Mr. Tompkins. I'm recovering from surgery."

"Yes, yes, I see." With a friendly smile, Mr. Tompkins shook Adam's hand, then turned to Marina. "What I need to discuss with you is of a rather personal nature." He shifted uncomfortably. "Perhaps you'd like to talk without . . . ?"

"Adam stays here," Marina said firmly. She indicated the easy chair. "Please be seated, Mr. Tompkins." Moving some of the gifts aside, she sat on the other end of the sofa. "Now, what do you have to discuss?"

The detective smiled briefly at both of them, then his expression became serious.

"Miss Prohaska, I represent Jadwiga Frederick Sonders, a well-known patron of the arts in Boston. Several months ago, Mrs. Sonders saw a picture of you and a gentleman—" He turned to Adam, "—in fact, Mr. Fletcher, I believe you were the gentleman—in the Boston paper. She was struck by your resemblance, Miss Prohaska, to her niece, Elena, whose maiden name was Prochaska, and also to pictures of Mrs. Sonders's sister, Anna Prochaska." He paused.

Marina rose, making no attempt to conceal her impatience. "Mr. Tompkins, I was an only child." She crossed her arms tight across her chest. "My parents died many years ago. This is pure coincidence. Now, if you'll . . ."

The detective raised his hand. "Please, Miss Prohaska, hear me out." He smiled patiently. "When Mrs. Sonders saw the picture, she asked me to conduct a thorough investigation of your background. I've been doing that since last fall. In fact, I've come by here a couple of times, but you were out."

Marina and Adam exchanged a look. "So that was you," Marina said softly. She didn't know whether to be relieved or unnerved. Well, no matter. He was wrong. "I appreciate your efforts, Mr. Tompkins, but I really must ask you to leave now."

"Not so fast, please." Sitting upright, he pulled out a notebook and opened it. "Let's see . . . ah, here it is. Your parents were Polish, is that correct?"

Marina heaved a restless sigh. "Yes, but that doesn't . . ."

"And your father was a professional clarinet player?"

"Yes, but . . ." She regarded him cautiously.

"And your mother was an accomplished pianist?"

"Well . . ." Her heart began to pound.

Mr. Tompkins smiled warmly and motioned toward the

sofa again. "Marina—I may call you that, may I not?" He ignored her lack of response and went on. "Marina, Mrs. Sonders escaped with her niece from Poland during World War II. Her sister, a concert pianist, and her brother-in-law, a world-famous clarinetist, were sent to a prison camp. They were to reconcile with her after the war, but never made contact."

He paused, his gaze settling on Marina's face. "My investigation shows that they traveled the country for several years, then settled in San Francisco, where a daughter was born. Mr. Prohaska died shortly after in a trolley accident, and Mrs. Prohaska died of pneumonia when the child was around five years old."

Marina felt the blood drain from her face. *Mama, mama, wake up—please wake up.* The memory hit her with stunning clarity. Stumbling backward, she dropped to the sofa.

"Marina, are you all right?" Adam pushed the gifts aside and slid close to her.

She clutched his hand, her heart pounding.

"Look, I think you'd better come back . . ." Adam began.

"No, I'll be all right. Let him finish." Not taking her gaze from Mr. Tompkins' face, Marina felt a tic start in her eyelid. She blinked, then blinked again.

With a gentle smile, he rose and stood before her.

"Marina, that child was you."

———————— THIRTEEN ————————

Several weeks later, Adam watched an Air Canada Airbus lumber over the tarmac of Vancouver International Airport toward the terminal. His heart quickened as the plane pulled up and stopped. It would only be moments before Marina emerged through the doorway into the waiting room—into his arms.

A shiver of anticipation shot through him. God, it would be good to see her. Although she'd spent just a weekend in Boston visiting her aunt and sister, he was as excited to see her as if she'd been gone months. Every moment alone had been pure agony.

It seemed an eternity before he finally spotted her. She was behind two elderly ladies, who doddered through the long tunnel at a snail's pace. She looked up at Adam, and their gazes meshed.

I can't wait to get my arms around you, he telegraphed.

I love you, she returned. With a rueful smile, she nodded toward the ladies ahead of her and shrugged.

At last the pair ambled through the door, and Marina was there. Adam caught her close, burying his face in the fragrance of her hair. She tilted her head back, and he kissed her. Lord, how he wished they weren't in the middle of an airport.

"Miss me?" she murmured.

"M-mm, I can't wait to get you home." He gazed down at her, hardly able to restrain himself from kissing her again. But he didn't dare. Not here, with everyone around. He needed privacy for what he wanted, and the promise in her eyes told him she had the same thing on her mind.

"Let's not waste time standing here," she whispered.

Adam felt his blood surge. "What are we waiting for?"

"So how was Boston?" He maneuvered around a VW bug and onto the freeway. With a smile, he glanced over at her, then back at the road.

"Wonderful." Marina leaned back in the seat and sighed. "I still can't quite believe it." She turned her head to look at his profile while he drove. His hair was nearly as long as it had been when they first met, but curlier. That same errant lock persisted in falling down his forehead. Smiling, Marina reached over and brushed it back.

"Watch that, lady," Adam growled. "You'll have me running off the road."

She laughed softly, and ran her hand down his neck.

He stretched his chin up, allowing her access to the buttons on his shirt.

She undid the first three, allowing her fingers to slide inside and play with the tangle of crisp curls she found there. One fingertip just happened to land on his right nipple, teasing it into a hard nubbin.

Adam caught his breath. "You're living dangerously, woman. I just may have to pull over and ravish you."

With a mischievous grin, she pulled her hand away and sat straight up, hands folded primly in her lap.

"Better?"

He looked over at her, a slow smile spreading across his face.

"Um-mm, for now. But when we get home . . ."

Marina's stomach muscles tightened. Who'd imagine

that just three nights away from him could create such a hunger? With effort, she forced her mind away from that dangerous territory.

For a time, they drove in silence. Then, Adam spoke. "You still haven't told me about the trip. Did all the relatives overwhelm you?"

With a laugh, she shook her head. "Would you believe it, Adam, I have two nieces and a nephew who are nearly as old as I am? In fact, I have a nephew-in-law and a couple of *grand*-nieces."

"What about your aunt?"

"She's a dear," Marina said. "She showed me the pictures of my parents and grandparents she smuggled out when she left." Marina turned, her eyes full of tears. "Oh, Adam, they were so young. If only . . ."

Awkwardly, he reached over and patted her shoulder. "I know, love. I know."

They were in Vancouver now. Marina lapsed into silence, her mind full of all she had learned about herself during the past days. She barely noticed when Adam pulled up in front of their building.

"Hey, we're home." Gently, he reached over and took her chin in his hand. She turned her head, and he leaned down to kiss her with exquisite tenderness. Tears brimmed in her eyes once more.

"Come on, Marina, don't cry." With the heel of his hand, Adam brushed the tears away as they overflowed and trickled down her cheeks.

Through the blur, Marina smiled. "Oh, Adam, I'm so happy. I have so much—you, my family, my music." She sniffled, fumbling in her purse for a tissue. "I thought I was happy before, but now—" Suddenly, a chill swept over her—a premonition almost. She clutched his hand. "Please, Adam, don't ever leave me. I couldn't bear living without you."

He gathered her in his arms and held her close. "Darling, darling, don't worry. We're together now. Nothing will ever separate us again.''

Once they were inside, the troubling thought receded into no more than a tiny shadow. As soon as the door closed behind them, Adam dropped her bag, then unbuttoned her coat and slipped it from her shoulders.

''Wait here.''

He left, and Marina heard the opening strains of *Chansons de la Nuit* coming from the living room. She started after him.

''What are you—oh, my.'' In the middle of the coffee table was the biggest bouquet of roses she had ever seen. She turned to Adam, who still stood beside the tape deck. ''They're beautiful.'' Walking over to him, she stood on tiptoe and put her arms around his neck, pulling his head down until she could capture his lips with hers.

His response was immediate and powerful. With a groan, he pulled her close. Behind them, the music swelled. ''I was going to bring out champagne and food, and seduce you with romance,'' he murmured, his lips close to her ear. With his tongue, he traced the shell, then continued down her neck, nibbling, kissing.

Marina turned her head, seeking his lips again. ''I love it. I love you,'' she whispered, punctuating her words with kisses. She pushed his jacket off his shoulders, and he shrugged it to the floor. Then she began undoing the rest of the buttons on his shirt, one at a time, with taunting slowness.

Behind her, the vibrant flute tones floated against the gossamer veil of the orchestra. The deep, rich sound of the cello replied, an invitation full of depth and promise.

Adam slid his hands beneath her top, lifting it up, taking his lips from hers just long enough to push it over her head and drop it to the floor. With trembling hands, he unfastened her bra, letting it fall free. When Marina nudged his shirt down his shoulders, he stood still, allowing her to tug it away, while their gazes met and clung. He glanced down at their nakedness, hers smooth and feminine, and his muscular and broad.

Slowly, suggestively, he drew her closer, following the tantalizing pulse of the music. Their bodies brushed against each other. Her nipples were thrusting and hard. Worshipfully, he took each into his mouth, tasting, running his tongue over the tip and around the aureole.

Marina sucked in her breath at the excruciating sensations he created. "Adam, I don't know if I can stand this much longer." In the background, the music rose, its passion contained, but threatening to burst out at any moment.

Adam let his lips travel upward, over the hollow of her neck, across her jawline, until she melted against him. He trembled with the effort to maintain control. That music, it tormented him, just as it had while they played. He wanted to love her, adore her. But he had waited too long for her return to let it be over with too quickly. God, that music. It was driving him beyond control.

"Oh, Marina, I love you so much," he breathed. Bending, he picked her up and carried her to the sofa, sinking down on it, his lips still moving over hers.

In a tangle of arms and legs, they undressed each other, their fingers clumsy with eagerness. At last they lay together, his hardness thrusting against her. The music surged in the background, the flute and cello rising toward the final triumphant climax. Marina threw her head back, her eyes closed.

"Now, Adam. I—can't—wait." Rolling to bring him above her, she opened to him.

Unable to resist his need any longer, Adam plunged into her waiting warmth. She wrapped her legs around his waist, and they allowed the tide of the music to carry them to ecstasy and beyond.

Marina lay in a sensual haze, replete with satisfaction. Adam's head was on her shoulder, his weight pressing her body into the deep upholstery of the sofa. The music faded, trailing off in wisps of sound. At last, there was silence. He began to move away, and she tightened her arms around him.

"Don't move yet," she whispered.

"But I'm heavy . . ."

"I love it. I'd love to stay here like this for the rest of my life," she said drowsily. She allowed her eyes to close, and the two of them lay motionless until she drifted off to sleep.

"Hey, sweetheart, time to wake up."

She opened her eyes. Outside the windows, it was dark. In the shadows, she could make out Adam's face close to hers. He kissed her, and she cuddled against his warmth, not wanting to move. "What time is it?"

"Nearly eight—dinner time," he said softly. "Or don't you want to try the special Fletcher quiche, created in honor of your homecoming?"

That got her. Lazily, she stretched and yawned. Sitting up, she reached over and turned on the lamp beside the sofa. Adam was beside her, still undressed. She leaned over and kissed him, running her hand lightly over his thigh. "Mm-mm, I like the idea of being served dinner right here." She tilted her head and regarded him for a moment. "I might even be convinced to toss together a salad."

He chuckled. "No need. With you gone, I spent my whole day in the kitchen. Everything's ready." Firmly, he moved her hand off his leg. "Unless the distractions are too great . . ."

Marina waved him away. "I wouldn't dream of spoiling a perfectly good meal."

"Then stay right here." He picked up the roses and set them on a table across the room, then went to the bedroom to find a pair of white terrycloth bathrobes. He tossed one to her and shrugged into the other one. "I promise, it'll be a meal you'll never forget."

It was. From the champagne and hors d'ouvres through

the Dungeness crab cocktail, broccoli and ham quiche, flaky croissants, caesar salad, and strawberry trifle. It was wonderfully romantic, with flickering candles and Ravel chamber music in the background. When they finished eating, they settled back on the sofa to drink their coffee, Marina nestled on Adam's lap.

He looked down at her. "Happy?"

"Ecstatic."

"Do you know what day this is?"

"Um-hm. It's the day I came home from Boston." Marina took a sip of her coffee. She set her mug on the coffee table and took his from him. "And the day we made the best love ever." Pulling his head down, she kissed him, long and deeply. "Did I miss anything?"

Adam laughed, then his face sobered. "Just one thing." He paused, and his eyes held a shade of uncertainty. "It's been four months and three days since I had the operation— and my last seizure." He caught her hand in a tight, urgent grip. "Marina, I know I'm cured. Marry me."

The laughter went out of her face, too. "Do you really mean that, Adam?" In the silence that followed, her heart pounded as if it would break through the walls of her chest.

"Marina, love, I've never meant anything more in my life. Through these last days, with you gone, I've done nothing but think." He shifted slightly to face her directly, and she could feel the tautness in his body. "I can't face life without you in it. Not now. Not when there's no longer anything to keep us apart."

Joy sang through Marina's body. He wanted her to marry him. She had a sudden urge to jump up and dance around the room, open the window and shout it to the roof tops. The emotion was so intense, she couldn't speak for a moment. Adam watched her, his eyes worried.

"If you don't . . ." he began, but Marina interrupted him.

"Yes, Adam, I'll marry you—" Irrationally, her eyes

flooded with tears, and she blinked them back. "Oh, yes, yes, my darling."

"Thank God."

He wrapped his arms around her, and she felt the tension drain out of him. He held her, and she clung to him, relaxed, happy, safe in the security of his arms.

In a far corner of her mind, the premonitory shadow surfaced again. She ignored it. She and Adam were together now. Nothing would ever separate them again.

The weeks following brought a madhouse of planning and activity. The chamber group toured eastern British Columbia and parts of Alberta. There were plans to be made for the wedding, plans for the coming year, decisions to be made.

Both received tempting offers from other institutions. Marina was asked to join the New York Philharmonic. Robert asked them to remain as members of the chamber group, now the Provincial Chamber Players, which was to receive permanent funding from the Foundation. Adam's agent contacted him with requests to perform in Paris, Berlin, Moscow.

"What are we going to do, Marina?" Adam waved a letter from London, inviting him to be a guest artist at an international music festival in October. "Hell, when will we have *time* for a wedding?"

He had just returned from a guest appearance in Los Angeles. It had been a harrowing trip, with late planes, missed connections, lost luggage. By the time he finally arrived at his hotel, he had only an hour before the concert. Between that, and the tight scheduling to get back to Vancouver for a performance with the Provincial Chamber Players, he was exhausted and on edge.

"Adam, calm down." She looked at her watch. "I have to pick up my dress for tonight, but after the concert we can sneak away to a nice quiet restaurant and sort things out." She gave him a quick kiss. "Don't worry. If we don't do another thing, we *will* have a wedding.'' She gave him a quick grin and hurried out the door.

But after the concert, they, couldn't sneak away. The Foundation wanted publicity shots for a brochure it was preparing, and the performers had to remain onstage, then attend the reception. Later, Annie insisted they come to her home for an impromptu party, from which they returned home at two in the morning.

The rest of the week was no better. Between student recitals, concerts, and Foundation demands, every spare moment was taken up with activity. By the time the weekend came around, Adam felt like a bow strung so tight it was ready to snap.

On Saturday morning, Marina woke to find him already up, practicing in the spare room. It wasn't like him. Usually, they spent a lazy hour making love before they rose, then lingered over breakfast until noon. She sighed. They were both stressed out. It was time to get things under control.

When she went to get him, he was intent on the music, a frown on his face.

She took a deep breath and smiled. ''Good morning, early bird.''

He looked up, his face softening at the sight of her. ''Did I wake you? I'm sorry.'' He shook his head. ''I couldn't sleep, worrying about this.'' He played a passage of a contemporary work for solo cello. ''No matter what I do, it doesn't feel right.''

Marina walked behind him and leaned down, wrapping her arms around his shoulders, rubbing her cheek against his. He turned his head and captured her lips.

''Why don't you leave it, and we'll go out for breakfast,'' she said softly. ''Today we'll get our plans straightened out, then we can both relax.''

They went to a small restaurant in the neighborhood and sat in the back booth. Over omelets and coffee, they talked.

"I'd like to stay here for one more year," Marina said. "Since we wouldn't be teaching, it would give us both a breather."

"But what about the other offers, my concerts?" Adam said. "I know it would mean time apart, but . . . ?

Marina leaned forward, resting her arms on the table. "Adam, those opportunities will be there next year, and the year after. You've said a thousand times you don't want to get caught in the rat race again, with constant jet lag and your life revolving around airline schedules." She smiled. "Besides, I'd like to spend my first married year with my husband."

The strain in his face softened. "You're right. I guess I've been on the concert track for so long I can't think any other way." He reached across the table and caught her hand. "Let's stay. And let's set the wedding day for the weekend after classes end." His eyes were warm and happy. "And now," he whispered, "I want to go back home and catch up on some unfinished business."

Marina looked at him questioningly.

He laughed. "I got up too early. Let's both go back to bed."

It was a wonderful afternoon. After a languid hour of lovemaking, they napped, woke up and made love again. Then they got up and went to the zoo at Stanley Park. Adam felt relaxed and at ease. Now that they had things settled, his mind was at rest. It felt good.

They reached the apartment, laughing and breathless, after a dash up the stairs, since the elevator was stuck on the fifth floor.

Marina started for the kitchen. "I'll cook and you set the table," she called over her shoulder.

Adam was close behind her. "Sounds good to me." He started for the silverware drawer. Just as he reached it, he felt the old, dreaded sensation.

No. No, it can't be—

But it was. He had a sensation of falling, then the familiar blackness closed around him.

Awareness returned slowly. As if from a great distance, Adam heard Marina's soothing voice.

"It's all right, Adam. You're fine. Just fine."

With effort, he opened his eyes. The blur before him gradually took the shape of her face.

"You've had a seizure, Adam. That's all."

He heard fear in her voice. Through the lassitude that claimed him, he struggled for control. He needed to reassure her, erase her anxiety.

"S'okay. Don't worry." He tried his hardest to act confident and assured, but the words came out slurred and indistinct. He heaved himself to a sitting position. Immediately, Marina was there.

"Easy, Adam, let me help you up."

Adam tried to wave her away, but he was just too tired. Without resisting, he allowed her to help him into the bedroom, then guide him to the bed. When she removed his clothes and covered him with a blanket, he hardly noticed. At once, he fell into a deep, dreamless sleep.

Marina closed the door softly behind her, latching it tight. She leaned against the jamb, her heart pounding. The seizure had come on with such stunning abruptness, there'd been no time to think. Her actions had been automatic.

Now, the impact hit her. She staggered to the sofa and dropped down on it.

Lord, what should she do? He'd sleep it off, but when he woke up, he'd be devastated. She had to help him, reassure him. Her mind whirled.

Dr. Johns. She'd call him.

Quickly, she went to the phone. His home number was on a card taped to the wall. She dialed, then nervously tapped her finger on the receiver.

"Dr. Johns, here."

Her shoulders sagged in relief. "This is Marina Prohaska." She took a deep breath. "It's Adam. He's had a seizure."

There was a beat of silence. "How long ago?"

"About ten minutes." Marina felt her self-control slipping. "There was no warning, doctor. It came on so fast . . ." Her voice broke.

"Now, now, Marina. It may not be significant."

His voice was calm and comforting. Marina felt her apprehension recede.

"Has he been under stress?"

"Well, we've been terribly busy trying to plan our wedding, and what we'll be doing next year." Marina thought back over the past weeks. "Yes, he's been under a lot of pressure." She hesitated. "Is that what caused the seizure?"

"It probably had something to do with it." The doctor paused thoughtfully. "He may never have another one. On the other hand, this could be the start of a new seizure pattern."

"I see." Marina swallowed back the lump that suddenly filled her throat. "Then he's not cured. Is that what you're telling me?"

"Marina, only time will tell. The tests we've done show no abnormal brain activity. We were able to remove all the scar tissue. But as far as the new scar is concerned—well, only time will tell." His voice was gentle. "Have Adam come in Monday morning. And Marina—" compassion warmed his words, "—Adam's going to need you now. More than ever."

Adam woke early. He lay beside Marina's still form, listening to the quiet rise and fall of her breathing. A potent surge of desire washed over him, and he rolled toward her, reaching out.

His muscles screamed at the movement. A dull pain pounded in his head, forcing him to fall back. The sensations were ominously familiar. He felt a sudden chill. A seizure. He must have had a seizure.

His mind raced, trying to remember. Through the haze, he had a vague recollection of Marina's voice, her helping him into the bedroom.

Oh, God. Not now.

His heart plummeted as the significance sank in. It was all over. His brief flirtation with normalcy was finished. He clenched his hands, swallowing back the bitterness.

You've been a fool, Adam. Only fools believe in miracles.

He closed his eyes against the pain that swept over him. There was only one thing to do now. Get out of here—out of Marina's life. Slowly, clenching his teeth, he pushed the covers back, and quietly slid out of bed.

Marina woke with a start. Where was Adam? His side of the bed was cold, empty. How could he have gotten up without her hearing?

Grabbing her robe, she opened the door. The normal, calming smell of fresh coffee assailed her. With relief, she started into the kitchen.

It was then she saw the pile of boxes in the hallway. Adam emerged from the guest bedroom carrying his cello and music stand.

Marina ran over to him. "Adam, what are you doing?"

He stopped, avoiding her eyes. "I'm leaving, Marina." His voice was quiet, resigned. "Don't try to stop me, please."

She stared at him. "No, Adam. You can't. I won't let you."

He started to move past her, but she stepped in front of him.

"Adam, it doesn't make any difference. I love you. We belong together."

"You say that now. But in a year, five years—don't you understand? I could have seizures every day, every hour. Would you still love me? Want me with you?"

Marina gave an impatient wave. "You're being ridiculous. That seizure could be the only one you'll ever have. Dr. Johns said so." She tried to grab his arm as he began to walk toward the door, but he shrugged her off. "And you, Adam. What if I got sick, or had an accident. Would you still love me?"

He stopped and wheeled. "Of course, I would, but that's different." He closed his eyes and took a deep breath. "God, Marina, why are you making this so hard? I'm not cured. It was all a dream. I've finally accepted that. And now I'm doing what I should have done months ago. I'm getting out of your life."

Throwing his shoulders back, he swung around and walked out the door.

The weeks crept by. Marina called Adam. She wrote him. But the phone calls only got his answering machine, and her letters went unanswered. At the Conservatory, he showed up for his classes and left immediately. They never encountered each other in the halls, or the lounge. Marina knew he planned his movements to avoid her.

Classes finished for the year a few days later. Adam wasn't at the graduation ceremony, and she overheard some of the other faculty members mention that he had already left.

Where had he gone? Marina longed to ask them. But she didn't dare. They'd only ask questions, or worse yet, look at her pityingly and change the subject. It was then she knew for sure. Adam was gone. The only thing she could do was go on with her life.

She tried. A few weeks later, when an old friend called and invited her to come to Seattle, where he was appearing in a special concert series, she jumped at the chance. But after only a few days, she returned to Vancouver, and her empty apartment.

A letter from the conductor of the Boston Symphony awaited her.

Dear Ms. Prohaska,

My attempts to reach you by telephone have been unsuccessful, hence this letter.

Adam Fletcher has graciously consented to allow the Boston Symphony Orchestra to perform the American premiere of the Debussy work, *Chansons de la Nuit*. Our board, of which Jadwiga Sonders is the chairman, has requested that I invite you and Mr. Fletcher to perform as featured soloists for this premiere, as you did in Vancover last fall.

I apologize for the lateness of this invitation, and I hope you will be available for this performance. Please contact me as soon as possible.

Yours, Charles Benedict

Marina sank down on the sofa, the letter falling from her hand. What could she do? She suspected that her aunt, romantic soul that she was, was behind this. Marina had never mentioned her relationship with Adam. Maybe she should have. The whole idea of doing the Boston premiere with Adam was impossible.

Her aunt, however, was determined, as her phone call later that evening proved.

"Marina, dear, isn't it just the most marvelous idea, you and that wonderful Mr. Fletcher premiering the work in *both* Canada and the United States?" Her aunt hardly paused for breath. "Of course, you'll stay here with me while you're in town. And I hope you'll plan to stay for at least a month, so we can really get to know each other."

Marina shifted uncomfortably. "Aunt Jadzia, I'm not sure I . . ."

"Well, dear, if not a month, at least plan on a couple of weeks. I'm terribly eager to see you, and to hear you perform in person."

Marina took a deep breath and opened her mouth to speak, but her aunt interrupted before she could get even one word out.

"Oh, goodness, there's the doorbell. I've got to run. But I'll tell Charles I've talked to you, and you've accepted. He'll be so pleased. Bye, dear." There was a click, then a dial tone.

Marina sat there, the receiver in her hand, feeling shellshocked. Like it or not, it appeared she was going to Boston.

The heat and humidity of the Boston airport hit her like a damp, soggy blanket as she left the terminal four weeks later. Her Aunt Jadzia and her sister, Elena, were at the gate when she arrived, and now they hustled her into the chauffeured limousine and swept her off to her aunt's huge Victorian-era home in Concord.

Marina tried to listen to Jadzia's plans for the coming three weeks, but all she could think of was Adam. He was here, in Boston. Soon, they'd rehearse together. The thought filled her with excitement and dread. How was he? How would he act?

"And I've got a wonderful surprise for you, Marina," her aunt was saying. "I've invited that nice Mr. Fletcher for dinner, and he's accepted. He tells me he left Vancouver two months ago, so I'm sure the two of you will have a lot to say to each other."

Marina's heart nearly stopped. "Adam? Here for dinner?" she gasped. "When?"

"Why, tonight, dear. I just told you." Her aunt suddenly paused and regarded Marina with concern. "That's all right, isn't it? You're not too tired for a dinner guest this evening are you?"

Marina felt the probe of sharp blue eyes, and noted a quick glance exchanged between her aunt and sister. She took a deep breath to still the pounding in her temples.

"No, I'm fine. I—I just wasn't expecting to see Adam for a few more days." She wasn't expecting to see him at *all*, except for rehearsals and the performance. Why had he accepted the invitation? What was she going to say to him?

The limousine pulled up in her aunt's driveway, and immediately Jadzia jumped out to supervise the unloading of Marina's luggage. Marina started to get out, too, but Elena laid her hand on her arm.

"Marina, Aunt Jadzia can be a bit overbearing at times." Her expression was warm and sympathetic. "I just want you to know, our cottage at the Cape is open. If things here become too much for you, you can escape there any time."

Marina threw her a grateful smile. "Thanks. I just may do that," she said softly.

"Come, come girls. It's nearly four. Mr. Fletcher will be here soon, and I'm sure Marina will want to get ready for him," Jadzia trilled. She waited impatiently while the sisters climbed out of the limousine.

As Jadzia turned to enter the house, the two exchanged a conspiratorial look. "Give me a call, if you need help," Elena whispered.

Marina nodded, the thought of Adam looming large. For certain, she'd need help. But not the kind Elena had in mind.

Marina lingered in her room until she heard the doorbell ring. Adam. It had to be him. The very thought made her knees weak. Lord, what would she say to him? How could she sit at the same table with him, eat a single bite?

There was a light tap at her door. "Marina, Mr. Fletcher is here." Marina recognized Elena's voice.

"I'll be right there." She took a quick look in the mirror. Her hair was smoothly coiled at the back of her head, her makeup impeccable. Except for the faint shadows beneath her eyes and the weight she'd lost, she appeared perfectly coifed, perfectly in control. She closed her eyes, willing her heart to stop pounding so.

When she opened the door, Elena was waiting. "Is everything all right?"

Marina gave her a strained smile and swallowed. "Just fine." With forced heartiness, she took Elena's arm and started toward the stairway.

When they entered the parlor, Adam was standing in front of the ornate marble fireplace talking to her Uncle Arthur and brother-in-law, John. Marina froze in the doorway, feeling dizzy and faint.

"Sure you're all right?" Elena whispered, tightening her hold on Marina's arm.

"I'm fine," Marina whispered back, willing her knees to stop trembling.

Just then Adam looked up, and their gazes caught. There was a flicker of nervousness in his eye, quickly gone. He set his glass on the mantel and started toward her.

"Marina. How good to see you." In five long strides he was in front of her.

Oh, Lord, how would she get through this evening? He bent to brush a social kiss across her cheek and her heart contracted.

"Adam, how are you?" She concentrated on keeping her face stiff and unemotional. "This is my sister, Elena Burke."

With courtly charm, Adam took Elena's hand. "Mrs. Burke, I've already met your husband." They exchanged a few words, then Elena murmured an excuse and left them.

"Would—ah, would you like to sit down?" Marina said, stammering slightly. She looked down. His gaze consumed her, as if he couldn't get enough of her. *Oh, Adam, don't you know what you do to me?*

He took her elbow and guided her to a velvet chaise on the other side of the room. Marina sat there stiffly, as far from him as she could get. Someone put a glass of champagne in her hand, and she drank thirstily, holding her glass out for a refill. *Careful, Marina. Remember what happened before.* Adam watched with sober eyes.

"How are you?" he asked, his voice gentle. "Are you all right?"

Marina set her glass on the table beside the chaise. "Do I look ill, or something? People keep asking if I'm all right." Impatiently, she turned to him, but her impatience faded at the haunted look on his face. "What about you?" she said softly.

"Marina, Adam—" They both looked up in surprise at Jadzia's approach. "We're ready to go in for dinner." With a twinkle in her eye, the older woman offered her arm to Adam. "Would you mind?" Uncle Arthur offered his arm to Marina. The couples led the small procession to the dining room. Elena and John followed.

Adam was seated across from Marina. The conversation went on around her, but she was aware only of him. Why had he agreed to come here tonight? Surely, it was as difficult for him as for her. She toyed with her food, ignoring the wine that sparkled in her glass. Her head was already light from the champagne. If she didn't watch out, she'd make a fool of herself.

At last the endless meal drew to a close. When the dessert dishes had been removed from the table, Jadzia looked at her watch and cast a significant glance at Arthur. "I hope you young folks will excuse us. All the excitement of your arrival has quite worn us out, Marina."

As if on cue, Elena and John rose. "We need to make another stop this evening," Elena said apologetically. "I hope you'll forgive us for leaving you two alone."

When everyone was gone, Adam turned to Marina. "I'd like to talk to you. Could we walk in the garden?"

"Adam, this is very difficult for me," she said quietly. "I think it would be better if you left, too."

He gazed at her, his eyes soft in the dim light. "Please, Marina. It's important to me."

Her throat was suddenly dry. Important to him? She gave him a hard look. "Well, in that case . . ."

His smile nearly did her in.

"Come on, then."

He held out his hand, and after a moment she took it. It was warm and strong, and he grasped her stiff fingers with gentle firmness. A lump rose in Marina's throat, his touch was so familiar and tender.

They wandered the garden in the twilight, neither speaking for a time. It was a wonderfully romantic setting, perfumed by masses of flowers in well-tended beds, shadowed by tall trees. Fireflies winked in the bushes beside the path.

Marina could make out a summer house through the trees. It was there Adam led her.

"Let's sit here," he said softly, guiding her inside to a bench.

She heard the gentleness in his tone. Her pulse began to pound. Why was he doing this? She dropped to the bench at his urging, and he took his place beside her.

"All right, Adam, now tell me what this is all about."

For a moment, he was silent, then he sighed. "I have a confession to make. I engineered this invitation to dinner tonight because I needed to talk to you."

"You mean you. . . ?"

He nodded, a faint smile on his face. "I called your aunt and asked her to invite me. She was thrilled at the idea." He hesitated, then gave a little laugh. "Jadzia is quite a lady."

"But I don't understand. Why have you gone to all this trouble?" Marina turned to him. His face was nearly hidden in the shadows.

"Marina, I've done a lot of thinking since I left you. As soon as classes were over, I went up in the mountains and spent a month in an old ranger cabin, trying to get things straight in my mind."

She felt his grip tighten.

"And. . . ?"

He gazed at her, his eyes dark against the faint lightness of his skin. "And I found I couldn't go back to that lonely, sterile existence I knew before I met you."

His hand gripped hers so tightly, she nearly cried out. Almost without realizing it, she reached out to touch his cheek.

"I love you, Marina. I don't know what's ahead, whether I'll have another seizure . . ."

"It doesn't matter, Adam," she murmured. "I told you that before." Joyfully, she slid her hand around to the back of his neck and tilted her head back, drawing his lips closer.

Suddenly, he wrapped his arms around her, clutching her to him, rocking back and forth. "Oh, God, how I've missed you," he whispered fiercely. He kissed her then, and the kiss had a desperate intensity. "Marry me, darling. Tomorrow. I don't ever want to live without you again."

Marina's heart was so full, she had to fight back the tears.

"You'll never have to, Adam. I promise you," she whispered.

Even Aunt Jadzia couldn't arrange a wedding on twenty-four hours' notice. But three days later, the family gathered in the summer house to hear Marina and Adam recite their vows. Shortly after, the couple escaped to Elena and John's cottage at Cape Cod.

Ten days later they performed the American premiere of *Chansons de la Nuit*. The critics gave it rave reviews. Aunt Jadzia scrupulously cut them out and mailed them to Vancouver.

"A stunning work and an equally stunning performance . . ."

The Boston Globe

"Prohaska and Fletcher surpassed themslves in the Boston performance of *Chansons de la Nuit*."

The Vancouver Sun

"Fletcher and Prohaska achieved new heights of depth and richness . . ."   *The New York Times*

Marina read the reviews aloud to Adam as he prepared dinner. When she finished, she looked up at him and smiled.

"I guess they liked us."

Adam came over and kissed her with slow deliberation. "But I'll bet nobody guessed our secret." His lips wandered along her jawline to her neck.

Marina gave a little shiver, closing her eyes as she felt his tongue trace her collarbone and begin to move lower.

"Secret?"

"Mm-mm," he whispered, unbuttoning the buttons on her blouse, one by one.

"What's—that?" She had to struggle to keep her mind on what she was saying.

He slipped her blouse over her shoulders and lifted her from the stool, allowing her to slide down his body. Lifting her in his arms, he started for the bedroom. At the door, he paused, his lips seeking hers again.

"That wasn't just any old music." The kiss left both of them shaken and breathless. Adam drew back slightly and smiled.

"It was the music of love."

ACKNOWLEDGEMENTS

My heartfelt thanks goes to the individuals and organizations who so generously provided research assistance during the writing of *DUET*. They include the Epilepsy Association of Western Washington, Epilepsy B.C., the Epilepsy Foundation of America, Vancouver General Hospital, the University of Washington Epilepsy Center, Dr. Richard Wohns and Kathleen McKane.

SHARE THE FUN ...
SHARE YOUR NEW-FOUND TREASURE!!

You don't want to let your new books out of your sight?
That's okay. Your friends can get their own. Order below.

No. 21 THAT JAMES BOY by Lois Faye Dyer
Jesse believes in love at first sight. Now he has to convince Sarah of this.

No. 22 NEVER LET GO by Laura Phillips
Ryan has a big dilemma and Kelly is the answer to *all* his prayers.

No. 23 A PERFECT MATCH by Susan Combs
Ross can keep Emily safe but can he save himself from Emily?

No. 24 REMEMBER MY LOVE by Pamela Macaluso
Will Max ever remember the special love he and Deanna shared?

No. 25 LOVE WITH INTEREST by Darcy Rice
Stephanie & Elliot find $47,000,000 *plus* interest—true love!

No. 26 NEVER A BRIDE by Leanne Banks
The last thing Cassie wanted was a relationship. Joshua had other ideas.

No. 27 GOLDILOCKS by Judy Christenberry
David and Susan join forces and get tangled in their own web.

No. 28 SEASON OF THE HEART by Ann Hammond
Can Lane and Maggie's newfound feelings stand the test of time?

No. 29 FOSTER LOVE by Janis Reams Hudson
Morgan comes home to claim his children but Sarah claims his heart.

No. 30 REMEMBER THE NIGHT by Sally Falcon
Joanna throws caution to the wind. Is Nathan fantasy or reality?

No. 31 WINGS OF LOVE by Linda Windsor
Mac & Kelly soar to heights of ecstasy. Will they have a smooth landing?

No. 32 SWEET LAND OF LIBERTY by Ellen Kelly
Brock has a secret and Liberty's freedom could be in serious jeopardy!

No. 33 A TOUCH OF LOVE by Patricia Hagan
Kelly seeks peace and quiet and finds paradise in Mike's arms.

No. 34 NO EASY TASK by Chloe Summers
Hunter is wary when Doone delivers a package that will change his life.

No. 35 DIAMOND ON ICE by Lacey Dancer
Diana could melt even the coldest of hearts. Jason hasn't a chance.

No. 36 DADDY'S GIRL by Janice Kaiser
Slade wants more than Andrea is willing to give. Who wins?

No. 37 ROSES by Caitlin Randall
It's an inside job & K.C. helps Brett find more than the thief!

No. 38 HEARTS COLLIDE by Ann Patrick
Matthew finds big trouble and it's spelled P-a-u-l-a.

No. 39 QUINN'S INHERITANCE by Judi Lind
Gabe and Quinn share an inheritance and find an even greater fortune.

No. 40 CATCH A RISING STAR by Laura Phillips
Justin is seeking fame; Beth shows him an even greater reward.

No. 41 SPIDER'S WEB by Allie Jordan
Silvia's life was quiet and organized until Fletcher arrived on her front
doorstep. Will life ever be the same again?

No. 42 TRUE COLORS by Dixie DuBois
Julian has the power to crush Nikki's world with the bat of an eye. But
can he help her save herself? Can he save himself from Nikki?

No. 43 DUET by Patricia Collinge
On stage, Adam and Marina fit together like two pieces of a puzzle.
Love just might be the glue that keeps them together off stage, as well.

No. 44 DEADLY COINCIDENCE by Denise Richards
J.D.'s instincts tell him he can't be wrong about his beautiful Laurie;
her heart says to trust him. If they're wrong, it could be deadly!
